SIDEWALKING

Nick Duerden

UNCORRECTED, UNEDITED MANUSCRIPT

FLAME
Hodder & Stoughton

First published in Great Britain in 2000
by Hodder and Stoughton
A division of Hodder Headline

10 9 8 7 6 5 4 3 2 1

British Library Cataloguing in Publication Data

ISBN 0 340 76619 0

Hodder and Stoughton
A division of Hodder Headline
338 Euston Road
London NW1 3BH

SIDEWALKING

For Elena, for everything

ACKNOWLEDGEMENTS

Huge thanks to my agent Judith Murdoch, my editor Philippa Pride and all the good people at Hodder; and to my mother, Natasha, without whom, no book in the first place.

PROLOGUE

My first instinct is to panic. My second, to bolt.

So I do. I bolt.

I hit the sidewalk running, somehow having managed to extricate myself from her grasp, squeeze around the tightly-packed bar, passed the drunken revellers, and out into the streets, which are heaving and sweating in celebration of the midnight hour. There are people everywhere. Some are singing, dancing, vomiting, and intermittently breaking out into half-fights that erupt and die like fireworks, while others are content to slowly walk home hand in hand, their heads on partners' shoulders, a look of love I immediately envy in their eyes. I weave in and out of them like a downhill slalom skier and, despite an intense curiosity, refrain from looking over my shoulder to see if she is following me, hot on my trail. Two blocks east and I cross a still-congested Broadway and 34th. Times Square remains out of bounds, mounted police patrolling every possible entrance, so I continue east, before commencing a zigzag movement through smaller streets and alleyways until even I feel lost, unable to pinpoint exactly where I am in my now otherwise familiar, adopted city.

My mind is teeming, a catastrophic pressure spilling from my ear lobes, and my chest is a balloon, inflating and deflating rapidly. How has she tracked me down so precisely, on tonight of all nights? My foot snags on an uneven slab of sidewalk, and up I go, flying through the fresh, damp air of a brand new year. During my flight, each limb assumes the point of a star, and there is nothing to cushion my fall but the cold, hard concrete paving that appears to rush up to meet me, fast. My hands draw in to protect my face, and I crash-land awkwardly, then skid along the rough road, tearing flesh. I come to an ungainly stop when I collide with what looks like two tree-like branches, long, knobbly, smooth and brown, sprouting from the tarmac up. They move uncertainly, first backwards, then forwards, clopping like a horse. There is momentary darkness, a cloak of impenetrable black. I blink, open my eyes, and look up.

The mounted policewoman peers down at me with disinterest.

"I hope we're not too inebriated to stand up, sir?" she asks in a chewy Brooklyn accent.

"No, officer," I respond, quickly finding my feet and explaining that I merely tripped.

"You wanna get those hands seen to," she says, before kicking

her ride in the guts and cantering off round a corner.

I look down at my hands and see two palms of ripped flesh,

mottled blood, and tiny chunks of sidewalk. I wince, brush then

gingerly on my shirt, and walk onwards. Suddenly, I realize that I'm

practically alone, that the normally busy streets are now deserted.

Unlike London, where revellers seem reluctant to leave the party,

and continue to occupy Trafalgar Square until night buses are

replaced by regular services the morning after, New York is entirely

different. Moments after the dropping of the New Year ball, people

disperse in every direction, all now homeward bound as directed by

a high visible NYPD who seem intent on stopping the party as

quickly as possible. And so, after wandering around aimlessly for

some time, I find myself on an unusually quiet 42nd Street, craving

something to eat, and have somebody fix me a drink for a change.

The city that never sleeps is largely bereft of life, and it takes

some time before I find a diner that is actually open.

Inside, there are just seven customers - one young couple,

while the rest are like me, sole stragglers with nowhere else to go.

The strip lighting is a harsh white, the walls bare. There are no

3

decorations, not even a hint of festivities, and no music, just an uneasy silence and the occasional sound of cutlery on cheap plates. I order some sausages and pancakes, a beer and a mug of steaming black coffee, and while I wait for it to arrive, I pay a visit to the bathroom. My visage looks haggard, still redolent of having suffered such a recent shock to the system. My black trousers are ripped at the knee, and my hands sting. I turn on the faucet and, when the limp stream of brown water loses colour and acquires enough temperature, I place my upturned palms underneath to clean my wounds. Glancing back up at the mirror, I notice that my eyes are red-rimmed, exhausted.

The pancakes, of course, don't compliment the sausages, and the syrup only confuses matters more when mixed with ketchup. But this is a uniquely New York dish and, as I'd discovered over the past few months, is far more satisfying a nocturnal feast than a lowly London kebab could ever hope of being. I eat with a suddenly ravenous hunger, and quickly polish off the first beer and order another. The couple upfront have rooted around in their pockets for loose quarters, and are now feeding the jukebox, which duly delivers the kind of haggard, blue-collared anthems that Americans appear so fond of.

A chunk of peppery sausage, a crescent of pancake, a dollop of ketchup, and a liberal dribble of sticky syrup. The fork is full, heavy, and is allowed access into my mouth only when I open it as wide as it will stretch. This is not a dish that necessarily requires teeth; just apply pressure with tongue to pallet and it soon acquires a mushy texture that you can soon swallow like so much lumpy soup. I wait for the glorious combination to slither down my throat and hit my stomach before loading the fork once more. Music drifts from beyond. The waitress blows bubblegum bubbles behind the counter, studying her fingernails with kohl'd eyes. An elderly gentleman two tables in front of me takes his teeth out and polishes them with his tie. He wears glasses that make his eyes appear ten times their normal size. I take another gulp of beer, thankful that my heart rate has returned to its normal rhythm. The food taste good, and the beer is so chilled it contains shards of ice.

From behind me, the chime of the front door bursts into life, and I involuntarily tense. Footsteps approach from somewhere over my shoulder. Before they reach me, they stop. The people beyond me look my way, briefly. Then, as I allow my form to slump into submission, a body swoops into the seat opposite me. Perfume assaults my nostrils.

"There you are," she says, allowing herself a wry smile, and clearly keen to play out this little drama for maximum effect.

A waitress arrives and takes her order of coffee and soup of the day. The waitress looks at the large clock behind the counter, and says, "Would that be today's soup of the day, or yesterday's? Because officially, what's written there on that menu is yesterday's."

"What was yesterday's?" she asks.

"Chicken," says the waitress.

"And today's?"

The waitress abruptly stops chewing her gum. "Hold on, I'll have to check."

"So," she says to me when we're left alone, now growing serious. "Hello there."

I reply with something similar, more a monosyllabic grunt than anything containing vowels and consonants, and ask her what she's doing here.

"We're here on holiday," she replies. We. So I had seen him, after all. "Thought we'd see the new year in somewhere different."

A latent sarcasm creeps into her voice. "Plus, we haven't been away for a while, because we've had some temporary problems with our passports."

I avoid eye contact, but can't help blushing.

"And seeing as we were here, well, we just had to come and look you up. Catch up on old times. How the devil are you?"

"Tomato," says the waitress, suddenly back at our table. Toe-may-doe.

"I'll have that, then," she says, smiling widely at her.

"How did you find me?" I asks.

She lights up a cigarette. "Diligence."

I finish off my meal in silence, aware that indigestion is already making its presence felt. She ignores her soup altogether. I order another beer, and drink it quick, desperate for the Dutch courage I hope it will afford me. It does, and eventually I tire of her game.

"Well, I won't say it was lovely meeting you again, because it wasn't," I say, in deadpan tones, "and I've better things to be doing. We haven't got anything else to discuss, have we? So goodbye, take care. Happy New Year."

Her voice raises in pitch slightly. She tells me to sit down, says that I am going nowhere. I ignore her and make to leave, feeling slightly drunk.

An anger I used to know so well flares across her face. "I've spent the better part of six months looking for you, so if you think you're going to walk away from me for a second time, then clearly you've forgotten me more than I have you." Of course I hadn't forgotten. That was never even an option. I sit back down. "Largely because of you, and that brother of yours, I've had a pretty tough time of late." She sweeps her hair back from her face, and just above her right temple is a long, thin scar from hairline to eyebrow, the flesh pink, still new. "In fact, it hasn't been easy at all, but then I'm not easily thwarted."

Her eyes, twin pistons of boiling fury, are now drilling into mine. She doesn't look happy. Deja vu swamps my senses. I feel my pulse throb in my solar plexus.

For her to have survived the past six months after everything we'd done certainly proves her tenacity beyond all doubt. I can't even imagine what she must have gone through - the endless fear, the ceaseless hunt, the ultimate escape - but, casting my mind back, perhaps I can hazard a guess. She always was resourceful. To have come away with only a minor flesh wound suggests that she is in fact indomitable. I'm deeply impressed. I want to ask her what happened to Short Order, but I'm not too sure of the etiquette here, so I keet quiet.

She starts, slowly, to smile. From the pocket of her suede jacket, she produces a gun - not the same gun, but a cowboy-style six-shooter - and trains it at me across the table. "If you run away from me again," she says through pursed lips, a heroine in her own B-movie, "then you won't get very far."

Suddenly I think of Tom, and wonder whether there is any way I can get hold of him. This time, however, it seems I'm on my own. Oddly, I experience very little fear, and once the initial surprise has subsided, I somehow feel calm, as if I'd been expecting this conclusion all along, a conclusion located somewhere between fate and destiny. I'd always known, at the back of my mind, that she'd catch up with me sooner or later.

"If it's about the money, then I can get it back for you no problem," I tell her.

"It has nothing to do with the money," she snorts, with

derision.

"So what exactly do you want, apart from catching up on old times?"

"I want," she says, "vengeance."

I look from her to the gun, and repress an instinct to smile. This is ludicrous.

"What, with that?" I ask.

She widens her eyes, curls back her lips, and contorts her mouth into a grin normally found on the clinically insane. I can see teeth, tongue. Then she cocks the trigger, seemingly in preparation to pull, her sanity careening into freefall.

"Look," I say, "isn't there any other way we can sort this out?"

The waitress comes back over to us, and the gun is quickly hidden under the table.

"Can I get you people anything else?"

"No thank you," she says, before I have a chance to speak.

Bubblegum pops as she walks away.

From under the table, I hear the barrel of the gun spin. It is directed at my crotch. The old man with the teeth looks up, smiles at me, then goes back to his coffee.

"Let's play a game," she says, her pupils huge. "Russian Roulette. There are six bullets in here. Four blanks, two live. Good luck."

She chuckles insanely, and prepares to pull the trigger. I tense every muscle.

Click.

Click.

Nine months earlier...

One. Hospital Corners.

The staff nurse's eyes fixed on my trainers, slowly panned up my body, settled on my face, and gradually focused onto my gaze. She gave me a stare that spoke a thousand admonishing words, an unspoken message I nevertheless failed to comprehend.

"Off," she said, her lips thin and taut, bloodless.

"Sorry?" I asked, nervously.

"Feet," she repeated. "Off."

Sheepishly, I removed my feet from the bed, dusted the covers and, as if back in school, sat up straight on the plastic orange chair.

"She's a fine woman, that one," said Grandad. "Probably spent my last jism on that lass. Reminds me of your grandmother, she does, God rest her soul."

Grandad looked terrible. He'd been prostrate on this hospital bed for two months now. It seemed unlikely he would make it into a third. The doctors weren't even sure what was wrong with him exactly, except that he was old and was dying. His skin had turned yellow, while his bed sores blossomed purple and crimson before bursting in mini explosions of blood red on the faded white sheets beneath him. Saliva was forever making a slow descent down his chin before coagulating around his prominent Adam's Apple. He croaked when he spoke, and wheezed when he breathed, which seemed less and less of late. His once baby blue eyes had turned to grey and the smile had vanished from his face forever. He smelt musty, like stale cabbage, as if he were well past his sell-by date. Which, of course, he was.

It wasn't easy looking at Grandad like this. However grave his symptoms, however harsh the reality of mortality, I still had trouble accepting that he could just lie there looking so thoroughly pathetic, so savagely wasted. Even at 72. This was someone I had grown up with, who had rescued me from my mother at weekends, my only father figure, the man whose stories took me away from Peckham, from home and school, and into flights of fancy that may actually have had little basis in truth, but which filled me with the thrill of hope and wonder and the delicious prospect of possibility nevertheless. When Mother was still just a daughter, and he just her father, Grandad was a local celebrity. He'd boxed, so he told me, with Henry Cooper above a pub on the Old Kent Road. He'd made plans and carried out scams with Ronnie Biggs - would've been in on the Great Train Robbery, too, had he not come off his Norton and smashed his legs to bits in the preceding weeks. It was he who afforded then likely lad around town, Frankie Fraser, with the prefix 'Mad'. He was in with the Krays and had spent years campaigning for their release from prison, and had even purportedly bedded Barbara Windsor, both before and after the Carry On movies, even if, he said, fame had spoiled her by then. In his lifetime, he'd both made and lost a fortune several times over. He was the kind of man who could acquire money from thin air, as if from nowhere. On a Monday morning, he'd be practically destitute, watching his last few pounds fritter away as the 10.10 from Kempton took a fall at the final hurdle. But by Friday, the drinks were on him, and the new suit he'd be wearing was tailor made and fit like a second skin. He'd held down innumerable jobs in countless professions. He'd been a nightclub doorman, a hospital porter, a casino manager, a pub landlord, a debt collector. He'd owned a fleet of limousines and had driven a number fifty three bus. His last job was street sweeper which had taken him up to year sixty nine, four years past retirement age on account that the local council manager was rumoured to be one of his many bastard offspring. That said, however, he remained loyal (after a fashion) to Iris, his wife for forty seven years. I was never quite as close to her as I was to him, which was probably due in part to an irascible temper that rendered her practically incapable of smiling when scowling was a viable alternative. When she died, aged sixty two, over ten years ago now, the only emotion I can remember feeling was one of relief. Grandad was almost destroyed over her passing. He spent the day of her funeral threatening hara-kiri until, at the reception later that afternoon, he came to a mutual agreement with Mavis over the road - concerning matters never discussed with me - that promptly put the sparkle back in his eye, leaving him suddenly quite capable to cope with his recent loss.

In his later years, Grandad's mind seemed to wander a lot, but he still made excellent company, especially if I'd arrive at his doorstep with a packet of twenty and a bottle of his favourite malt whiskey, which I inevitably did. This last year, however, I'd almost ceased my visits altogether, mostly because I was busy assisting in the total collapse of my own life, which seemed to take a lot of my time.

Now that he's in here and I'm sitting before him feeling awkward, the guilt is slicing right through me. I apologize constantly for not visiting him lately but all he does is pat my hand and tell me not to worry, that he understands, and that he's fine, just dandy. "I still remember what it feels like to be young," he says, attempting, in vain, to force his long flat mouth into a crescent smile. I just blush and fight back the tears.

As if to compensate, I've been here, by his bedside, an hour a day for the past two weeks solid. Mother has popped in on occasion, a feat in itself and worthy of some celebration, but otherwise, I'm his only visitor. I listen to his repeated stories, and make up some of my own, but mostly I watch him drift between sleep and semi-consciousness. Every time he mutters his late wife's name - "Iris? That you, Iris?" - my eyes well up and I have to turn away, taking long measured breaths, and look instead out the window, at the passing tube trains, the building opposite dressed up with scaffolding, the brick wall infested with weeds and graffiti, the grey sky up above, and the dark clouds fat with raindrops choosing their moment to open up. Then, shortly after the nurse's rounds, during which time she deposits a white pill into Grandad's mouth, and strokes his cheek the way she would a child's, I bid him farewell and take my leave, feeling an instant relief as I step back out into the real world, the living world.

Then, one day, I arrive at my usual time to see Grandad sitting up in bed, his face beaming as he sees me approach.

"Ah, there you are at last, my lad!" He ruffles my hair, something he hasn't done for at least seven years, and I sit beside him, my young hand holding his arthritic, liver-spotted one.

"Come closer," he says, beckoning me. "Closer."

He still sounds weak, and looks just as frail, but there is something in his eyes that suggests in a parallel world, Grandad is up and about, dancing, frolicking.

"It's time, son," he says, and I look at my watch.

"Um, 2.30, Grandad."

"No, you fool. It's time."

"That's nice, Grandad, that's just fine."

My eyes scan the room and I see other decrepit patients with members of their own family huddled around the narrow NHS beds. Everyone looks either concerned or bored, occasionally both.

Outside, the rain has broken earlier than yesterday. Grandad suddenly has another of his coughing fits and I jump to my feet, whip out several Kleenex tissues from the box on his bedside table, and wipe away the sticky green phlegm from his pyjamas.

"That's it!" I say, and I reach a hand down beneath the bed covers, under his pyjama bottoms, brushing against his sores, and retrieve a packet of Silk Cut. Only three cigarettes remain. "These are coming with me. This is the last packet I'll ever buy for you. I mean it this time."

Grandad ignores this and starts to speak, his voice reedy, growing weaker.

"Listen to me, boy. I haven't much time left."

He pulls me towards him with his skeletal claw and whispers in my ear, showering spit into the lobe. Only respect stops me from pulling away and balking. I listen intently. Then, as instructed, I turn to retrieve his holdall, which is stuffed deep down in the bedside table, and give it to him. He opens one zip slowly, then another, then another still. His lips are moving as if he is talking to himself. Presently, he lets out a sigh of relief, clutches something tight into his right hand, and tells me to put the bag back. I obey.

"Now," he says. "Come closer." He spits some more into my ear.

"The allotment," he says.

"What about it?" I say.

He wheezes violently. "Lad," he says, straining, "shut up and listen to what I'm about to tell you. It's important. Go to the allotment. Inside the shed, in the left-hand corner at the back, behind the mower, the spades, the shovel, the pick axe, underneath the tool box, the stack of magazines and the football programmes, there is a concrete slab." He wheezes more and I strain to pull away so I can peer into his eyes, just to see if he is dying or not, but his grip on my shirt collar is vice-tight. "Lift up the concrete slab and you'll find a trap door. It's heavy, mind, so lift it with care, slowly, like. Underneath that is a box. A metal box, briefcase-sized. That box, son, is yours. Understand.?"

My brow frowns. "I suppose, yes."

"But you're not to say anything about it to no one. Not ever. Keep your mouth shut, be wise, be clever. Anyone ever asks you any questions about it, you're to play dumb which, no offence, shouldn't be too hard for you. And don't, whatever you do, tell your mother, or that brother of yours. Keep schtum. Never talk ill of the dead and go enjoy yourself. Don't be like your father, son. Use the

box, think of me."

He lets go of me, wheezing slowly like a flat tire. His eyelids

flicker. He murmurs, groans, and turns a deathly white as he sinks

back into the pillow. Tears stream down my face, and I'm about to

scream for the nurse when suddenly he opens his eyes wide.

They're very bright indeed.

Slowly, he extends a clenched fist towards me. "Open your

hand," he says, croaking.

I open my hand and reach over until it's directly underneath

his. He opens his fist and a small metal object drops into my palm.

A key, rusty, slightly bent. I look up, a quizzical expression on my

face.

"Use the box, think of me."

The bell goes and it's time for me to leave. I lean over and

kiss Grandad on the forehead and tell him to take care, that I'll see

him tomorrow. He murmurs an unintelligible reply. When I reach the

swing doors at the end of the ward, I turn and squint through my

glasses. Grandad is smiling widely at me, his head raised above the

pillow, his blue eyes bluer than I can ever remember.

I offer him a half wave, turn on my heel, and am gone.

At 7.12pm that evening, so too is he.

Me, up until this point.

"Hi, hey, not busy are we? Great, super. Fancy a game of Monopoly? Got the board here, see, so how about it? Monopoly, I mean! Tee hee!"

She sits down on my bedroom floor, crosses her legs, and makes vague allusions to her knickers, which are white, lacy, and tight, and which her short skirt is making a poor job of concealing.

"You can be the iron," she says, giggling. "You're a New Man, after all. I'll be the top hat, yes?"

It is a typical weekday afternoon. The agency has failed yet again to make my telephone ring. Consequently I have no job to go to, and nothing to do. Nothing to do, that is, except play Monopoly with Katkin. Katkin is five feet five inches short, with bobbed blonde hair, chocolate brown eyes, chubby cheeks, and a permanent electric glow. She has brought tea and biscuits and, before long, she has bought Pall Mall and Park Lane to my Old Kent Road and Lambeth. She is winning, as she always does. As much as I loathe her presence, her perkiness, I secretly lap up the attention and admit to more than a passing attraction for both her and her white and lacy knickers, and for what lies beneath. It is a temptation, however, I am adamant to resist.

Two and three quarter hours later. The sun is now setting, a lamp has been switched on.

"I win! I win!"

I, meanwhile, feel a wave of relief. I can sense my impending freedom.

"Wait there! Don't move a muscle!"

Katkin rushes out of the room, Monopoly stuffed under her arm, leaving me sitting there alone nursing my backache. I'm gripped with fear. The don't move a muscle directive suggests her return is imminent. I half expect her to walk back in wearing something more comfortable, and I try to imagine whether I will finally consent to her intended seduction. Such optimistic contemplation, however, proves to be entirely in vain as she returns some moments later, now proffering Scrabble.

"You're good with words," she teases. "Maybe you'll have better luck with this."

More hours pass. Eventually, nighttime falls, preceded by

another interminable afternoon and a torturously long evening.

"Hard luck," she says, at the game's conclusion. "I must say I was very lucky. Oxymoron was the most amazing word I've ever had. And double word score, too! What about Snap?"

"No, really. Thanks, but my back is killing me. I need to rest."

I am stripped naked to the waist, lying flat on my stomach, my face nestling into the shagpile. From somewhere north, Katkin's hands are kneading my bare back like dough. Despite earlier protestations, it is admittedly a glorious sensation. If I crane my neck around a little further, I can see that Katkin, who is sitting on my bottom, has pulled her mini skirt up around her waist, and is therefore positioned on my jeans with only her knickers for protection. Try as I might to stem the craving, I am more than a little aroused by this. My groin leaves its imprint in the carpet.

But I'm destined for yet another cold shower, it seems, as from somewhere downstairs, a door suddenly slams shut.

"That must be Mummy!" squeals Katkin. "See you tomorrow." And off she trots.

Frustrated, yet also relieved, I roll onto my back, sigh theatrically, feel my erection wane, and stare up at the ceiling.

Mummy.

Katkin's Mummy, a fiftysomething insurance clerk possessed of a permanently glum disposition who I know only as Ms Crombie, is my landlady. I live on the top floor of her three-storey semi in Shepherd's Bush, in a small room that's badly decorated and poorly furnished with items that probably were all the rage twenty years ago. I've done little to assert my own identity here, realizing that it isn't, nor will it ever be, a proper home to me. I have, however, created a micro kitchen in one corner, consisting of a kettle, toaster, a coffee mug, two plates, and a tin opener, which means I don't have to suffer mealtimes in the company of people I'd really rather not have to interact with. I have lived here thirteen months, in abject misery. There is another tenant, a thirty-year-old Moroccan man called Jaz, who preceded my arrival here by three weeks, and who has yet to utter a single word in my direction, friendly or otherwise. The rent is sixty-five pounds a week, a sum I can never quite afford without sacrifice. Katkin is a fairly recent addition to the household, a university student who, upon graduation, returned to London to seek gainful employment, and moved back in with her mother largely as an excuse to break up with Simon, her longstanding student boyfriend, and lay herself open to new experiences. Hence her vague interest in me, which as yet has amounted to nothing more than playful teasing. (She has so far expressed a distinct lack of interest in Jaz. "Not that I'm racist or anything," I have heard her tell the telephone. "Just that I'm afraid of the unfamiliar.") Katkin's half-hearted wooing of me takes place usually during daylight hours, and roughly twice a week. The rest of the time, she's out job-hunting or meeting up with friends while steadfastly avoiding Simon, before usually caving in and inviting him to stay on alternate weekends.

I, incidentally, am twenty-five, and my name's Jake. I've the kind of surname that either elicits confusion or raucous laughter, so I employ it as infrequently as possible. Honesty propels me to describe myself as something of a loner. I wear glasses, read paperbacks, am more at home in cafes than pubs, have few friends, and have yet to hold down a full-time job since dropping out of college four years earlier. In those four years, however, I've had even more temporary jobs than my late grandfather. I've worked in offices and warehouses. I've answered phones and delivered mail. I've sold encyclopedias at suburban shopping centres and kitchen utensils door-to-door. I've worked on market stalls selling fruit and vegetables, records, and underwear. I've delivered newspapers and cleaned swimming pools. I've been a motorbike courier and, for one summer, a flu carrier (for research, for money). I've donated blood for my overdraft and sperm for fun. I've been sacked, let go, made unemployed, promoted (once), and I've walked out so many times that I've lost count. My extra-curricular activities include a fondness for music, books and films, but I haven't really got anyone to share these enthusiasms with, despite my general affability and GSOH. As a result, I fear that my tastes in the aforementioned may be rather mainstream and not particularly in touch with those of a similar age and outlook. This is something that causes me trouble. In attempt to compensate for my lack of acquaintances, I write incessantly in notepads, filling page after page with reviews and thoughts and musings which reveal, I feel, a sharp mind just waiting to be properly taxed in life.

And so it is that I pass my time slowly, frustratingly, simultaneously fending off Katkin while desiring her incessantly. Which brings me, somewhat reluctantly, to the subject of girls. I haven't had one for some time, though this is of course a situation

I would dearly love to remedy.

My father, if sources are to be believed, is inside somewhere, serving three-to-five years for various insurance scams, his lifelong pursuit for riches still failing badly. I haven't seen him since puberty, so his incarceration doesn't unduly concern me. My mother, after nurturing me throughout adolescence in a manner that has left me in touch with my feminine side (or so I'm reliably informed), had something of a nervous breakdown a few years ago and, upon recovery, immediately became obsessed with finding herself another husband and starting her life anew, an activity which means she goes through a succession of ill-suited boyfriends with shocking speed. My older brother Tom, meanwhile, who may well be the devil incarnate, works in computers in the city and goes through two tubes of hair gel, at least ten Cuban cigars, and several blonde girlfriends a month. Aside from Christmas and the occasional birthday, I keep interaction with the family down to a bare minimum.

*

It is another weekday evening, it could be any one of seven. A television soap opera is fading into the background on my portable television set as Katkin bursts, unannounced, into my room, an inane grin on her face, with a nose as rosy as her mother's.

"Hi, Jake," she says, draping her arms around my neck, clearly under the influence of the sherry which resides in a corner of the dining room. "Mummy's tucked up in bed," she informs, hiccuping. "Not feeling too well. But not to worry, she'll be fine in the morning. Anyway, I've a backgammon game downstairs awaiting a re-start. Fancy it? I'll be lenient, promise!"

Katkin careens out of my room, and before I can check myself, I find I'm following her downstairs, switching off the light as I go and pulling the door to.

Three. Grave Misgivings.

Anyway, Grandad's key.

I hadn't visited Grandad's allotment in at least five years,
maybe longer. But back in my childhood, I'd meet him there every
Saturday morning where, among other things, he introduced me to
Bovril, and to pornography.

"Get your laughing gear round that," he'd say, handing me
this month's Razzle, while my hands clutched a mug of thick,
steaming black liquid that smelled like Marmite and tasted even
worse.

The allotment was a tiny rectangle of churned soil that nestled
around a thousand others on a site about half a mile east of
Peckham Rye park, behind an old peoples' home and underneath the
railway line. Although small, he'd organized it meticulously and had
divided it up into four separate squares. Upon the first, he had
planted daffodils which, when in bloom, he'd sell to men in pubs
suddenly desperate for last minute presents or peace offerings to
the women they'd left at home. Upon the second, he grew
cauliflower, the third lettuce, and the fourth a combination of irises

and roses. Around the perimeter was some shabbily erected netting entwined with barbwire to keep out, he said, foxes and rabbits - who subsequently had little trouble in either jumping over the two-foot frame or burrowing underneath. As insignificant as this minuscule plot of land was, it was nevertheless the old man's pride and joy, a place to come for solace, for contemplation, for a proximity to nature.

The shed, meanwhile, was a ramshackle palace of magnificent clutter, with a small doorway and two square windows so caked in dirt and dust and mud that sunlight had been unable to penetrate within for several decades. And outside the shed's door sat two colourless deck chairs, one more horizontal than the other due to a design fault, upon which we'd park ourselves for much of every Saturday, under Peckham's slate-grey sky. If it rained, we put up umbrellas. We were immovable in ritual.

Thursday afternoons was when I would start to get excited about my imminent visit. Quite why I'm not entirely sure. I've never possessed green fingers, nor do I have a particular affinity for plantlife. But I viewed my Saturdays spent there in my grandfather's small garden as liberation from all my weekly anxieties, anxieties brought on by the ritualistic bullying and evil mind games exerted upon me by my older brother, and my perennial inability to truly mix at school. The teachers saw me as something of a disappointment when I quickly proved myself incapable of living up to Tom's scholastic excellence, while my peers seemed to regard me as curiously unappealing, either in the classroom, on the football pitch, in gangs, or as potential date material. One afternoon in the third year, on a glorious Spring afternoon, we had a class photograph. After almost thirty minutes of being arranged and preened for the camera, everybody huddled together for the collective cry of cheese! Somehow, I ended up separated from the rest, standing a little to the left, looking in the wrong direction, mildly upset.

Come the weekend, however, I was the star attraction around the allotments, where Grandad and his similarly grizzled cronies haggled to show me their bulbs, buds, sprouting stems, and blossoming blooms, me feigning an interest which betrayed a seemingly genuine respect for my elders. When all horticultural topics had mercifully fizzled out, the old men would then lecture me on the infinite wonders of smoking, prodding me with their tobacco tins, encouraging me to help myself, clambering to offer me a light.

On average, I'd go through fifteen cigarettes in a day, and in the evening would have the cough to prove it. After a packed lunch of corned beef sandwiches and yet more cups of Bovril, Grandad and I would settle down on the deck chairs alone, and he'd begin to regale me with stories from his past, most of which would inevitably come down to his myriad sexual liaisons with women from every corner of the world, all of whom had somehow found themselves astray in a dank Peckham pub (for Grandad had never travelled further south than Dover in his entire life). By mid-afternoon, the hip flask would come out and he'd start talking about his life of crime, the money he'd made and lost, the heists he was currently planning. And then, later, as the whiskey began to take effect, his eyelids lowering, his words slurred, he would drum into me his Ten Steps To Proper Manhood.

One. Make them beg. Never give yourself too freely to a woman. Always make sure it's her what does the chasing.

Two. Never remain faithful to a wife in the biblical sense. Sex with the same partner is, by definition, as boring as bowls after the three month honeymoon period, so play the field, dip your wick, bag as many birds as you can. A good wife will stick by you all the same, and she's good to have around the house when you're hungry or need someone to sound off on.

Three. Be strong. Never back down from confrontation. Anyone what gives you the stare, deck them quick. Get in there with the first punch. Aim for the throat.

Four. Or, if the bastard's bigger than you, run like the clappers. Unless you've got a gun, of course. If you've got a gun, it don't matter his size. Just pull the trigger. Then run.

Five. Always remain faithful to your friends. A friend in need is a friend indeed. Especially round this manor.

Six. Don't turn into a poofter. Ain't natural.

Seven. That said, give anal a go - with a woman, mind. You may be pleasantly surprised.

Eight. If you can't afford it, steal it.

Nine.

Ten.

This little speech of his was first recited to me upon my twelfth birthday, which fell on a Saturday, and was regularly repeated thereafter. He'd even get me to say them back to him to prove I was taking it all in, and to emphasize just how important they were to

a successful, fruitful life. But he never once managed to get past

eight. Either sleep would steal him away, or one of his friends would

saunter over and interrupt us. At first I thought he was saving

Nine and Ten because they were the best, most important points and

he only wanted to disclose them when he felt me good and ready,

but after the first few years, I began to doubt their very existence

in the first place.

*

The phone call came early the next morning, shortly before nine.

Apparently, they'd tried my mother several times the night

before, but were unable to get through.

"Hello?"

A voice at the other end asked me if I was me.

"I am."

"I'm afraid I've rather bad news."

I was told that my grandfather had passed away yesterday

evening, just after dinner, which he had apparently consumed with great gusto. He appeared happier, they said, than he'd been since his admission. He had mentioned to the man in the next bed that his last transaction had been completed and that he was now ready at last. Around seven o'clock, he lay down and slowly drifted into sleep. He looked peaceful. He didn't suffer. At 7.12pm he expired his last breath.

"His last words?" I ventured, my voice a whisper.

"Hold on, I've written them down somewhere," said the nurse. "Here they are. They may not make any sense, I'm afraid. He said, 'It was mine short, mine to do with as I will. Mine, not yours short.'

"Right, I see. Thank you."

I replaced the receiver and went back upstairs to bed, where I lay for some time, staring up at the ceiling. I shed very few tears, having prepared myself well for this inevitable conclusion. Instead, I felt strangely peaceful, as I'm sure Grandad did the night before. He had died in his sleep, a smile on his face, content in the knowledge that his good lady wife was waiting for him on the other side, as foolishly faithful as ever.

There were many things now to be done, arrangements to be made. I'd have to notify Mother, contact an undertaker, get the ball rolling. I had no idea where to begin, however, so I just lay on the bed, very still, not moving, not blinking.

*

I rose a little after one in the afternoon, padded slowly downstairs, hoping not to run into Katkin. I was feeling tired and drained, in no mood for any board games whatsoever. Fortunately, Katkin wasn't in the kitchen, but Jaz was. He looked up as I entered, our eyes briefly meeting, and he quickly looked away. "Hello," I said into the silence, and waited, pessimistically, for an echo, a response, but none came. Jaz was eating lunch, which consisted of kidney beans on brown toast and an exotic-looking salad that contained many green things that I didn't know the name of. He was drinking a bright yellow energy drink of his own concoction. Again it struck me just how little I knew my flatmate.

Upon opening the fridge, my heart sank in the realization that I hadn't been shopping in over a week. On my shelf sat one jar of pickled onions, a half-eaten Scotch egg, and an unwrapped pork pie which could well have passed its sell-by date. Jaz's shelf in comparison was stuffed to capacity, its contents looking much like Holland & Barrett. I took out my morsels, found a clean plate, and set my lunch upon it. I sat opposite Jaz and began to eat. Occasionally, I'd grunt or look up at him or try some other vague attempt at communication, but each fell on deaf ears. Jaz was consumed by his food, engrossed in the tangle of spidery leaves, the yolk-coloured drink. He chewed with his eyes shut and his mouth open, so I did similar. Again, he registered nothing, and so I gave up.

The Scotch egg had a violent vinegary taste, and so to disguise it, I accompanied each mouthful with a large gulp of water, and swallowed everything whole, without chewing. The pork pie, meanwhile, had hardened in its wrapperless state, and so I was forced to masticate like a cow, grinding it down with my teeth until I felt able to swallow. The pickled onions made me burp, until one particularly voluptuous example went down the wrong way and left me choking, attempting to fold my arms origami-style behind my back in order to thump it free. Tears sprang from my eyes, my face flushed red. Jaz glanced up at me, a look of scorn in his eye, and began clearing away his plate in haste. He then stalked out the room, leaving me alone.

Back upstairs, I placed Grandad's key inside a Kleenex tissue, wrapped it up carefully into a tiny little bundle, and placed it deep into the front pocket of my jeans. Searching the sofa and the floor underneath the bed for any remaining coins, I eventually came up with sufficient bus fare, and began to prepare myself for an odyssey south of the river. I wondered whether I could remember the route. It had been some time since my last visit.

At Shepherd's Bush Green, I awaited the 94 bus with a strange sense of exhilaration. What would the key lead me to? I wondered. My initial suspicions were that a stack of vintage pornographic magazines were awaiting me, suggesting that my grandfather still thought of me as a wanker, albeit a grown-up one. But his final words to me still rang in my head. Use the box, think of me. Keep schtum. Make something of yourself. I drew a blank, but mounted the bus with the kind of excitement I've not experienced since childhood, when I still believed, no matter how improbable, that Father Christmas worked his way down our chimney in the dead of night once a year to leave presents in a stocking at the foot of my bed. We never had a chimney.

The bus journey was torturously slow, weaving through London's afternoon traffic at a snail's pace. By the time we reached Westminster Bridge, I'd changed buses and was now sandwiched between two number 12's, a convoy in frozen motion. Once successfully over the bridge, I was back south of the river and it all came quickly flooding back to me. The grey roads, the crumbling rows of identical narrow houses, Elephant & Castle's idiotic shopping centre, daubed a shocking electric pink, and the maze of ugly back streets that make up Peckham's inglorious facade.

As soon as I disembarked, the heavens opened and rain poured. Within seconds, I was soaked. I walked around the park's interminable perimeter, crossed over two estates, and managed to find the old peoples' home, confirming I was on the right track. Then, into the alleyway that took me under the railway bridge until finally, I'd arrived, drenched through to the skin, shivering.

Every allotment was deserted, unsurprisingly since the weather had turned so adverse so quick. I walked passed countless mini plots of land, passed endless rows of inner-city vegetation, wilting flowers, and a huge array of willfully unruly weeds which paid little heed to where one plot finished and another began.

And then I found it. My dead grandfather's plot, his minuscule

pride and joy. The weeds here were now approximately two feet high

and were scattered over all four squares. The shed leaned towards

the left, looking as if collapse were imminent. The deck chairs were

in a heap in front of it. The rainfall increased, slanting horizontally.

I approached the door with extreme caution, unable to quell the

feeling that I was trespassing and that my furtive footsteps would

result in the nearest witness punching 999 into the nearest phone

box forthwith.

And then I discovered a major setback. The shed door was

bolted shut with a huge rusty padlock, for which the delicate key

in my pocket offered little solution. I cradled the lock in the palm

of my hand, its heavy weight depressing and somehow very

emphatic. Why on earth hadn't the old man given me a second key?

To come all this way, with hope and anticipation practically

constricting my breathing, only to be obstructed now - and in the

pouring rain - seemed doubly cruel. My fists curled up in anger, I

raised one and banged on the door hard, creating an instant bruise

that would cause me pain for several weeks to come.

And then, a very funny thing happened. The door creaked,

and slowly, very slowly, tilted backwards, then began to fall, the hinges disintegrating into dust, the nails freefalling through the air. The door hit the ground with a dull thud and, quickly checking that no one was watching, I dipped inside, into its dark, dank lair.

The torch, mercifully, still hung in its usual place, and while the batteries were clearly failing, it did afford me a meagre beam. Initially, all it picked up were striplights of dust; everything else remained cloaked in a midnight gloom. The smell was fetid, stale, elderly. I couldn't put a single step forward without dislodging something, sending one or other rusting implement crashing to the ground. But, powered on with an extreme sense of urgent anticipation and nervous energy, I haphazardly made my way over to the left-hand corner. On the shelf above, I found three candles and a box of matches which lit, despite the damp, first time. I removed the tools, the boxes, the yellowing newspapers and magazines, the rubbish. A rat suddenly darted out from the abyss, sending my heartrate instantly careening towards cardiac arrest. Composing myself for a good ten minutes, I then resumed my work until I eventually cleared the area of all its abundant clutter.

I blew hard and shut my eyes as a carpet of dust lifted from the floor and floated in the artificial light. I felt for the concrete

slab, found it, and attempted to move it. Just as the old man had

forewarned, it was a dead weight. Unable actually to lift it, I

dragged it towards me instead, then off to one side. I pulled open

the stiff trap door wide enough until I could see below. And there,

sitting in the torch's faltering glow, was the metal box, slightly

smaller than your average briefcase, its many dents and scratches

bearing the passage of time. I crouched down, reached into this

secret storeroom, and grabbed hold of it with both hands, pulling

it up and out. My heart, was racing, thudding rhythmically in my

temples. Sitting on an old pile of Razzles, I positioned the box on my

lap, removed the key from my pocket, unwrapped it, and, aware that

I was applying as much mental drama to this as I could, slid the

key into the lock. It fit perfectly. But nothing happened. The lock

wasn't catching. I tried again, then again. Then, getting desperate,

I removed the key, brought up some phlegm, and spat into the lock,

hoping it would act as a lubricant. Rather surprisingly, it did.

There was a clicking sound. Then, as I pulled it open, it

buckled and made a loud pop! I used a little more force until,

finally, the box, my grandfather's dying gift to his favourite grandson, was wide open.

In slow motion, I lowered my gaze, and peered in.

I next started to tremble, to shake. I put the box aside, ran

to the door to check that no one was about, that no one would

suddenly intrude, and ran back to it to contemplate the contents.

The box was filled with banknotes of every denomination. They

were not bunched together, nor arraged and stacked neatly like in

briefcases in the movies, but stuffed in carelessly, any which way,

as if in extreme haste. My eyes floated dreamily, heavy with

disbelief, over ten, twenty, and fifty pound notes. There seemed to

be hundreds of them. Some had been scrunched up like discarded

tissue, others were ripped, almost torn in half. But it was money

nevertheless, and it was very probably dirty money. But from where

exactly? Grandad's well-worn tales of his connections with gangland

London had about as much truth to them as a fable, or so I always

thought. A win on the horses, perhaps? A very big win? Or did the

evidence now before me lend an immediate, and belated, veracity to

his lifelong tall tales? Perhaps he really had been criminally active,

as he'd always claimed? I was dumbfounded, had difficulty

breathing. Tears welled in my eyes, and butterflies performed intricate dance rituals within my stomach. The torchlight kept flickering on and off, and I had to shake it hard to maintain a semi-steady beam.

Suddenly, I felt panic bolt right through me. I needed to get out, to flee the scene. The rain continued to pour outside so, with the box jammed tightly under my arm, I ran through the allotments and the various alleyways at breakneck speed, until I reached the main road where, with a flourish of sudden impetuosity, I hailed a black cab, and sank back into the expansive upholstery, my legs stretched out before me, feeling deliriously light-headed, and not quite sane.

"My first time in a cab," I told the driver, giggling foolishly.

"You don't say," said the boil on the back of his neck.

Four. The Art Of Acquisition.

(i)

"And this, sir, as you can see, is the bedroom, complete with en suite bathroom. Power shower, sunken tub, bidet, and coral tiles for that underwater effect. And here, just take a look at that view. That green you can see is Holland Park, while over here, if you'll permit me to lead you towards the window in the lounge, is the Portobello Road. There's a lovely market here Saturdays, very popular with the tourists. I'm sure you'll agree it's a lovely place and, more importantly, its location is to die for. Convenient for the underground, the buses, there's more restaurants here than you could ever possibly visit, and it's positively teeming with famous people. A highly desirable neighbourhood, sir. What's that? Oh, yes, yes sir. It's available immediately."

I took it and moved in tout de suite.

(ii)

It had been an active few weeks. My life quickly transformed beyond all recognition. My grandfather's bequeath was put to instant - and exceedingly good - use. I became a changed man.

When the taxi dropped me off in Shepherd's Bush that first evening, I rushed up to my room, closed the door, and began to count the money. I estimated thousands, maybe even in excess of ten. But it proved an even greater sum than that. After repeated calculations, by which time I was surrounded by piles and piles of cash, I reached a grand total. I was now in the possession of œ142,750, in what I gathered were untraceable notes. It was therefore mine to keep, to spend as I saw fit, with no comeback from anyone either living or dead. If I played my cards right and, as my late relative suggested, kept schtum, I could now begin the process of getting my life on track, acquiring myself a purpose, a direction. While I didn't for a second regard money as the solution to all problems, I also wasn't one of those people convinced of its inability to bring happiness. Right there in my squalid little bedroom - which I was very soon to move out of into something far grander - I had never been happier, and that was as a direct result of all that filthy lucre. And this was just the beginning. I could use this cash to buy things, go places, do stuff. I could afford anything I wanted, within reason - and my life has always been dictated by reason.

Therefore, I limited my immediate celebrations to a Chinese takeaway and a bottle of wine, which I polished off alone while watching a travel programme on the television. At one stage, Katkin knocked hard upon my door, asking whether I fancied a game of Cluedo. I replied in the negative, telling her I needed time to myself to mourn a death in the family. She was surprisingly understanding, and left me to my devices. I fell asleep sometime after two, slightly drunk, on an eiderdown of banknotes, the Queen's face staring impassively at me from every conceivable angle.

The next day, I got to work.

First thing, I put in a call to Letitia at the job agency and told her to take my name off the list, as I would no longer be requiring employment. Oh, why? she enquired. Because I've won the lottery, I told her. She laughed. Whateveryousay, she replied quickly before offering a singsong goodbye and replacing the receiver.

Next, I telephoned my mother to alert her to her father's death. She didn't appear to be in, so I hung up and called Tom instead. Tom's PA told me that he was in a meeting and not to be disturbed. I told her of the gravity of the situation, and got his

VoiceMail. In a burst of vocal gunfire, I told him of the death and

asked whether he could contact mother and then make arrangements

for the funeral, as I neither had the means nor the strength to do

so myself. I told him to return my call if he so wished, but if he

was too busy, then I perfectly understood. I started to tell him

something else, but a piercing beep alerted me to the fact that I

had been cut off.

Then I bounded enthusiastically upstairs, passing Jaz on my

ascent, to my bedroom where I dressed in my least impoverished

clothes, applied a comb to my hair, and made preparations to go out.

I called a mini cab firm and booked a taxi for fifteen minutes hence.

Almost an hour later, it finally arrived and transported me, at an

excruciatingly slow twenty miles per hour, to my local building

society where I opened an account which I seem to remember was

called Liquid Gold For The Filthy Rich. At first, the Deputy Manager,

who I encountered in an office the size of a small cubicle, appeared

wary of my box full of money, but once I'd proved my grandfather's

recent death and informed him that my late relative had a deep

mistrust of banks - hence the readies - we were able to proceed. I thanked him and offered my most sincere smile. He said, "Build a better future with The Halifax, where the customer is always a priority." I noticed flecks of scrambled eggs in his moustache.

Next, I proceeded up into Notting Hill, threw another bundle of cash into the bank, thereby widening my debit and credits options, then endeavoured to visit every estate agent until I found my dream apartment.

This proved slightly harder than I had at first anticipated.

(iii)

My first day of proper flat-hunting had led me to one very emphatic conclusion. All estate agents are cunts. While generalizing can, in the main, be a prejudiced and dangerous thing, each one I encountered was a virtual facsimile of the one before. Each was outstandingly rude, unfailingly arrogant, publicly-schooled, pompous, condescending, oily. I would walk into their offices, gliding gently upon plush carpets, feeling happy, radiating positivity. But in the time it took them to look up from their leather Filofaxes and down their noses at me, I was suddenly shrunk to dwarf proportions, feeling wholly insignificant, utterly unworthy.

"Ah, yes, sir. And how may I help you?"

"I'd like to rent a flat, one bedroom, around here, please."

"Would sir perhaps like to look at our brochure first?"

"Actually, I'd rather see some flats immediately, if possible."

"I only suggest this, sir, because our properties tend to be rather select."

"What do you mean?"

Typically, around this point in our discourse, a telephone would ring, the caller taking immediate precedence over me. So I would sit and wait patiently while my agent fawned over a more desirable client or, far more likely, their partners, who appeared to call solely to reiterate plans for drinking Pimms in Chelsea later that evening. Presently, my agent would look up at me and smile helplessly with an exaggerated shrug, but make no noticeable effort to end the conversation and turn their attentions back to me. So I waited.

"I'm awfully sorry about that. Now, where were we?"

"Select."

"Select, right. Yes, our properties tend to be rather expensive.

We rent out only the finest Notting Hill properties."

"Yes, and I'd like one please."

"May I ask whether you're a student?"

"You may."

"And are you?"

"No, I'm not."

"Oh. What is your profession?"

"Actually, I'm currently between jobs."

The already dim light in the eye dies. "Right, I see. And how much can you stretch to a week, rent-wise?"

"Well, what's the going rate?"

"I really think sir should take away our brochure. If any of our properties appeal to you and are within your financial boundaries, then do give me a call on the old telephone. Otherwise..."

"Look, I can afford the going rate."

The estate agent would then frown, pull a face that betrayed a growing frustration, and sigh theatrically. "If sir doesn't mind, we really are rather busy at the moment."

So at the next place I visited, I adopted a different approach.

I walked in stridently, gliding once more upon plush carpet, and sat before a heavily made-up woman whom I judged to be in her early forties.

"Hello," I said.

"Good afternoon. How may I help you?"

"I'd like to rent a flat, one-bedroom, around here, please."

"May I ask if you are a student?"

To this I offered no vocal reply. Instead, I reached into my pocket and brought out my account book, opened it at page one, and held it in front of her nose. My index finger pointed at the column marked Balance. Then I said, "I'd like to rent a flat, one-bedroom, around here, please."

Her face lit up like electricity, her foundation cracked, emitting a small explosion of dust. "Yes sir, of course, sir." She reached for a colour brochure. "We'll start with these, yes? Come, my car is just around the corner."

(iv)

My new address was located midway between Portobello Road and Holland Park. My neighbours were lithe young people who earned their money acting on the big screen or writing songs which they later played before thousands of people a night. Every restaurant window possessed an instantly familiar face, and the local 7-11 employees often found themselves in the presence of greatness at the confectionery counter late at night, the time when the munchies hit. The flat was exquisite, a top-floor, two-level place delicately furnished with designer items, while the walls were home to various works of art from up-and-coming local artists. Everything was fitted for convenience, comfort was paramount to the design, and the view at either end was delightful. A series of discreet lamps enabled me to control the atmosphere with a flick of a switch, while various complicated cooking apparatus allowed me to do similar with food in the kitchen. The sofa was a vast ocean of leather, the TV screen cinema-sized, and various ingeniously-placed speakers meant that I could listen to music in magical surround-sound in any room I set foot in. The owner, who is currently on an eight-month work transfer in the Far East, has exquisite taste. I silently applauded him for his faultless sense in interior design. The weekly rent was extravagant by anyone's standards, and the figure would put pressure on my lump sum in time. But for now, I intended to spoil myself, to initiate myself in the ways of financial opportunity, so the flat was, temporarily, perfect for me, home.

It's a shame I was unable to show the place off properly, for I felt very house proud.

(v)

Next, wary of my lack of fashion sense, I decided to spruce up my wardrobe and sent off an application form to a daytime television programme in which contestants are given a makeover. My hopes of success weren't particularly high as this show was very popular among the unemployed, househusbands, and the elderly, and I wa sure that if I didn't get rejected immediately, then I'd be placed on a lengthy waiting list. But, bizarrely, success appeared to side with me as, a mere week later, I received a call on my new mobile phone informing me that the old lady booked in for tomorrow's programme had suffered a stroke and therefore they needed to fill the position quick. They asked if I could come up to their Birmingham studio the following day for the recording; it would be screened two weeks later.

And so up I went, first class carriage at the television company's expense, and came back a new man.

Despite initial reservations to the contrary, they proved to be lovely people. I arrived feeling much like one does when already strapped into a rollercoaster before experiencing grave doubts about just what they've let themselves in for. As soon as I was ushered into the inner sanctum and introduced to various people whose names I didn't catch, I wanted to turn and flee. This, I feared, was a terrible mistake. Having never previously appeared on television, the prospect of making my debut performance on daytime TV seemed colossal, insurmountable, plain idiotic. I would clearly be rendered a fool, a laughing stock to all those who knew me.

Stuttering my hellos, I quickly made excuses about a sudden overwhelming need for the bathroom, and rushed out into the corridor, from where I fully intended to find the nearest fire exit. Instead, I ran straight into an attractive young woman wearing oversized headphones, bouncy Nike trainers, and some kind of two-way walkie-talkie attached to a chunky leather belt.

"Good God, love," she said, "you look like you've seen a ghost."

With little heed for etiquette, I blurted out the reasons for my current state peppered with panicked expletives, to which she laughed throatily.

"Just calm down," she said, maternally. "You'll be fine, I promise. Here, have some of this."

From one of the many zipped pockets of her jacket, she produced a small square wrap of tracing paper. Cool as ice, she unfolded it, licked her middle finger and rolled it around in the modest pile of white powder. Then she pushed her finger into my mouth, between my taut lips which acceded helplessly, and rubbed the stuff on my virgin gums. She then used the same finger to apply more of the same into her mouth. Within seconds, my brain was trampolining in my skull, my eyeballs stretching their sockets. I stood there and gawped at her for several moments, this beautiful, kind woman, with an inane grin on my face, until the activity inside my head levelled out to a pleasing rush, like a battery-operated buzz.

The girl smiled profusely. "There," she said. "You'll enjoy yourself now. Ciao."

The studio lights were hot, boiling. I was talked through my requirements over the next forty-five minutes, told what to expect, what to do. I shook hands with the hairstylists and makeover folk, all of whom appeared radiant to my sparkling eyes. I exchanged pleasantries with my fellow contestant, an old lady from Manchester who wanted something special to celebrate the night of her fortieth wedding anniversary, and together we met the host, whose tan was the colour of mahogany. Then we were announced to the studio audience, which consisted exclusively of blue-rinsed, infirm women above the age of sixty, all of whom were probably booked onto a package holiday to Lourdes the following day.

Suddenly, there was movement, barked orders, and people walked purposefully in every direction. The show had begun. From somewhere unseen behind me, I was approached by the host who told me to explain to the camera what I normally wear. I looked down at myself - clad in blue jeans, grey T-shirt, Adidas Gazelle trainers - and replied, "This." She asked me which look I now desired and I replied that I wanted my wardrobe to make me look like an upwardly mobile, successful twentysomething male and not the eternal teenager I have resembled since I turned thirteen. For some reason, this response illicited a laugh from the audience, and I felt myself turn crimson. I was then wheeled towards the hairstylist, a bulky man in a tight ribbed T-shirt who ran his thick fingers between my hair, the bangles that hung from his wrist jangling melodiously in my ears. Then he picked up a pair of scissors and went to work. Halfway through this process, the presenter reemerged with a beauty consultant who informed me, the studio audience, and the viewers at home, that my nose was home to far too many blackheads. For the next twenty-five minutes - slimmed down to just two when broadcast - I was pinched, prodded, pummelled, plucked, polished, waxed, squeezed, clipped, scrubbed, massaged and manicured. It was at once relaxing, painful, stimulating, and almost erotic, like a close approximation of heaven with just a smidgen of hell thrown in. I was then transported to Wardrobe where I was dressed in Shelly's black brogues, a charcoal grey Paul Smith suit, no tie, a deep blue YSL shirt, and opal cufflinks. I felt peculiar, I felt not quite me. Then came the show's climax, which required me to walk the studio catwalk, the ghosts of

Helena, Kate and Eva beside me, while the elderly studio audience clapped as enthusiastically as arthritis would allow. The host reminded viewers that there were no mirrors backstage and so when the big stage mirror spun round, I would see the new me for the first time. She asked if I was ready, and the sweat upon my brow told her yes. The mirror turned, and with it my stomach. I looked alien, as if a proper grown up now stood in my place. My hair had been styled rather than cut, and swept back over the ears, giving my face a disarmingly raffish frame. I blinked hard and smile beatifically. I told the host I loved it, and I thanked everyone profusely. Then my co-contestant, who looked elegant in mauve, did similar, and together we bowed to the camera with greater elegance than we ever did before. I got to keep the suit.

On my way out, I bumped into the girl in the bouncy Nike trainers who said, "Told you", and as she gave me a friendly peck on the cheek, she slipped another little wrap into my Paul Smith breast pocket. "Compliments of the BBC," she said.

Lovely people.

(vi)

In order to further cultivate my understanding of style, and much more besides, I next paid a visit to my local newsagent. Browsing through the mens' magazines, I came across an incredible number of titles, many of which looked like the same magazine, only with a different naked woman splayed across each cover. One was subtitled For Men Who Should Know Better, another The Original Magazine For Men, another still 4 Men Who Like It On Top. One magazine featured a close-up of a perfect male torso, six-pack flexed, which bore the plain fabrication, It's true - working out can give men the body they want. Inside such magazines - magazines which previously I had paid very little attention towards - were features on film, music, television, fashion, celebrity, sports, cars, fitness and sex. There were two-page articles on cider drinking, holiday romances, the latest drug of choice, penis enlargement, cosmetic surgery, call girls, football players. I gathered together as many as my arms could carry, and made my way over to the nearest till, proffering my gold card. Then I took a taxi home, sat at my large dining table, and began to read.

What an education. I read about breasts - also referred to as

61

tits, melons, boobs, jubblies, airbags - and saw an awful lot of them, in colour and black-and-white, breasts big and small, pert and pendulous. I read about vaginas - also referred to as pussies, snatches, beavers, fannies, cunts in some magazines, c**** in others - but saw distinctly fewer of these, as most models kept their underwear on. I read about premature ejaculation, multiple orgasms, impotency, sex therapy, and the Kama Sutra. I learned about the rumoured private lives of a myriad Hollywood stars, who they are doing it with, for how long and, occasionally, why. I learned how to turn my body into a temple, what to eat, and how to lose weight, stay fit, and transform myself into a fine figure of muscular masculinity. I detached a fold-out wall chart on fitness and stuck it up on my bedroom wall. It instructed how and when to do sit-ups, press-ups, squat thrusts, and stretches. It also counselled on how to get the best out of swimming and jogging. This, in turn, encouraged me to join a gym to further help tone my body towards perfection. I also gleaned vital information on how to meet the perfect girl, how to woo, what to cook, what to wear, how much to spend, what to do in bed and for how long, what to say the morning after, how to survive the morning after, and when, if necessary, to place the follow-up call. I bought a variety of sex education videos

and placed them on heavy-rotation on the Sony. I followed

instructions on which clothes to buy and from what part of town,

and subsequently used my gold card heavily in Covent Garden, Bond

Street, Knightsbridge, Fulham and Chelsea. I bought fourteen pairs

of shoes and trainers, some with laces, others with zips. I bought

face creams, body lotions, pore cleansers, sponges from the Indian

Ocean, puff ball sponges, natural sponges, a pumice, a loofah, a

blackhead remover, a stylist's hairdryer, a comb carved from ivory,

an electric toothbrush, and various gizmos to test my virility, my

heartrate, my fat intake. I bought a shiatsu mattress, a foot spa, a

palm-top computer. I filled the fridge with Japanese beer, isotonic

NRG drinks, Scottish steak, lots of fruit and lots of vegetables. I got

Sega and Nintendo, a satellite dish. I threw out my paltry CD

collection - old Christmas presents from distant family members, all

of which suggested that I shared a similar taste in music to someone

fifteen years my senior - and bought new ones instead, albums by

younger, more tortured artists who bore the faces of confused

young men whose inability to successfully integrate in society had

produced in them a surfeit of creativity. I tried everything from

63

pop to dance, ragga to drum'n'bass, ambient to electronica. I bought books, lots of them. And I threw out my glasses, and acquired some contact lenses.

I appeared less me than ever, and yet I knew it was a successful transformation. I became better.

(vii)

Soon after, my newly-developed self-confidence was then given a further supersonic boost when I unwittingly stumbled upon a new career. It all happened quite by accident. During one of my many visits to the newsagent, I came across a magazine called Zeitguy, a new title for men indistinguishable from the others save for its cover price which, for one month only, was just one pound. I bought it, took it home, opened it up. Inside were yet more features about sex, stamina, film and music, but after every feature, there was printed the following blurb: Think you can do any better? If so, then drop us a line, including an example of your writing. The most promising entrants will then be taken on for a three-month trial. It could be you!

Immediately encouraged, I went direct to Tottenham Court Road and bought myself an iMac, with all the various multimedia trimmings and a very attractive colour printer. When I returned home, I began setting my new toy up, which took me the better part of an afternoon. By nightfall, I had successfully located the ON switch, and was ready to wax lyrical upon computer screen for the first time since my aborted course in IT at school years before.

The first hurdle encountered was what to write, exactly? A feature? A review? What I Did On My Holidays? Having spent most of my adolescence scribbling various thoughts and critiques into notebooks, I didn't envisage this as much of a problem. I started by practicing my typing skills, but they were such that they barely warranted the word skills at all. I then attempted to write about one of the recent albums I'd bought, but ended up practically copying word-for-word the review from one of my music magazines, so I scrapped that and was faced with the blank screen once again. A film review, perhaps? It dawned on me that I hadn't actually visited a cinema in some time, and, anyway, couldn't remember the name of the last film seen, much less its content. The first full paragraph I completed was about the weather.

Today was a distinct improvement on yesterday. Although we're in mid-May, the weather has so far been more typical of late-March. There has been wind, some rain, and the clouds rarely part for long enough to allow sunshine to stream through. But rising this morning, I was greeted by blazing golden rays, which poured into the bedroom as if in celebration. Summer has arrived, I thought. And, indeed, the sun maintained its glow, unhindered by the intrusion of clouds, all day, until, reluctantly, it was forced to set upon the horizon. Its presence filled me with optimism. Tomorrow, I thought as I watched it dip out of sight, it will return just as emphatically. It will be hot.

I read over these words, feeling sick to the stomach. I'd spent thousands of pounds on some state-of-the-art technology here, and all I was capable of achieving was 120 words of pure piffle. I got up, made some coffee, and walked over to the window. And then it hit me. I knew exactly what to write about to get me going, in the mood. Before attempting to review anything, I'd simply put down a few thoughts about my grandfather's last few days, his life in reevaluation, the money he left me, and where it could have come from. Perhaps it would help me come to terms with his passing. And perhaps once the words started flowing - as I was sure they would - then they'd continue to flow, and I could then approach writing something suitable for Zeitguy. It was a little after eleven o'clock at night, but I suddenly felt wide awake.

*

Four hours later, I managed to print, then save the file, and switched the computer off. My back ached a little, but this was somehow a good feeling. I'd done some respectable work here. The words certainly did flow, and I'd written wisely about my relative. Although quite unwittingly, I realized that while writing it, I'd embellished many points. For example, I displayed no doubts as to my grandfather's supposed gangland connections. I wrote in glowing terms about his honour, his bravery, the lengths to which he would go for his family. I wrote of his money, and how he had acquired such sums. I cast myself in the piece as a grandson in awe of his grandfather, not only aware of his criminal activities, but proud of them too. I even suggested that I assisted him in a couple of minor jobs, and relayed the thrill that accompanied them. Like The Krays, Grandad was ultimately a good man who rarely, if ever, hurt anyone in his quest for quick cash. The bigger the corporation he robbed, the less he was to blame. The country was forever screwing the ordinary working man, anyway. Here was one working man who wasn't ordinary, and who was instead quite capable of screwing right back, and then sharing his ill gotten gains with a wide circle of friends and family. He had died, I concluded, as something of a folk hero. I felt honoured to be related to him.

When I'd finished reading it, I sat back and basked in a sense of achievement, something I wasn't normally privy to in everyday life. I was very pleased with this slice of fiction. By its close, even my typing had picked up.

It must have been sometime after three in the morning, and I now felt very tired. The thought of next having to write an appropriate article for Zeitguy filled me with dread. I needed sleep. Why not just send the piece on Grandad to the magazine? I thought. It certainly gave an example of my writing which, at this stage, was all they needed anyway. Yes, why not? I found an envelope, a first class stamp, and sent it the following morning.

A week later, I received a letter from Zeitguy, requesting my presence in their Soho offices on Monday morning, 11.30am. Elated by this news, I soon had to put it to one side in favour of more pressing matters. On the Friday before, I had to bury the dead.

Five. Woof.

Two days ago, Katkin reached me on the mobile as I was making my way back home from another successful shopping expedition. Her news stopped me in my tracks. My grandfather was to be buried at the end of this week at a church in Peckham Rye, at the distinctly ungodly hour of nine am. She'd received this information via a telephone call from my mother, who was still unaware that I'd changed address. When my mother asked to whom she was speaking, Katkin introduced herself as my girlfriend, to which my mother was reportedly overjoyed, and was heard to mutter the words at last. Katkin hoped I didn't mind this little indiscretion, and I issued back the appropriate white lie.

"I'd like to come with you, if you don't mind?"

I wondered why. Since moving out, Katkin's phone calls to me had become as frequent as her previous invitations to join her in a game of whatever she had closest to hand. While this at first appeared a mere continuation of her earlier flirtations, albeit more concerted, more determined, I also became suspicious that she was now drawn to me specifically because of my windfall. While I of course wasn't so stupid to divulge the exact amount, I did confess to her that my grandfather had left me some money. I felt I needed to explain the opulence of my new apartment should she ever visit, which seemed inevitable.

"Why?" I asked her. "You didn't even know him."

"I'd just like to offer you my support," she replied with solemnity. "And I'd love to meet the family."

For some reason, this made me feel uneasy, but the idea of female companionship appealed.

"I'll pick you up Friday morning," I told her.

She squealed with what sounded like rapacious excitement.

*

The taxi arrived at my place at seven in the morning, and we were over in Shepherd's Bush within five minutes. Katkin exited the house and made something of a flamboyant entrance into the back of the cab. She was a vision in black, complete with a widow's veil, which struck me as ridiculously comic, and not just a little morbid. She clearly relished her appearance. I, myself, looked far more appropriately subtle, in a black Hugo Boss suit, a white shirt, black silk tie, and leather brogues from Jones. My hair was combed back and held in place with a spurt of industrial-strength hairspray.

Katkin kissed me upon my cheek, and while the cab made its way over to Croydon, to where my mother was living with her latest boyfriend, she attempted to remove the lipstick marks from my face with a combination of persistent rubbing and saliva.

We arrived within the hour, where I immediately came face to face with my brother Tom, whom I hadn't seen for upwards of six months. His first words were rapid-fire exclamations, stunned by my appearance.

"Rob a bank?" he asked, eyebrows scaling forehead.

"I'm doing well at work," I replied in monotone.

"You don't say?" he said sceptically. "And who's the pound of flesh?" he added, eyeing Katkin lasciviously.

Tom has always been bigger than me, taller and more muscular, handier with his fists, and had more than a fleeting knowledge of the rudiments of karate. I know this because he spent most of my adolescence proving such prowess to me upon the living room floor. However, although I'd only been attending the gym for just a few weeks, I had gleaned far more physical confidence than I'd ever had before. Also, he looked a little red-rimmed around the eyes, tired, vulnerable. So, for no longer than a couple of seconds, I imagined hitting him with all my might square on the bridge of his nose, then watching blood explode down his mourning suit. A righting of past wrongs. But then my mother came out, a flurry of tears and kisses, unashamedly ecstatic that she now had both her sons together, a tight family unit once more.

"Duncan!" she shrieked to her latest boyfriend, a balding man in his fifties wearing an ill-fitting suit and an uncomfortable expression. "Take a picture of us. Me and the boys."

Only mother said cheese.

Then she turned all her attentions toward Katkin, whom she loudly proclaimed to all as Jake's new girlfriend. Tom looked at me, disbelief etched into his features, as well as suspicion. He promptly strode past me, shouldered my mother to one side, and presented himself.

"Kat-kin," he said, savouring both syllables, "what a

wonderfully exotic name. I'm Tom, Jake's older brother." He outstretched his palm. "Charmed."

Katkin looked up at him, into his eyes, and appeared to melt, if only for a second.

"Hello," she replied. "Jake never mentioned you before."

"Well, he's always felt a little jealous of me," he said, chest thrust forward, "especially around beautiful women such as yourself."

Katkin appeared to suddenly gain some extra height. "Can't think why. Jake has nothing to fear from you, if first impressions are anything to go by." Then she smiled and retreated, happy to have issued words laced with poison, and watched his expression fall.

Tom looked as if he'd just been dealt a punch to the stomach, turned violently, and took out his mobile phone.

"Where the fuck is Pamela?" he said in loud, emphatic tones, while impatiently jabbing a digit onto the dial pad.

"His girlfriend," mouthed my mother, out of his view. "She's late. Anyway, Jake and Katkin, may I introduce you to my new friend, Duncan. Duncan, this is my son and his girlfriend, Katkin."

Duncan shook hands and blushed deeply. Katkin looked empowered, strangely regal.

While we awaited the arrival of Tom's latest blonde, and the hearse, I felt obliged to indulge in small talk with my mother, explaining that I'd moved into another flatshare. She wanted to know whether Katkin and I would move in together, and Katkin - turning the deception I fed my mother into a tool for her own rhapsodizing - said that undoubtedly we would and that happiness was now an emotion with our names upon it which she pressed tight to her breast. She clasped my hand in hers, and stared lovingly into my eyes. Mother, always a sucker for cheap poetry, kept bursting into tears of pride, and it continued in such fashion until I reminded everyone why we were here in the first place.

Eventually, the hearse arrived, followed by a black stretch Mercedes, into which my mother and her man, Tom and his woman, and me and mine, all bundled. We then embarked upon a torturously slow journey across South London towards Peckham Rye.

When we pulled up outside the church, several old people were milling about aimlessly, all dressed uncomfortably in black. Among these people may have been Grandad's old allotment friends, were any of them still living, but I recognized no one. My mother worked her way through them, crocodile tears spilling appropriately down powdered cheeks, taking some by the hand, while others she clasped to her bosom, seemingly overcome with emotion. Tom, meanwhile, took Pamela - a tall blonde whom I momentarily mistook for one of the women I'd seen modelling in one of my many mens' magazines - to one side to berate her for one reason or another. They concluded this exchange with a deep-throated kiss, friends again, blind hands seeking out various hidden body parts, until the sound of a church organ suddenly intruded and everybody slowly shuffled in.

In the church, hymns were sung halfheartedly, followed by a sermon from the priest, and then Tom took the pulpit to deliver a ridiculously dramatic speech about the gaping hole left in a family's life when a valued relative suddenly dies. For this, he got a standing ovation from Pamela, until scolding eyes forced her back into her pew. In the absence of an encore, Tom was replaced at the pulpit by a squat old man, with a robust torso and a face like a grizzled pitbull, walked up and began talking in gruff tones about loyalty and friendship. He was small, stocky, and looked somewhere between sixty and sixty-five. He was dressed in a shiny grey suit, and his huge feet were encased in black-and-white leather shoes which gave him a mafioso look. Upon several fingers were fat gold rings, on his right wrist a chunky gold bracelet, and around his neck, on a very long chain that finished halfway down his tie, he wore a gold crucifix. He concluded his little speech with a mumbled, "...we had a lot of unfinished business, but I suppose we'll have to take care of that later", and, as he walked back to take his seat, he shot me a look so menacing that my blood chilled instantly.

After the burial, we all transferred ourselves to the local British Legion, where my grandfather was a member, for the reception. Once there, I allowed myself several stiff drinks, one after the other, prompting in me a bloated bladder which required immediate relief. When I emerged from the cubicle, the old man from the church was standing by the sinks, arms crossed. I walked around him and rinsed my hands.

From behind me, I felt him approach. I looked up, shook my hands dry, and there in the mirror, just over my shoulder, he stood. Our reflected stares met. He smiled curtly, nodded once, and said, Young man, by way of introduction. His voice sounded like gravel spread with honey.

"Hello," I replied, my voice strangely high.

Slowly, I turned to face him.

He thrust out his right hand, and I flinched inadvertently. Uneasily, we shook hands.

"We've not met," he said, almost with accusation.

"No," I said. "Were you a friend of my grandfather?"

"In a manner of speaking. We was business associates from way back."

"I see."

In the ensuing silence, my eyes drifted over the urinals, the sinks, and, I noted with some surprise, a liberal daubing of graffiti, something I didn't expect to see in a British Legion club. GODBER IS A POOF. MFC SHIT SHITE ON CHARLTON. WOGS OUT. When I turned back to face him, his eyes intruded into mine with venom.

"I've heard much about you, son, much about you. It's good to finally see you in the flesh. You're much as I expected."

"Oh?"

"Nice suit, by the way. Must have cost an arm?"

I found no reply. Instead I shrugged. Eventually, I suggested we go back out to the others.

"Not a good idea," he said. "What say you and me go for a little drive?"

My calm dissipated in an instant. "A drive? Where?"

"You'll see."

"Sorry, but I'm not going anywhere. I've a reception to attend. My grandfather has just died, remember?"

He placed a solid oak hand on my shoulder, squeezed until pain shot up into my brain, and smiled.

"I want to talk to you about your grandfather, son. And I'm going to do it now."

"Can't it wait?"

He steered me out the toilet, and through a side exit, unseen by the others. We approached a metallic green Jaguar XJS - his. He unlocked the passenger door and, with one hand on the top of my head, pushed me into car. Then, he slowly walked around to his side, and got in. The motor started first time, sounding like a contented cat, and we sped off before I'd managed to locate the seatbelt.

I looked over and saw steely determination in the tightness of his jaw. The vague friendliness he'd shown back in the WC had now all but drained from his face. He lit a cigar, his features lost in a cloud of smoke, and we proceeded in total silence.

*

The car weaved its way through South London, passing through various places that recalled my youth. From Peckham, we bore right towards New Cross, where I went to school, through myriad backstreets, and up into Deptford, where I'd spend lunch hours in one of many video game arcades. Away from the High Street, we made our way through a succession of smaller streets, until we pulled up alongside a cluttered skip and a fence that looked over a small park. With a neat flick of his wrist, he disengaged the engine, and got out the car. Again, with much deliberation, he walked slowly around to my side, while my heartbeat, sounding like someone dragging a tin cup up and down my ribcage, echoed with emphasis around my ears. As soon as he opened my door, I spoke.

"Look, what the-"

He brought a nicotine-stained index finger to his lips - shhh! -

and I immediately fell silent. After looking both left and right, in front and behind him, he ordered me out, and I reluctantly complied. He then stooped back into the car and retrieved a small plastic packet from the glove compartment.

Then, with his hand on the small of my back, he directed me to walk forward, through the park, and up towards a small pond, upon which glided a family of malnourished ducks. We reached a bench and sat down side by side.

"Nice day for it," he said, shaking the plastic packet and opening it carefully. Reaching a hand inside, he brought out a small pile of breadcrumbs which he proceeded to throw in the direction of the ducks. Within a minute, we were surrounded by pigeons, a few sparrows, and four helplessly outnumbered ducks, all scrambling for the proffered food scraps. The old man snarled abruptly, like a bull to a matador, brought up some phlegm into his mouth, and spat it out in the direction of a cluster of faded grey pigeons.

"Hate pigeons," he said. "Fucking scavengers."

I considered my options which, when properly examined, whittled down to just one. There was nothing I could do but wait until he decided to speak. While feeding the ducks and verbally accosting the pigeons, however, he made no effort whatsoever to break any ice that may have lingered between us.

Eventually, he did speak. He asked me whether I like birds. I replied that I'd never considered whether I had any feelings for or against them. Wrong answer, it seemed, as he felt himself moved to spit again. When the last of the breadcrumbs were now scattered on the tarmac before the flapping birds, he very carefully folded up the plastic packet and placed it back inside his outer pocket. Then, without warning, he rocketed to his feet and began frantically kicking at the pigeons. In an instant, the air around us was a scene of pure chaos, carnage, wings flapping, heads bobbing, strange, urgent sounds emanating from somewhere within the frightened birds. Most were able to escape, to soar up and away from this sudden burst of violence, but my eyes focused on two pigeons who appeared to be flying at very strange angles. They flew straight up with considerable velocity, but just as quickly seemed to lose pace, then tumbled down into the pond, flailing desperately in the water until their wings wound down and stopped beating altogether, their heads lolling to one side, bobbing gently in the murky water.

Cleaning his mafioso footwear with an embroidered silk

hankerchief, the old man chuckled to himself.

"Daft fuckers," he said.

He turned and looked at me. "I said, daft fuckers."

Reddening, I began nodding in agreement. "Yes," I said.
"Completely stupid."

His twisted mouth broke out into an ugly grin.

A yawning emptiness then followed as I watched the family of
ducks swim in the pond, giving a wide birth to the dead pigeons.

Some more time past, but eventually, he started talking.

"You was close to your Grandad, weren't you, son?"

"Yes. Yes, I was."

"What I want to know is, how close?"

I considered this awhile, then shrugged.

"Want me to repeat the question, son?"

"I was close to him, he was my grandfather. What do you want
me to say?"

"What I'm saying is, he took you into his confidence, didn't
he?"

"I suppose so."

"Ever mention me?"

"I've no idea who you are."

He told me he was known as Short Order, on account that he used to be a short order cook in the immediate years after WWII, and the fact that he's vertically challenged.

I tried to think whether I'd ever heard that name before. It didn't ring any bells, until I suddenly recalled the nurse's reading of my grandfather's dying words: It was mine short, mine to do with as I will. Mine, not yours short. Short. Short Order? Possibly. If so, then his ramblings almost made sense, although quite what remained mine, mine to do with as I will continued to mystify.

"No," I told him after much consideration. "I don't recall that name at all. Would he have known you by any other name?"

He suggested it was unlikely.

"Fact remains, however, that he died owing me money."

If my gulp was audible, then it was accidentally so.

"A lot of money from certain business propositions we carried out."

I blinked rapidly, involuntarily.

"Whatever we made during our partnership, right, we split it fifty-fifty, straight down the middle. But turns out that he was on the fiddle for our last couple of jobs, the sly old bastard. I confronted him, of course, along with a slap to the side of the head, but he claimed himself all innocent, like, and accused me instead. Reckoned it was me what was pocketing on the side. Maybe I was, maybe I wasn't. But if I was, it's only cos he was too. See what I'm saying?"

I began to shrug, but immediately thought better of it and started nodding instead.

"A breakdown of communication, happens all the time. But he still did me wrong whatever way you look at it, and that gets my back up. Dead or alive, I'm still narked at him, and I don't forgive easy. I happen to know he left you some money when he went, not a fortune, but a tidy sum nonetheless. Much of that money is rightly mine, but as I'm not the sort of bloke to deny the dead a final wish, I've decided to let you keep it. Call me soft in my old age, I don't know. Bygones. Anyway, you get to keep the money on one condition. You want to know what that condition is?"

A quick, sharp nod of the head - yes.

"My condition is that you behave, you don't do anything stupid with it, you keep quiet, you lie low. And anything you do know about our business transactions, then you naturally keep very quiet about it. That money, son, wasn't earned toiling a nine-to-five, if you know what I mean, which means that someone somewhere is missing it. They're probably searching for it, too. And if they're not, then the boys in blue certainly are. They've got their eyes peeled, and they're just itching to come asking me questions. A whole pile of questions. They'd ask your Grandad too, had he not snuffed it, but now he's gone, it's me they'll come looking for. But they'll only come looking if you encourage them to, if you go shooting your mouth off. Don't forget you were related to him, so even idiot police can put two-and-two together. You act all flash bastard, they'll come a-sniffing. And if they arrive at my door, then I'll pay you a visit, of that you can be sure. I even get called in for questioning, then it'll be down to you, and you won't walk again. I'm an old man, son, and I want to see out my days in the open air. Understand?"

I told him I did.

"Keep your head down, keep out of trouble, and you're fine, I'm fine, we're all fucking fine. Enjoy your good fortune. Do otherwise, son, and you'll have me to answer to. I've made myself crystal, haven't I?"

He had.

"Good, then. Good."

He placed a hand on my shoulder and applied pressure again.
"Sorry about him dying. All told, he was a good man. I'll miss him."

He then stood, bones cracking, and stretched. Before leaving,
he offered one last parting shot.

"Oh, and you looked a right tit on that makeover programme.
Don't go on TV again."

Then he walked slowly back to the car. I watched until he
became an indistinguishable blob, and I watched him disappear into
the green sports car. And although I didn't hear the engine, I
heard rubber on tarmac as he sped off. Then I turned back and
looked at the dead pigeons, floating beaks-down on the pond's grimy
surface.

*

I took his advice immediately and, instead of taking a cab home,
suffered the agony of a never-ending bus journey back over the

river. I arrived home later that evening to three worried phone messages - from my mother once, and Katkin twice, enquiring what on earth had happened to me. I made a mental note to make placatory calls to the both of them as soon as I could, but first went over to the computer. I turned it on and called up its only file. As I sat reading the perhaps not so fictitious tale about my late grandfather's life, I felt a shiver go up my spine, equal parts nervousness and excitement. This, I realized, had to go. Were it to fall into the wrong hands, then it could effectively work as some sort of confessional. I moved the cursor to the top of the pile and gingerly placed an index finger on the delete button, and watched with relief as it gobbled up the feature word by word until nothing was left but a blank screen.

Uneasy with my own company, unsure what to do next, I packed my gear into a bag, and went out to the gym. The gym is a rather depressing place to frequent on a warm Saturday night. Those of us without anything better to do or, more pertinently, without a date with whom to share a Chinese meal and a video, ends up in here, alone, working off countless frustrations on the rowing machine until exhaustion removes feeling altogether. Predictably, the place was practically empty. There were just three of us, two large men with their backs to me, and myself. First, I began on my warm-up stretches, then transferred onto the treadmill where I spent an all-time high of twenty minutes. From there I managed half an hour on the bike, then just five on the rowing machine, which turned my arms to putty. Next, I got changed and eased into the swimming pool which succeeded in disguising the muscular pain, if only temporarily. Never the strongest of swimmers, I found myself close to drowning after just ten lengths and so, from there, I dragged myself into the sauna, where I roasted in the kind of dry heat that makes nostril hair sizzle. Finally, before a glorious cold shower which would bring me back to at least half my senses, I switched to the steam room and inhaled its menthol air until I felt high.

The health club bar was also deserted. I fetched myself a beer and sat in front of the television and watched an obscure rerun of an eighties detective show starring David Hasselhoff and a low black sports car that not only talked back, but was able to solve all manner of complicated crimes. There was poor reception, and the colour looked as washed out as I felt. Regardless, I stewed and I watched, utterly engrossed in this ridiculous show. At key moments in the plot, I even felt my heartbeat increase, but tried to force from my mind the image of a single man, drinking alone in a health club, and watching dreadful television, for the picture was simply too depressing, too real.

Imagine my undisguised glee, then, when someone approached, asked if this seat was free, and sat down to join me. I'd long heard that health clubs were the new singles bars, a place where young men and women of similar disposition met, fell in love, married and kept fit together, but I imagined this only happened at more exclusive places and to more deserving of members, for in all the times I'd visited this place, I found myself incapable of even making eye contact, much less enquiring whether a particular woman - whose beguiling leotard transformed into dental floss around the buttock area - would care to dine out with me. But, somehow, here she was anyway.

Her name was Sarah, and she'd been a member here for four years now, which would account for the perfection in the tone and muscle of her body, visible to me through tight white cycling shorts and a trim grey T-shirt. She bought me another drink and we sat talking small talk, while both of us made no mention whatsoever as to what, exactly, either of us was doing in a place like this, alone, at the weekend. From her general demeanour, however, I guessed that she'd recently come out of a possibly longterm relationship and was looking for a little fleeting company. Ideally, I would have opted for more than a mere fleeting acquaintance, but I was eager to fulfill any roll that she may have wished me to play.

"Do you fancy coming back to my place?" she asked presently.

I, of course, heartily agreed, and within five minutes, courtesy of her gleaming purple Ka, which looked more like a cough sweet on wheels than a bonafide car, we were now sitting in a heavily fragranced front room, lighted candles flanking either side of the large green sofa. She lived in a small one-bedroom flat on Queensway that bore few traces of a recently departed man. The walls were magenta, the art prints Matisse, and everything appeared laced with the scent of femininity, including her male cat, George. At this point, we encountered a little awkwardness, the magic back at the club having been interrupted by the sudden change of venue. Sarah, sensing a slight rift, produced a couple of bottles of white wine from a huge fridge in the kitchen, and as the alcohol flowed, so too did a reformed bonhomie, and before long, our bodies were entwined horizontally, her lips hovering below mine, my tongue eager, both our eyes wide open, a collective delirium mounting, and an eventual consummation not spoiled by a certain drunken clumsiness but actually enhanced by it. We both awoke the following morning, alarmed by one another's unfamiliar faces, and had to be re-introduced all over again. An uncomfortable atmosphere prevailed, however, an atmosphere that was not, this time, to be alleviated by a stiff drink at eleven am on a Sunday morning. She offered me a courtesy coffee nonetheless, but brought me tea instead, and by its conclusion, I had already been ushered out the front door, which slammed behind me without a final goodbye.

I decided to walk back home as the sun was blazing, and I had nothing better to do. I took a detour through the park, sat by the lake, and promptly decided to resurrect my nicotine habit which I'd successfully kicked a couple of years earlier. I quickly procured a packet for myself and enjoyed a Silk Cut while watching rich young children sail model boats on the shimmering water. Remembering the new mobile phone that nestled somewhere within my light jacket, I switched it on and discovered several VoiceMails demanding to know my immediate whereabouts. Mother threatened to call the police if she didn't hear from me by midday, while Katkin threatened excommunication. I called them both immediately and explained that a sudden sadness had consumed me, prompting my disappearance yesterday. I just needed to be alone, I attempted to explain. My apologies were profuse, and reluctantly I was forgiven.

Then I turned all thoughts to tomorrow, to my appointment with the editor of Zeitguy magazine. Although my underlying emotion was excitement, the overriding one was an inexplicable fear. I smoked six cigarettes back to back, and returned home, coughing, alone once more.

Six. Ashes To Ashes.

I awoke after a fitful sleep at three am, the luminous green of the alarm clock radio displaying the evil hour with unarguably bright certainty. I shut my eyes again, buried my head under the pillow, and willed myself to sleep once more. It worked, but only haphazardly. I awoke again at 3.37, then at 4.07, then 4.48, 5.17, 5.29, 5.59 and 6.12. Sixty seconds later, I gave in and got up, stood under a steady stream in the shower, and padded into the kitchen where I breakfasted on cereal and coffee. Briefly, I entertained the idea of surfing the net but came to the emphatic conclusion that such technology continued to exist beyond my limited realm of understanding, and so I activated the remote control instead and settled down to be cosseted into the world of morning television. I watched mini features on beleaguered politicians, fashion, and the world of footballers' wives, then, dazed, realized I was now ready for more sleep. Unfortunately, at nine am, it was already time I left, and so, reluctantly, I did.

*

The cab made light work of the early morning traffic and weaved expertly through countless backstreets towards Peckham. The presentation of a ten pound note into the driver's clammy hand allowed me the privilege of lighting a cigarette within his prized No Smoking carriage, and I made a concerted effort to enjoy every lungfull.

At the funeral parlour, located close to the church from which I was kidnapped, I waited patiently at the reception while a middle-aged man with a twitch and a particularly cruel neck rash attempted to locate the ashen remains of my grandfather. Twice he had returned empty-handed, politely explaining that the casket had apparently gone missing, and it was only when he employed the services of his immediate superior that Grandad was eventually found, safe and sound, in a box made out of wood and painted a sombre black.

Thirty minutes later, I was back outside, now aware that if I didn't get a move on, I'd be late for my appointment with Zeitguy. I impressed upon the cab driver - again with a little financial persuasion - the urgent need for haste, and we sped towards Soho with little heed for crossing pedestrians or red traffic lights.

Grandad, or what remained of him in a plastic Marks & Spencer bag by my feet, rocked with every sharp turn.

Zeitguy magazine is located above a pornographic book shop in Berwick Street, and surrounded on either side by shady flats with red lights in their windows. As the cab pulled up sharply on the pavement, I suffered grave misgivings. Perhaps I should just leave now? I approached the door and pressed the appropriate bell. A robotic voice told me to push the door hard when the buzzer sounds, and I scaled three flights of stairs with ease. On the top floor was a large black door, closed, and covered with stickers of various bands, as well as the Zeitguy logo. A sign above the bell read: RING ONCE AND STAND WELL BACK! This I did, only nothing happened. So I ventured again. Still nothing. Then, feeling increasingly tense, and gripping tightly on the plastic bag, I knocked hard until somebody screamed back a garbled directive which I took to mean come in! The receptionist looked up at me as I entered as if instantly repulsed by what she saw. I announced myself, wiping sweat from brow, and told her that I was here to see the editor, who was expecting me five minutes ago. She told me to sit, pointing towards a sunken couch opposite her desk, and punched a few digits into a red telephone. I lowered myself into the couch, and it promptly swallowed me whole until my knees had risen to my direct line of vision. I sat there feeling stupid, patently unable to rearrange myself into a position that wouldn't prompt immediate hysteria on sight. I waited some time, possibly upwards of half an hour, in extreme discomfort. Sweat continued to pour off me, while Grandad sat obediently in my lap, almost taunting me by his very presence.

Eventually, a large man came into sight at the end of the corridor. He was six foot plus, mid-thirties, with a red, whiskey-sodden face, dancing grey eyes behind designer frames, and was dressed in a loose-fitting khaki linen suit that he filled with a stomach that was customarily used to excess. He beamed a huge smile at me, suggesting that this was perhaps the editor.

"Many apologies for my tardiness!" he hollered. "I've been tied to the bastard phone all morning! Meetings, meetings, meetings!"

I struggled to get to my feet.

"Here, grab my arm."

I did as instructed, and was immediately hoisted into a

standing position.

"Susie, darling, get that sofa replaced, will you?" he said to the receptionist. "Our friend here almost drowned in it!" His laughter boomed right through me and out the other side.

He introduced himself to me - "John Sultan, charmed" - and led me into his office. He offered me a chair, then sat down behind his desk, and eyed my plastic bag with curiosity, but said nothing.

"Tea? Coffee?"

He ordered us both a hot drink, which Susie brought within seconds, and he continued to smile expansively at me, his eyes looking me up and down, appraising, checking me out. I smiled meekly and waited for him to say something.

"Loved the piece," he said eventually. "Really got to the heart of the subject. Good style, too."

I thanked him and asked if this meant that I was to be taken on for the initial three-month period.

"I think we can safely say that, yes, you're hired. Write more stuff like that for us and we'll soon appoint you as our resident gonzo journo. We can send you out to Ibiza, up to Manchester, over to Belfast. Hard news with an underlying feature style, yes? Music, drugs, culture, and, of course, crime, your particular speciality."

I was stunned.

He asked who else I wrote for, as he hadn't seen my name before, and I admitted that I was just a beginner. This pleased him hugely.

"Terrific!" he said. "All the better for the magazine. A great new writer, and it's us who discovers you!"

I took a large gulp of coffee and attempted to restrict my inane grinning to a more appropriate smile.

"Want to see something?" he then said, like Father Christmas asking whether children want a sneak preview of their presents. "Wait there."

He left me alone inside the small office in which his impressive ergonomic desk took proud centrestage, and upon which sat a sleek black laptop, two telephones, a micro-sized fax machine, several executive toys, a couple of sporting trophies, and a photograph of him sharing a glass of champagne with Michael Caine. Intermittently, the phone broke the silence and burped into life, while the fax silently vomited reams of printed paper.

"Here it is," he suddenly cried, bursting back into his office, a chaotic bundle of kinetic energy.

Under my eyes, he placed an A3-sized piece of shiny plastic which looked like an oversized magazine spread. Which is exactly what it was. Text ran across both sides, while in the middle was a shadowy black-and-white photograph of two men in overcoats standing under a lamppost at night, exchanging a wad of banknotes. My eyes surfed these images back and forth, and presently came to settle on the lurid headline: GROWING UP IN LONDON'S UNDERWOl - ONE MAN'S STORY. Underneath that was my full name, written in big bold letters which started dancing hideously before my eyes.

Sultan patted my shoulder with brutish enthusiasm, while I turned to liquid. Blood drained from my head, I started to rock slowly, and fully expected to pass out.

As fruitless as it may have been, I posed the question anyway.

"What's this?" I asked.

"That, Jake, is your debut feature for Zeitguy magazine. What do you think?"

The emptiness within my head meant I was unable to think anything at all. I swallowed hard, Adam's Apple plundering to my stomach and back, and cleared my throat.

"You're not going to put this in the magazine, are you?"

Sultan had by now resumed his position behind the desk, hands behind his head, his smile growing ever wider.

"Of course we are!" he said. "Already gone to print! It's out next Monday."

"But," I began, "but I thought that this piece was just meant to give you an idea of what I'm capable of?" My voice was pitched high, thin.

"True, true," he replied, looking ridiculously pleased. "In every case so far, the pieces we've received from readers, such as your good self, merely give us an indication of that person's potential, or otherwise. None of them were publishable as they stood. Yours, on the other hand, was perfect, exactly what we were looking for. Not only was it well written - I have of course tarted it up here and there, given it the benefit of my editorial expertise - but the subject matter was absolutely terrific! Our readers will love this. Zeitguy is all about ensnaring new readers and tempting them away from all those other inferior titles. To do that we've got to smack them right between the eyes. This piece should help do that nicely. My job, Jake, you see, is to spot talent. Welcome aboard!"

101

Pride jostled with white fear. I had suddenly shrunk to the size of a gerbil, squirming about in this gigantic chair, unable to find my footing, unable to flee the premises, burning in a bonfire of vanity and impending doom. Sultan appeared now to be laughing at my helplessness, saliva frothing from his enormous mouth. His eyes widened, his cheeks reddened, his whole body vibrated with convulsions. Images burst into my head, a succession of grizzly suicide attempts. Perhaps I should fling myself in front of a train, a speeding car. Or jump from a tall building. An overdose? Drugs. Or maybe I should buy a plane ticket and distance myself as far as possible from an undoubtedly encroaching Short Order.

My head swam in concentric circles, faster and faster. I started breathing deeply, attempting to regulate my oxygen intake. I needed to speak, to make something very clear to Sultan, and very quickly.

"You can't print this," I told him.

"Already done, my friend. I thought you'd be pleased?"

"No, you don't understand. This feature, it's ..." think, think, "... it's fiction. I made it all up. It has no basis of truth whatsoever. I just wrote it as an exercise, just to show you that I could string together a sentence. If I had any idea that you'd print it, then obviously I would have alerted you to this fact earlier. I'm really very sorry." My bottom lip quivered.

John Sultan beamed even brighter than before. He was obviously a complete idiot. He took out his cheque book and wrote one out for œ250, payment for the piece.

"Jake, my friend, you're a natural!" he laughed. "My motto, Zeitguy's motto, is: If The Facts Don't Cut It, Fake It. In other words, Jake, lie, exaggerate, fabricate whenever required. As long as you don't finger anyone in particular, defame or libel anyone, then you're completely safe. Nothing to worry about at all! That's what journalism's all about. Obviously, a little truth here and there is preferable to abject lies, but if all else fails, then who cares? You've written a great piece, you've pleased your new boss, so now go out and spend your earnings. But first, a celebratory drink."

He picked up the phone and punched four digits. "Susie, darling, a bottle of bubbly." He listened to the receptionist's reply and frowned. "What? No, no, that's fine. Pomagne will do just fine. Bring it in."

He turned back to me, and through his beaming smile was unable to detect that I was now feeling markedly unwell.

Involuntarily, my eyelids flickered, then snapped shut.

*

When they opened, some indeterminate time later, I found myself on a train bound for the South Coast. How I got to be here on this deep blue British Rail seat I neither knew nor, at that point, cared. The mere distance that had sprung up between me and London afforded me welcome relief. I, rather naively, felt safe, as if mere distance in miles were to grant my ultimate salvation. A hostess walked down the aisle serving an assortment of sandwiches and crisps, and I bought a couple of each, along with a scalding black coffee and a small pot of cream. Outside, green fields rushed towards me at speed, then left me far behind.

I'd visited Brighton twice previously in my life, once on a school trip aged eleven, our geography teacher feeling it necessary to introduce city kids to the sea and the dubious joys of pebble beaches, and once on an unwise attempt at a romantic weekend with a former girlfriend. Rain, in every sense, stopped play on both occasions. I didn't envisage this trip to be any real improvement.

Upon arrival, the gathering clouds suddenly parted and afforded the town a delightful early summer's sunshine, which prompted a predictable response in many of the locals, but especially the elderly who immediately made haste towards the beach, stripped off naked, and lay down beneath the glare as if offering their withered bodies as sacrifice.

I walked down until parallel with the sea, then walked along the front until I reached the pier, a grim phallus that thrust out Francewards, its paint peeling, its once grand facade long since faded to grey. I worked my way past the pensioners gathered before slot machines, through the miniature bingo hall, and made my way to the funfair at the pier's edge. The sea beneath me churned with its usual mixture of boredom and anger, and wave after wave of brown sludge hit the pier's posts. I lifted Grandad free from the carrier bag and held him tightly between both palms. I muttered a few words which were instantly swallowed by the sea breeze, then eased open the lid and scattered his ashes into the wind. He streamed out before me, rising into the air, then sharply dipping, hitting another gust, and disintegrating into a million particles. He had now gone forever. I replaced the empty box into the bag, turned, and walked back through the arcade.

As I retraced my steps back towards the pier's exit, I stopped to buy some sugared donuts when I caught sight of a uniformed official who came bounding over towards my general direction. His voice was raised, a fist waving, and I momentarily thought his apparent anger was directed at me. A second later, I realized it was. When he reached me, now doubled over and panting hard, his face bright pink, his few remaining grey hairs resembling the after-effects of a particularly strong electric shock, he struggled for words.

"Don't ... don't move," he puffed, an authoritative hand on my shoulder. "Wait right there."

I did as I was told, attempted to avert the stares of passers-by, and forced one of the donuts into my open mouth. Sugar coated my lips, the tip of my nose, and I ate another.

"What were you doing up there?" he asked rhetorically. "You can't do that. There's by-laws about that sort of thing. It's not allowed. You should have come to me first, and I would have told you so." He continued to gasp for air. "I would have told you that it's not allowed, what you did up there." He continued his fight for breath. "There's by-laws for that sort of thing."

I looked down at this elderly official, silently wondered exactly what post he held within Brighton's council, and considered what kind of punishment he was about to unleash. He rubbed the tears from his eyes, caused by running into the wind, and fixed me with his deadliest stare.

"So?" he probed.

"What?" I shrugged, wiping the back of my hand across my sticky mouth.

"What have you to say for yourself? You're not allowed to scatter ashes into our sea. There's by-laws about that sort of-"

"I'm very sorry," I told him, interrupting, then added, "I was merely carrying out the dying wishes of my grandfather - a war hero, incidentally - who wanted to spend eternity in..." and here I struggled, trying to work out quite what to say next, "...in salt water."

The man continued to stare at me, but now with softer eyes, clearly empathizing with my plight.

"Navy man, was he?" he asked.

"Navy, yes. He was a navy man."

"Oh, I see," he said. "In that case, I suppose an exception can be made. Still, there are by-laws which, by law, we are bound to keep and abide by, but in this case, I'll grant you an exception. You're free to go, young man."

He patted my shoulder in condolence and I thanked him.

"I myself was a navy man," he then added. "Which regiment was he in?"

*

With as much clear thinking as I employed for the trip down here and the impetuous, motiveless decision to cast my grandfather out to sea, I commandeered a local taxi to drive me back to London which cost, approximately, the equivalent of an air fair to Southern Italy. Despite the fact that the back seat of this particular Nissan Sunny was about as comfortable as a milk crate, and that it was covered in a thick plastic sheet which suggested that it was the site of many unpleasant nocturnal emissions, nothing could shake the sudden tiredness from my shoulders, and within minutes I slumped sideways, fell into a deep sleep, and didn't re-surface until we careened violently around Marble Arch some hours later.

Back at home, I faced further messages from an increasingly frantic mother. I picked up the phone, and dialed.

"Yes?" I said as she answered before the end of the first ring.

"At last," she replied, exasperated. "Listen, they've found a will left by Grandad, not an official one, just a pencilled scrawl on a piece of paper which he had witnessed by a nurse. They found it in his holdall."

My eyebrows scaled my forehead. Apparently, he'd left no money - in fact, he died leaving several debts which, my mother informed, Tom and her boyfriend would have to clear. But he'd left me some photographs, a clock, and some old magazines.

"And he also expressed a wish to have his ashes spread on that beloved allotment of his," she added, to my horror. "I know you picked them up this morning, so we may as well get it over with now, this evening. Tom is free, so we'll meet you there in, say, two hours."

She replaced the receiver with a clatter, and I fell back into the nearest chair, winded.

An hour later, I hailed another taxi, and made a brief stop at my local 7-11 where I bought a family-sized box of teabags and several bottles of ground pepper. And, as we made our way south towards Peckham, I hastily set about recreating Grandad for the imminent ceremony.

I arrived slightly late to find my mother and Duncan, and Tom with a different girl, standing impatiently in the middle of the allotment, as dusk fell on London. Several allotments away, three old men sat around a boiling kettle and viewed us with a mixture of suspicion and infinite boredom.

"Who's the pound of flesh?" I whispered into Tom's ear, to which he smiled broadly at the reference and informed me that after Enya witnesses his sensitive side, she'll be jelly between his sheets. Enya was as tall as Tom, elegantly dressed, with long fingernails and a longer nose, flowing blonde hair, and a cluster of freckles that gathered neatly on either cheek. She smiled politely at me and mouthed a silent hello.

Without prior permission, Tom relieved me of the casket and began intoning some very familiar words.

"When a valued relative, such as our dearly departed

grandfather here, leaves this earth for a better world..." he began,

essentially repeating his funeral speech for the benefit of Enya's

fresh ears. He prattled on for some time before reaching a sombre

conclusion. "...We can at least be sure that he has now gone to a

better place, to meet his heavenly maker, and to be reunited with

his dear wife, our own much-remembered grandmother."

He looked up at me and winked. I tensed.

As he concluded, he took it upon himself to unscrew the lid,

which he passed on to Enya to hold, while he scooped the substitute

ashes into his hands and scattered them liberally over the allotment.

He repeated this action several times until the casket was almost

empty, then tipped the remaining ash into a small heap at his feet,

which he then dispersed with the tip of a handmade leather shoe.

Into the respectful silence, Enya then issued an almighty

sneeze, followed by another, and another. The force with which she

did so sent blood rushing to her head and her cheeks soon looked

on fire. Snot flew from her nose as she grappled with various

pockets, desperately seeking a tissue. Once located, she buried her

face in a Kleenex and offered repeated mumbled apologies. Ever the

gentleman, Tom helped her regain composure, then offered her his arms into which she gratefully fell. From just over her shoulder, Tom offered me another wink, but then I too was swallowed up in a hug from my tearful mother. Duncan, standing awkward and alone, waved at the three old men still watching on, then resumed his hands-in-pocket pose and stared at his feet.

Commiserations finally dispensed with, I finally saw an end - an escape - in sight until Tom, with obsequious kindness and, naturally, an ulterior motive, offered to drive me home. Mother thought this a splendid idea, and while I desperately attempted to suggest otherwise, everyone was agreed that we'd all go back to have a look at my new abode, and for coffee and contemplation.

*

As I opened the door to my flat, jaws fell open and then, cartoon-like, onto the floor.

Tom was first with the profanities.

"Fuck me," he said, before receiving harsh vocal condemnation from my mother.

Duncan refused to take his hands from his pocket, but also

looked similarly impressed. Enya, nonplussed, asked as to the whereabouts of the bathroom, while instinctively my mother headed straight for the kitchen, and opened every cabinet to check up on my eating habits.

"Darling," she said, contentedly holding a packet of brown rice in her hands, but also clearly confused by my sudden opulence, "where on earth did you get the money to pay for such a palace?"

"Yes," said Tom, suddenly right by my side. "Do tell."

Once again, my mind was required to perform intricate mental acrobatics. Cleverly, I reached for a cigarette and lit up, which stalled matters a while as I then fielded counter accusations over my weakness for nicotine and the fact that I was giving myself lung cancer with every puff. I suggested we all repair to the living room. I'd join them just as soon as I'd made the coffee, and would then explain everything.

When I appeared five minutes later bearing a tray heavy with beverages, Tom was simultaneously playing with the hi-fi and the television, a remote control in either hand, a dazzled smile on his face. The computer was also on and he was, I believe, surfing the net. My mother and Duncan were admiring the nighttime views of

Portobello Road and beyond, while Enya, who had only just now returned from the bathroom, perched herself delicately on the end of the couch.

I told them that I was merely flat-sitting for a friend, that of course this wasn't my new place. This elicited much confusion as Katkin had already told my mother that I had moved out of the place in Shepherd's Bush, and why on earth would I move out if I was only flat-sitting? This particular friend, I informed, was away for six months, that's why. While this appeared to placate everyone, Tom remained alert and suspicious. When I went back into the kitchen for more milk, he came too.

"A friend, is it?" he asked.

"What?"

"This place belongs to a friend of yours?"

"Yes, that's right Tom. You heard correctly."

"What friend of yours would live in a place as flash as this?"

He refused to believe me.

"You're lying."

"And why would I do that?"

He frowned. "That, I don't know. Yet. But I'll find out."

Tom wasn't used to being outdone by me in any respect, least of all financial. When the question of employment came up, I managed to fob them off by telling them that something promising was in the pipeline, which was all that I was prepared to say right now. Again, Tom refused to take the bait, and asked how I suddenly could afford all these new clothes, and who was it that managed to introduce me to style. I said nothing, and quickly changed the subject.

"Look, Tom," I said, flicking channels onto a made-for-TV film. "Shannon Doherty."

While growing up, Tom and I may have shared the same house, but otherwise we inhabited different planets altogether. Tom was outgoing, good in the classroom, excellent on the sports pitch, popular with boys his age, revered by girls up to three years his senior. From the age of ten onwards, he had a vibrant social life, and rarely came home before nine o'clock in the evening. Weekends were his favourite times, however, and wherever it was he actually went during these two inevitably heady days and nights, the upshot was that we saw increasingly little of him. Once, aged fifteen, he disappeared on a Friday night, and came back late Sunday evening with a suntan, but refused to say where he'd been. His popularity being what it was, his actual relationship with our grandfather was therefore practically non-existent. He'd heard the old man's tales as a bored prepubescent, yawned incessantly, and thought him senile and rather sad, and subsequently viewed time spent with him as wasted time. Grandad, for his part, was equally unenamoured with Tom, and so they shared a mutual dislike which grew more pronounced with each passing year, making each subsequent Christmas increasingly unpleasant.

"There's something not quite right here, something you're not telling me," he said, brow furrowed.

I looked at him, pint of milk in hand, then looked right through him.

"You've been watching one too many bad movies," I told him as I headed back to the living room.

He followed me, still unsatisfied, still suspicious.

"Look," I told him, pointing at the screen. "Tori Spelling."

My mother then shut us both up by firing a succession of probing questions over at Enya, who blushed with every reply. She was a receptionist in Tom's firm, she was a year younger than me, and wanted children just as soon as possible, as she had come from a family of twelve, she being the youngest. She currently lived in a bedsit in Mile End, but admitted with considerable embarrassment that she had recently been spending a lot of time with my brother in his Docklands flat.

"The central heating in my flat is broken," she said, attempting explanation.

"But it's summer," said Duncan out of the blue. "Why would you need heat?"

Enya blushed, while Tom smiled broadly.

Apparently satisfied with her answers, my mother then turned to me.

"And how's Katkin?" she asked.

Truthfully, I replied that I didn't know, but was sure she remained just fine.

"I thought you two were a happy couple?"

My next response was directed more to Tom.

"I'm going out with someone else now," I said. "Sarah. She lives just down the road, in Queensway. We met at my gym."

Tom's reaction was, again, the most vocal.

"Gym?" he said. "You're a member of a gym? Good God, now I've heard it all."

Duncan then chose this moment to finish his coffee with a loud slurp and placed both cup and saucer down onto the coffee table with finality.

"Well," he began, clasping his hands together as if poised for action. "It's getting late, and we don't want to be on the roads when the pubs close, eh? Work in the morning."

He stood up and put his corduroy jacket on. My mother followed suit.

"Look after this lovely place," she said to me at the door. "And take care. Keep in touch, won't you?"

Enya presented her cheek for me to kiss, the sudden intimacy prompting another of her rather charming blushes. She mouthed goodbye.

"Come Tom," she said.

Tom grabbed his jacket and followed his girlfriend, his eyes locking onto mine as he passed.

"Let's meet up sometime," he said. "Sometime soon. Have a chat, yeah?"

118

I closed the door behind him, and fell onto it gratefully, slowly exhaling in utter exhaustion, both physical and mental.

Then I went to bed and dreamt bad dreams.

Seven. Grave Digging.

Tom left school at eighteen, a bunch of impressive exam results to his name and a glowing reference from the headmaster. He received offers from three universities, which he temporarily considered, but a Saturday job in a computer hardware store quickly led to an irresistible position in a software company, and, by twenty, he was earning enough to keep himself in the manner to which he was quickly becoming accustomed. He was now as familiar with the language of technology as priests are with the good book. There appeared nothing he didn't know upon the subject, and his ascent within the ranks was swift enough to make him profoundly disliked by everyone in the firm who saw him as a threat to their temporary seniority. Now, still two years shy of his thirtieth birthday, he was on an obscene salary, and poised to become the youngest partner the company had ever appointed. His success in a career which, everyone asserted, was the most significant in a world hurtling towards a future entirely dominated by technology was mirrored in his taste for recklessness and danger. In this and many other ways, Tom was a walking cliche:

his ability to conquer everything that fell before him gave him a similarly ravenous hunger to slay everything else in his wake, too. In the decade since leaving school, he'd worked his way through countless women, claiming monogamy impossible and, moreover, inhuman. Rarely did he bother with condoms, as skin on skin was absolutely paramount in his quest for the perfect orgasm. Aside from a dose of crabs when he was nineteen, he'd procured no further STDs, and if he'd spawned any children along the way, then he remained blissfully unaware, as rarely would he divulge personal information to the women he bedded, least of all how to trace him afterwards. For the first few years of his professional life, holidays were spent in increasingly exotic and out of the way climes, but since he turned twenty-seven, he turned his vacational interests towards climbing precarious peaks, skydiving in war-torn countries, hunting endangered species, and descending barrier reefs. He'd worked his way through marijuana, then cocaine, then heroin, before wiping drugs from his life almost overnight, and now he veered between being a happy drunk, and a health fanatic high only on life and isotonic drinks. He'd even dabbled in football hooliganism when it became briefly fashionable a few years ago, and was more than willing to protect a date in a London club by introducing any passing trouble maker to the intense power of his fist. Ultimately, he appeared profoundly in control of both life and destiny. He only ever mingled with those more powerful if he could then later steal some of that power for himself; otherwise, friends, girlfriends, and associates were inevitably a few rungs lower down the ladder than he.

And we, the brothers, hated each other. Although our contact was fairly minimal during adolescence, Tom was around enough to inflict a strict discipline on me, demanding respect, or dishing out wholly inappropriate, often acutely cruel, punishment. As we both grew into adulthood, our hatred thawed minimally and he began to view me much like one would a street beggar, with condescending condolences. He was, of course, secretly thrilled that my life remained in neutral while his sped off in fifth gear, because in this family, there was room only for one success story. His achievements, he thought, were even greater given the circumstances - the fact that he'd been the product of such a weak, unspectacular seed. If there was anything to bring us together, then it was the mutual disdain with which we viewed our absent father. Our mother also regarded Tom as something of a miracle, wondering just how he could prove so accomplished when her ex-husband was such a thorough waste. While she certainly didn't view me with my brother's same sense of condescending dismay, she nevertheless felt underlying disappointment, and although she never said as much to me, it was always there in her eyes. More than love, she afforded me a bottomless well of sympathy, always hoping that I'd start to prove myself sometime soon, or, if need be, sometime later.

The flat, then, was a good start. As was the new wardrobe, the hairstyle, and my general air of confidence, hitherto conspicuous by its absence. It pleased my mother enormously just to see me in such surroundings, but it sparked off in my brother a suspicion that would not rest until he'd come away with some satisfactory answers.

And it was this that formed his most prominent weak spot - an unquenchable desire for information, power, conquest. Like a racing driver desperate to be first over the line, my brother craved dominance and control over everything. Once achieved, he then required a new danger in his life, another hurdle for him to focus all attention on, to pursue until he triumphed again. But as these cravings - both professional and personal - became more hazardous, each possessing a greater degree of risk, then it seemed, to me at least, that he was heading for a fall. Prosperous he may be; infallible he is not. Anyone who runs that fast, and for that long, must trip up sooner or later.

*

I awoke the following morning to the gentle trill of my slimline telephone. It rang three times before I swallowed back a yawn, cleared my throat and found my dormant voice. I offered it a mumbled hello, and listened to a babble of breathless words reply. After replacing the handset, I sank back into the pillow and considered my good fortune which, if you discounted the mounting worry over the imminent publication of my incriminating article, was absolutely buoyant. The call was from John Sultan offering me my first commission, to interview a band called Chemical Cosh, whose recent turbo-boosted album of dance and cartoon rock had taken them to the top of the charts on both sides of the Atlantic. I was to accompany them on the first three nights of their UK tour and write an on-the-road piece consisting of several thousand words.

I knew absolutely nothing about them, something I'd have to quickly remedy.

I grinned throughout my first morning coffee, then right through my second. But the smile was quickly wiped from my face with the arrival of the morning's post. In a large brown envelope, suspicious in itself, I found a copy of Zeitguy magazine which, over two pages, offered further conclusive proof of my new career.

I sat down and read it, feeling drunk and sick, and re-read it a dozen more times, focusing with extra concern on Sultan's ridiculously flamboyant embellishing, feeling increasingly worse each time.

If he sees this, I thought to myself, that's it, I'm done for.

GROWING UP IN LONDON'S UNDERWORLD - ONE MAN'S STORY

Last month, another chapter in London's underworld closed with the death of my beloved grandfather. A one-time accomplice of

The Krays, Mad Frankie Fraser, and the late Lenny McClean, my grandfather ruled South East London with an iron fist throughout the 50s, 60s and beyond. A legend in his own lifetime, his long association with crime bore none of the unnecessary violence of today's inept criminals. Instead, the man was a folk hero, looked up to by everyone he knew, who pumped the money he amassed back into his beloved Peckham for the benefit of everyone. And, throughout my childhood, I was privy to this life on the other side of the tracks, and was trained effectively to take his place when mortality took his.

I was eleven years old when I first realized that I was different, that my lineage fully came into play. It was a lunchtime in early summer, an overcrowded playground, the temperature up in the thirties, tempers flaring, balls flying in every direction, jumpers for goalposts. I was involved in a game of football in which the only rule was there were no rules. I caught a lob on my right thigh, brought it down with my hand onto my right foot, and ran with it, weaving past several opposing players, a group of girls skipping on a rope, and a teacher with a mug of tea in her hand, then ran squarely at the goal. Only the keeper kept me from the moment of sheer glory, the kind which infused my nightly dream: scoring the winning goal. The keeper was bigger than me and, crucially, several months older. In the unwritten rule book of the playground, which every pupil must keep to if they value their continued existence, the younger bow unequivocally to their elders without exception, and never attempt to get the better of them. For me to score a goal against this particular keeper was effectively me taking life into my own hands. Revenge would be his before the day was out and I would live to rue the moment I decided to go for glory without considering the consequences. So, momentarily, I wavered. My run with the ball thus far had been little short of miraculous, not least because none of their team's sixteen defenders had managed to wrestle it from me. I'd never be able to forgive myself if I didn't take the run to its logical conclusion and plant the ball in the top hand corner of the goal. And so, wantonly, I leant back, positioned my right striking foot just so, and kicked the ball with force, watching it soar past the keeper and slam emphatically onto the crumbling wall which doubled, at lunchtimes, as the back of the goal net. Blood rushed to my head, I turned, ran, and started screaming, while my many teammates all came to congratulate me for nabbing the last-minute winner, making the final score 18-17. I felt euphoric, a giant among the small people of primary school.

Before reaching the classroom, however, the keeper had caught up with me to exact his inevitable revenge. He dragged me into a small storeroom and punched me across the face. When I fell into a heap on the floor, he began kicking me in my stomach until my cries were satisfactorily tortured. As a final punishment, he spat on my face and suggested that if I ever caused him similar embarrassment, then I'd walk with a limp for the rest of my life.

From the sick room, my mother was called and soon came to pick me up. I refused to tell her exactly what had happened other than mumble the words a fight, but when I saw my grandfather later that night, I told him everything, desperate for as much paternal compassion as I could glean. His sympathy, it transpired, was in fact rather minimal. He thinned his lips, narrowed his eyes, and blinked repeatedly. Stress lines bore down on his elderly forehead, and ever so faintly, he began tutting to himself, then mumbling methodically. He patted me on the head, told me I'd be fine, and went out.

Two days later, I returned to school and immediately sensed

that something had changed. I was suddenly afforded a wide birth from those children who had previously bullied me, and I was given space on the football field to be as audacious as I liked. The goalkeeper, meanwhile, was nowhere to be seen, and when I enquired as to his whereabouts from a friend, all I was told was that no one had seen him since the day he'd hit me.

It wasn't until two weeks later that I finally saw him during a visit to the local park with my grandfather. He was hobbling awkwardly on a pair of crutches, his knees - visible under his baggy shorts - bandaged thickly. When his eye caught mine, he went white as a sheet, quickly turned and hobbled off in the opposite direction.

"No one'll ever mess with you again, son," said my grandfather. "Our friend with the limp will see to that."

The years that followed saw me enroll as a junior member in my grandfather's circle, an unofficial club in which every member had served time and boasted the scars, mental and physical, to prove it. They were a circle of friends as loyal to one another as masons, and every member came equipped with pistols, sawn-off shotguns, knives, knuckle-dusters and baseball bats. Everyone there could break into a car within seconds, all could pick locks, and there wasn't anyone who didn't have contacts in police stations, prison cells, and court houses. Associate members were working as night-watchmen in high street banks, building societies, and rich law firms across the country, while others still had access to factories and warehouses, could crack safes, convert bonds into hard cash, melt down gold, smuggle priceless paintings across any border, and were capable of stashing drugs in parts of the body so unobtrusive that even the the most attuned canine nose was unable to sniff it out. Everyone was capable of manslaughter, most had already proven so.

And when they'd all converge together, approximately once a month, crime was turned into an art form. They'd plot, scheme, and carry out heists, robberies, burglaries, never getting caught, and would split the resulting cash equal ways, a true democracy. My grandfather, however, was the man to oversee everything, to impart upon matters his years of expertise, to grant an ultimate say so on whichever job they were discussing.

Initially, I was there to fulfill no greater role than grandson to the guvner, but in time, I was included on various, smaller scams, having learned everything there was to know. I'd perform roles as the look out, and, from sixteen onwards, the getaway driver, the latter proving even more illicit fun, garnered from the fact that I was breaking the law twice, as also an underage driver.

But as the years passed, so crime became dirtier, uglier. A new breed of criminal was attempting to usurp my grandfather from his position, by which stage he was old enough to be content to take more of a backseat. Eventually, he distanced himself from such people altogether, claiming that things had changed for the worse, that violence itself had become the sole currency, the only motivation. Crime, he said, was now lost to criminals. Were it not for the occasional dalliance in relieving Securicor drivers of their postbags full of cash and the like - and then only for old times' sake - then he'd have retired altogether.

Inevitably, once I'd left school and moved on with life, my grandfather and I grew apart. He remained busy, naturally, but I wasn't quite none the wiser. I still kept tabs. Then, a few months ago, he was taken into hospital and later died. I had visited him several times in the previous weeks and although ill, he retained the vitality for life that had always made him so admired. He had, he assured me, kept his hand in, and suggested, with a wink, that I would soon see the evidence for myself.

When he died, I learned - via the kind of will not executed by lawyers - that he had left me some money, undoubtedly the profits of ill gotten gains, specifically his last job on a subsidiary post office in South East London. He always said charity begins at home. Since putting that money to good use, I've ensured it continues to do so.

For someone reputedly happy with what I'd written, Sultan's editing of my piece proved considerable. He'd tampered with it endlessly, transforming what was essentially a personal elegy into some kind of gratuitous tabloidesque confessional. I was doubly displeased with it, initially because it bore little similarity to my original piece, but, far more importantly, because it effectively signaled what I could only imagine was my death sentence, active immediately. The subsidiary post office job in South East London - which wasn't referred to in my original piece - had happened about six months previously, and the local news was still asking witnesses to come forward as no one had yet been arrested. The police believed the gang to have consisted of three elderly men, all known locally, though they had no proof. Sultan had put two and two together, and come up with six.

I may as well start digging my own grave, I thought while hyperventilating on the bathroom floor and attempting to flush the offending magazine down the toilet.

*

The next day, I went to my local record shop to acquaint myself properly with the band Chemical Cosh. I was surprised with just how much I found, and bought their entire back catalogue which consisted of three albums, twelve CD singles, and twenty old-style twelve-inch remixes. As I returned home, a motorbike courier was waiting for me, demanding a signature in exchange for a huge package. I signed and went upstairs, and placed the package on the coffee table. I then gave it a wide berth, walked into the kitchen, and viewed it from a safe distance of several feet. Still acutely aware that if Short Order were to see my article then he'd promptly come after me, my nervous system was now in overdrive. At every sound I jumped, convinced that this was the signal for danger. Out on the streets, shadows stalked me, while at night, dreams haunted my semi-conscious state. The delivery of a mysterious package, therefore, did little to abate my current mood. Eventually, I plucked up the courage and approached it, aware that I was now breathing a little too quickly and sweating just a little too profusely, despite the heat of the day. Picking it up with a pair of clammy hands, I shook it gently. I heard what sounded like plastic on plastic. No ticking, which could only be good thing. Then I tore it open, rapidly before bravery deserted me, and discovered, with no little surprise, Chemical Cosh's entire back catalogue consisting of three albums, twelve CD singles, twenty old-style twelve-inch remixes, along with a preview cassette of forthcoming material, a wad of press cuttings the size of a telephone directory, a handful of band stickers, and a mouse mat with the band's logo emblazoned across it. There was also a letter, on record company-headed paper, signed by someone called Annabel, the band's press officer, saying, You're editor asked me to send you this. Enjoy! See you tomorrow at 11. Ciao!

I spent the rest of the day in a relatively calm mood,

preparing myself for tomorrow's interview. Although the prospect of spending time with a band whose fame was now almost on par Coca Cola filled me with a certain dread, it was nothing compared to the expectation of Short Order's retribution, and so I readied myself with a level-headedness that would have impressed John Sultan. I placed their blaring electronica on heavy rotation on the hi-fi, and by midnight, I was not only ready for them, but secretly already quite sick of them.

*

I was awoken the following morning by a sound so insistent, it pierced my eardrums. From under the duvet, I vaguely recognized the noise but was unable to quite place it. Lifting my head from pillow, and my body from mattress, I followed it with bruised senses into the front room until I realized what it was. Somebody was buzzing the intercom, their finger seemingly stuck on the button, for there was now no interruption whatsoever, just a persistent monotonous cacophony. I lifted the receiver and shouted an annoyed, What?

"Police," said a tinny voice. "Open up."

"What?" I replied, incredulous.

"Open the door please, sir. It's the police."

I blinked into the early morning sun.

"Is this a joke?" I asked.

The terseness of the reply suggested otherwise, and I buzzed them up.

While they made slow progress with the stairs, I performed my morning rituals in seconds. I splashed water on my face, brushed my teeth, then ran directly into the bedroom, and threw on some clothes. By the time I answered the forceful knock on my door, I was out of breath.

The two policeman whose faces greeted mine were not smiling. Both in plain clothes, waving their identification in front of my nose, they had a creased, lived-in look that suggested satisfaction was something forever just out of their reach. They were in their mid- to late-thirties, with vague, undefined features, and the smell of stale cigarette smoke hung heavy in the air. One asked my name, and as they walked in and straight past me, an air of resignation followed them. Without a word of introduction, they looked around the flat, one with his hands behind his back, the other with his stuffed into his pockets. They looked deeply suspicious, and the one whose face hadn't been acquainted with a razor that morning looked increasingly frustrated. Clearly, patience was something he mislaid on a regular basis. He told me that this was a purely unofficial visit. It would not be noted down, not recorded. They came, he said as his lips curled up into a thin, bloodless smile, in peace.

Presently, they came together and introduced themselves. The unshaven officer was Detective Banks, the other Detective Russell. I told them my name again and was about to ask exactly how I could help them when Banks suggested coffee. I left them alone in the living room while I quickly made us all a drink, managing to spill both boiling water and milk as I poured. When I returned, Russell was sniffing around the living room, opening and closing drawers, while Banks was coming down from upstairs. When they saw me, they smiled tersely and sat on the sofa. And while Russell was dropping three white sugarcubes into each cup, Banks opened the briefcase he'd brought, and carefully took out a copy of Zeitguy. Involuntarily, I gulped down a lungful of oxygen and pulled at the neckline of my T-shirt, suddenly finding it constricting.

Russell thanked me for the coffee with a vapid expression, while Banks leafed through the magazine until he found what he was looking for.

"Interesting," he said, his yellowed fingers tapping my gangland article. "Very interesting."

I said nothing.

"This," he said in slow, sardonic tones, holding the magazine in mid-air with the tips of two very disdainful fingers, "arrived in the post, anonymously, yesterday morning. One of those yellow Post-It notes, which was stuck on the cover over the naked model's breasts, alerted us to the specific pages. And so I sat down with it, had a coffee from the machine, and read your, your ..." and here he snorted, pig-like, "article." He looked up and fixed me with a stare that set goosebumps on a race down the length of my back. "I remember thinking to myself that this could provide us with a lot of clues to some currently unanswered questions. But it also disturbed me, disturbed me a lot, that this could be printed in a magazine in a manner that unarguably glamorizes crime. If you'll permit my honesty, I thought it very bad taste, very bad form..."

Here, I interrupted his flow.

"It's fiction," I said. "Pure fiction." And attempted to explain.

But he wasn't listening, and talked right over me.

"...And so did your editor, a Mr. John Sultan. Well, eventually he agreed that it was in bad taste. But then it's amazing what several hours questioning in Paddington police station can achieve. After our little chat, Mr. Sultan told us that he only allowed it printed in the first place so as to lead the guilty towards the law. You to us, in other words. He saw it as his duty, so he said." He paused to sip on his coffee, and winced at the taste. "A good citizen, your Mr. Sultan, full of care for the community."

They then proceeded to ask me about my grandfather, about whom they appeared to know far more than I. They wanted to know the extent of his involvement on several recent building society robberies, his and mine, as well as several other crimes, some of which dated back years. I was unable to tell them anything. I told them I was no wiser than they, the truth. They didn't buy this at all, however, and so their questions were repeated, in a loop, for what seemed like an awful long time.

"Sir, may I point out to you that you've written a feature here," said Banks, "that practically reads like a confession. It's right here in black-and-white. Here, take another look, refresh your memory." He tossed the magazine carelessly into my lap. "For you to then suggest that you know nothing, that you're innocent, is a little like suggesting you think that we're completely stupid. To our faces. Which, I must make clear, I do not take kindly to, and neither does Detective Russell."

I pointed out that if the feature were indeed true, then I would have to be mad to willingly write it in the first place, much less submit it for publication.

"Well, sir," suggested Russell, "maybe the weight of your crimes proved too much to bear, and you wanted to ease your guilt through confession. It wouldn't be the first time something like that has happened. Even criminals have a conscience."

"Exactly," added Banks. "So stop wasting our time and start talking. Either that, or we'll take you down the station, make our enquiries a little more official."

After almost an hour like this, back and forth and back again, they showed me a series of photographs of weather-beaten old men with prison numbers under their faces. Since my grandfather was now deceased, they explained, he could no longer be tried for any of the crimes he may or may not have committed, and eventually the two detectives conceded it unlikely that someone of my rather nervous disposition had indeed colluded with either he or his associates. There were, however, several other people, still living, that they wished to question further on various connected charges, and thought it distinctly possible that I could identify them, and furnish them with more information on them and their activities. Finger them, they said.

"Call it an act of good will," said Banks. "For the time being, we will believe your story, your tale of innocence. And we haven't dragged you down to the station for any unnecessary unpleasantness, have we? So take a look at these faces, see if you recognize anyone. Point one or more of them out to us and we'll leave with our mutual respect intact. How's that?"

He smiled at me, the gaps in his teeth and the crookedness of his grin conspiring to convey pure malice.

Eight A4-sized photographs were spread out on the coffee table before me, and each pictured a man near to pensionable age. Despite their advanced years, they hardly bore signs of withering, or of mellowing. Instead, they looked like the kind of people who ate reputations for breakfast, perennially belittling those around them in order to maintain absolute command. Were they Italian, they'd be Mafia bosses. Instead, they were South East London's equivalent, more cockles than canneloni, but deadly all the same.

"Take your time," said Russell. "Take as long as you want."

Seven of the photographs meant nothing to me. In fact, each one could have been the same face, the same man. When you see evil up close, individual features become insignificant. All you see is the evil. But the eighth one I recognized immediately as Short Order. Somehow, his evil was more pronounced, more personal due to our recent contact: a prevalent feature in the solid cut of the jaw, the cauliflower ears, the bulbous nose, and the eyes that beheld a stare of stone. Inwardly, I shivered, remembering his earlier threat. If I finger him now, he'll be banged up, then perhaps I'll walk away with my life intact, I thought. Under the table, my hand flexed, and my index finger extended, preparing itself for identification.

"Recognize anyone?" said Banks gruffly.

"No," I said softly. "No, no one." The finger retracted. "Sorry, but I've never seen any of these people before." I shrugged helplessly.

Banks collected up the photographs slowly, never once removing his eyes from mine. Russell put them, along with Zeitguy, back into the briefcase and stood to leave. Banks followed him, but turned back to inform me that investigations would not stop here, and that I would be required to help them further, should need arise.

"And it will," he said. "It will. Don't leave the capital without informing us first. I hope we've made ourselves clear."

When they finally left, I ran a bath, got in, and submerged myself completely under water. With my eyes open and my hearing blocked, suddenly my world had shrunk, consisting now only of bubbles and pale green water. I blinked, and the bubbles bounced before my pupils. I blinked faster and enjoyed the effect it produced. Then I started counting in my head, eventually managing over a minute and a half until I reemerged back into the wider world, gasping for the taste of oxygen.

As I was about to go under once more, the intercom began buzzing, again with as much insistence as before. The police had returned. With a towel at my head, wiping away excess water and foam as I walked, I offered the intercom my weakest hello.

143

A voice barked back at me with garbled enthusiasm, and after requesting the voice to repeat itself several times over, I finally understood who it was. It was my ride to Chemical Cosh's headquarters, somewhere in Essex. My time with the band would take me across the country, first stop Manchester. Five minutes after being cautioned by police not to leave London without their prior say-so, and already I was forced to do otherwise. Does this constitute breaking the law, I wondered?

I dressed in seconds, grateful that I'd had the foresight to pack my bag the night before, and ran out the front door, taking with me - in case of unforseen circumstances - my credit cards and passport, a whim and a prayer.

Eight. Public Relations.

We sped through London's streets with the windows open and the

wind in our hair. With every set of traffic lights we zipped past,

I felt freer, and allowed myself to relax more. The driver, a boy

called Del in his very early twenties with gigantic, wraparound

sunglasses, a crewcut, and a slight visual reminder of teenage

acne scarring both cheeks, was clearly prone to hyperactivity,

slipping the new Chemical Cosh album into the CD player, pumping

up the volume while depressing a single button which opened

every window in the sleek black Renault Megane, and, while

retaining just a single finger on the steering wheel, also managed

to free himself from his oversized, unseasonal puffa jacket, and

tell me, in loud barking tones, who he'd chauffeured recently.

Then, in mid-sentence, mid-action, his free hand dug about in one

of the many velcro'd pockets on his cargo trousers and brought

out some Rizlas, a tin stuffed with tobacco, and some marijuana,

which he effortlessly fashioned into a spliff while negotiating the

roads without really looking where he was going.

When he lit it, and took down a huge gulp, he asked me

whether I was cool with this.

"You cool with this?" he said, practically shouting over the music, and grinning inanely.

I told him I was and he banged an open palm on the steering wheel in demonstrative appreciation. He then passed it onto me, but I declined, wanting to remain clear-headed for a whole number of reasons.

As we descended into East London, before heading out towards Essex, he put on a compilation CD of classic Northern Soul, a kind of music which prompted in him a reaction normally reserved for women upon presentation of the baby they'd just spent eighteen hours delivering. At first, he would sigh, then moan softly, before making a noise that veered between wild laughter and manic howling, his face contorted into all manner of pained positions.

"Oh, ooh," he said at one point, his breathing growing rapid, uncertain, "I fucking love this bit." The volume was raised further still, and at the next set of traffic lights, we received admonishing stares on either side of us from early morning drivers for whom Northern Soul prompts nothing but irritation. Del, however, remained oblivious, and in a near state of ecstasy.

I was vaguely aware of the sound of sirens before I realized what they represented. I swivelled in my seat until I could see out the back window, and through the rotating blue neon flash, saw a police car practically mounting the back bumper. Epileptic hand signals suggested we pull over.

The speed at which we were travelling, combined with the intensity of the music, and the panic of the situation, all conspired against my vision, and I was unable to tell whether the police car contained Detectives Russell and Banks or not, but I was pretty sure nonetheless. They'd told me quite unequivocally not to leave the capital without informing them beforehand and I had blatantly contravened the instructions almost immediately. And now I was to be arrested. It was really quite simple, and I had no one to blame but myself.

"Fuck!" Del, too, finally realized what was going on, cut the music, took a sharp left, stubbed out the spliff, popped it into his mouth, swallowed it, and produced from another pocket a tiny cannister of menthol breath freshener.

"Open up," he said, spraying the fresh minty liquid into both our mouths and into the air around us. He then slowed down

147

quickly, mounted the curb, whipped off his sunglasses to reveal baby blue innocent eyes, and disengaged the motor.

The police pulled up sharply behind us, then slowly got out of the car. In the rearview mirror, I discovered that these were merely uniformed officers, and not my two detective friends. My sphincter loosened considerably, and I began to breathe regularly once more, really quite gloriously relieved.

"Step out of the car please, sir," one said to Del, while the other peered over the body of the Renault and talked into a two-way radio. I remained seated, as instructed, and stared ahead, attempting to clear my mind of all thoughts, all panic. Out front, meanwhile, Del was quite clearly charming the officer questioning him, actually provoking a smile at one point. Driving license, tax disc, and insurance details were checked, and I made out a very polite, law enforcing request to please keep the volume down to an acceptable level.

"Sweet as," he said, as he slid back into the driving seat, giving me a quick wink before those eyes disappeared once more behind industrial-sized sunglasses.

We ploughed onwards, the music no longer bouncing off my

diaphragm.

*

Annabel was waiting for me upon our prompt arrival, an eager, rapacious smile spread across her face. She had bright green eyes, rosy cheeks, dyed blonde hair that was brown at the roots, pierced ears and a silver stud in her left eyebrow. A tight white Lycra top hugged her generous figure like a second skin, and she was wearing a pair of sandy coloured linen trousers that sat low on her hips, revealing just millimetres beneath her pierced navel a line of white elastic upon which I read the words alvin Klein Calvin Klein Calvin Kle. She had a mobile phone positioned at her trim waist, and a black wire that led up from it into her ear, with a tiny microphone level with her mouth. She was able to greet me - "Hi, lovely to meet you, be with you in a sec" - while simultaneously continuing with her conversation on the Nokia.

Her phone call appeared nowhere near an end, and so she led me by the arm towards the band's headquarters, a labyrinthine studio complex situated underneath a large clothing factory, while talking with increasing volume into a handset that was, by now, out of range.

"Shit," she said breathlessly. "I hadn't finished talking there! Typical, eh?" Then, switching attention onto me, she inquired how I was. "Found the place alright? Good. You'll love the band, by the way. They're chilling out downstairs, and they're in a really good mood because they've just gone up four places on the American charts. Great, eh? You a fan? I am, I love them. I can't tell you just what a thrill it is to work with them, they are just so..."

We walked through a dank corridor filled with the screams of a thousand sewing machines, then took the staircase down three flights, until we reached another, darker, corridor. At the end of that was a large black door which, when closed, locked out any remaining noise from outside. In here, everything was silent, save for a low murmur off in the distance, which Annabel suggested we follow. She then continued to babble on about various subjects, each one delivered with a disarming amount of enthusiasm. She appeared to love everything around her, everything in any way connected to her, her job, the whole wide world itself. I was wonderful, she proclaimed ten minutes after meeting me, the band were better still, while she herself was feeling in excellent form after cutting down on the alcohol and taking to the step machine at her local gym, which cost a hell of a lot of money but was, like, well worth it due to its overwhelming fantastic-ness. It felt as if she were robbing this underground lair of all its remaining oxygen and I wished that she would fall silent, if only temporarily. Her words were bouncing around my brain, making me nervous, nauseous.

Eventually, we reached the murmur, and the band's windowless studio. This consisted of three large rooms tattooed with faded posters of myriad bands from the past few decades, each of which boasted members with an excess of lank hair and phallic guitars which protruded from groin regions. One room consisted of a small stage, several boxes and crates, discarded guitars and drum machines, microphone stands, and a huge bank of computers. In another was the recording equipment which looked as vast as it did complicated. And in the other room was a small kitchen, several chairs and sofas, a snooker table, a television and hi-fi system, and various members of Chemical Cosh - as well as several unidentified others - lolling disinterestedly in seated and sprawling positions.

Annabel introduced each of the four members to me, as well as the three friends, but none of them looked up, nor offered any vocal reply. Instead, their gazes remained fixed squarely onto the television, where their latest video was being screened on MTV. They didn't look particularly happy; indeed, they looked blandly bored, wallowing in a stupor so soporific it suggested that a vocal greeting required far too much effort, an effort that no one was willing to exert. The smell of skunk wafted through the room like body odour in the gym.

Annabel then led me back into the rehearsal room, where we parked ourselves on a box each. She explained that they'd been mixing all night long and were now understandably a little tired. "They'll warm to you, no fear," she said, her optimism undinted. While we waited, I heard their video come to a conclusion. Then, just as the VJ was in the process of introducing the next track, there came a loud squeal of tape being quickly rewound. Thirty seconds later, the sound ceased and was replaced by the familiar crunching opening bars of their single. They were watching themselves on video over and over again.

"When do we leave?" I whispered to Annabel.

"Well," she began, "the tour bus has been here all night. The driver's sat there, ready and waiting." She shrugged. "We leave,

basically, when the guys want to leave. But don't worry," she

added, smiling with inane ebullience, "I'm sure it'll be soon. Soon

enough."

Three very long hours later, the bus pulled out of its parked

position, and pointed itself north, Manchester-bound.

*

Manchester proved little improvement on Essex. We arrived after a

slow five hour journey to a torrential summer downpour which

showed no signs of abating. While Annabel ushered us off as soon

as the bus pulled up outside the venue, the band made no similar

movements, and so the two of us ended up in a grim pub, alone.

Over drinks, she explained that the band needed time alone, as much

as possible sometimes, to mentally prepare themselves for a stage

show which, she explained, gives new meaning to the words, um,

really energetic. Right now, they were probably soundchecking, but

I was not invited to watch. The interview could take place later,

after the show, or tomorrow morning perhaps.

153

"What, when they finally start warming to me, you mean?" I asked her sarcastically.

Annabel said nothing, and went to the bar to procure some more drinks.

This was not going particularly well. In fact, it was proceeding significantly worse than a bad nightmare. During the bus journey, I succeeded in making no contact with the band whatsoever. Designed like a lavish hotel suite on wheels, the front of the bus consisted of four large armchairs, which was where I was allowed to sit and wallow in front of a video of Chemical Cosh's recent performance in Los Angeles, while the band themselves disappeared behind a drawn curtain halfway down the bus, behind which, I was later informed, were six bunk beds, a mini kitchen, a shower room, and a so-called chill out room consisting of large sofas and more TV screens. While Annabel regularly disappeared behind the curtain herself, it was suggested that I stayed put until invited to do otherwise. I waited a long time. The invitation didn't come.

After what must have been a couple further hours in the pub, my stomach now replenished with several jars of ale and packets of salted peanuts, Annabel had run out of things to say to me and had instead immersed herself in several women's magazines, one of which

had a survey that required unswerving concentration for upwards

of half an hour, and the use of a blue ballpoint pen. Intermittently,

she checked the reception on her mobile phone, which was to ring

as soon as the band were ready for us. At one stage during our

incarceration, the photographer arrived, having made his own way

up here a day earlier, and mumbled a greeting, then left to fit in

another appointment before heading on to the venue. Otherwise, both

Annabel and I sat there in silence, she reading, me staring aimlessly

into smoke-infested space.

And then a mobile phone did finally chime into resplendent life,

but it was mine, not hers. She looked crestfallen. The small

rectangle screen informed me that the caller, whoever they were,

had withheld their number. I pressed the appropriate button, and

brought the phone up to my ear. Before I had a chance to speak,

a gruff, truculent voice flooded my canal.

"Your first mistake," it said, before promptly cutting off.

Suddenly alert, Annabel looked up at me expectantly.

"Work?" she asked.

I nodded.

As she went back to perusing the beauty pages, my body went into rigor mortis. While the call could well have come from one of the police detectives - the voice was fairly indistinguishable, the reception poor - I was nonetheless in no doubt as to who it was. How he had acquired my mobile number was something I was never to discover, although this did set a precedent. No matter what I did, or where I went, Short Order was always one step ahead of me. The old man didn't merely have eyes in the back of his head, he had them all over the country.

That's it, then. He'd seen the magazine article. I was now beyond salvation. My life would never be the same again.

Annabel made movements.

"Just off to the loo," she said, all smiles.

Thrown entirely off balance, unreasonably convinced that my grandfather's enemy was about to pounce on me from behind the bar or around the next corner, I made a sudden, rash decision. Picking up my bag and throwing it over my shoulder, I stood up and hurriedly made my way over to the door, squeezing myself passed all the mid-evening regulars. As I reached the exit, I turned to see Annabel reemerging from the toilet, a confused look on her face as she saw first the empty table, and second my retreating figure. I shrugged helplessly to her, then disappeared back out into Manchester's sodium-soaked dusk. Once on the pavement, I broke out into a run, taking great long strides that carried me further and further away from where the phone call had intruded upon me, and I didn't stop until I collapsed back into a train seat, huffing and puffing, sweating profusely. Minutes later, the train pulled out of the station, due in at Euston three hours later.

Why London? I had no idea, but then I wasn't thinking at all clearly. I experienced a sudden compulsion, though, to return to familiar sights, to the vague security of home, something I clearly wasn't going to glean from remaining in Manchester a moment longer. And anyway, it was obvious that my time with Chemical Cosh was an absolute disaster, and I'd little doubt that the interview would be aborted entirely, sooner or later. They'd taken an instant dislike to me, and I felt incapable of reversing their opinion. But then I also no longer cared either way. I'd deal with my career - if I still had one - sometime later, in an uncertain future. My immediate survival was now of paramount, sole concern.

Just passed Birmingham, I received another phone call, this

time from Katkin.

"Long time no see," she said, amid a chuckle that betrayed a certain irritation underneath.

I made usual excuses, and promised to rectify things soon. Very soon, it transpired.

"Let's meet," she suggested.

"Okay," I replied. "Meet me in Euston Station in approximately ninety minutes."

This she appeared most eager to do.

We had a date.

Nine. Hunted.

Due to the kind of excuses privatized rail companies always tend
to fall back on, the train didn't pull into Euston until almost
midnight, an hour late. As I emerged onto the concourse, tired
and irascible, I spotted Katkin immediately. She looked similarly
hassled, washed out and weary, standing with her back against a
snacks machine. A beggar was directly in front of her with his
hand thrust under her chin, demanding it be crossed with gold.
He smiled derangedly. With the other, he clutched at his emaciated
frame, complaining that an empty stomach had removed from him
all shame. He didn't care what she thought, he just wanted some
money, and wouldn't leave her alone until she relinquished some.
As I approached, his insistent whine grew in volume into a
belligerent holler. I felt my blood boil and, wound tight as a coil
anyway, decided that I had at last found an appropriate victim.

"Come here," I said to him, making brief eye contact with
Katkin before pulling him roughly to one side, and feeling satisfied
as he stumbled.

He was younger than I first thought, and reedier. Up close, he looked scrawny, and no older than eighteen. He was also several inches shorter than me. "Do yourself a favour," I told him. "Piss off out of here immediately, or I will rip you to shreds. I'll beat your face so fucking bad that even your own mother won't recognize you."

He blinked slowly, obliviously, and opened his mouth to respond.

"Don't," I said sternly. "Don't say a single word. I'm serious. Open your mouth one more time, and I'll inflict more violence on you than you could ever imagine. And believe me, no matter how drunk you are, you'll feel pain. You'll feel a whole load of pain."

He grinned up at me, revealing no more than nine teeth, all of them stained, shrugged his shoulders, and shuffled off. As I watched him retreat, I felt disappointed that he hadn't provoked me further. I had suddenly found myself consumed with what I took to be violent intent. The need to control a situation, any situation, was huge, but it wasn't about to be sated.

Not yet, anyway.

Katkin appeared before my eyes, and hugged me hard.

"Oh, I'm so glad to see you," she said, her eyes two pools of tears. "Yours is the friendliest face I've seen in ages." She hugged

me tighter, and I reciprocated, melting into her warm embrace.

In the taxi, she told me that she'd finally severed relations

with her boyfriend completely, and that she'd hit a sticky patch

with her mother. She berated me for disappearing from her life just

when she needed me most, and I disguised the feeling of suffocation

that abruptly consumed me by looking out the window, focusing in

the middle distance, and breathing deeply. But within another

heartbeat, I changed emotion again and asked her if she fancied

spending the night in a hotel. I told her, my treat, I could well

afford it. Her eyes brightened, and she nodded with childish glee.

"I just have to pick up a few things," I said, as the taxi

pulled up outside my flat, "Wait for me here, I'll be back in a couple

of minutes."

She sat tight.

*

I walked up the staircase to my front door in darkness, scared to

turn on the light, just in case someone was waiting for me. If I was walking into trouble here, then I'd rather do it blindly, was my illogical reasoning. When I reached the top, there was no yellow police tape obstructing the entrance, no evidence that the door had been forced. I slipped the key into the lock, turned it to the left, and opened it. I stepped inside and proceeded, illuminated only by the light of the moon, to the bedroom upstairs where I would pack a few more essentials. When I entered the room, the door suddenly slammed behind me and the light went on. Startled, I turned to find an ugly young woman, trussed up in a garish, lime green shellsuit, smiling widely at me, revealing crooked, nicotine-stained teeth. She looked about twenty, maybe slightly younger, and had brown, greasy hair parted in the middle, and large brown eyes. Several earings dangled from each ear, and she wore large gold rings on each finger of either hand. She was very pale, and had a hint of a moustache on her upper lip. She chewed gum loudly, and blew a huge bubble that burst and smeared all over her chin.

"Wotchya," she said, in broken cockney, a sing-song element to her voice.

"Who are you?" I said.

Wordlessly, she approached me - my height, bigger build - and placed a large hand on my shoulder, gripped my T-shirt tightly, and dragged me back down the stairs and into the living room, where she deposited me messily onto the couch. She turned on a table lamp, then squatted down opposite me until we were face to face. She removed her chewing gum and placed it behind my left ear. Then she spoke, her breath rancid despite the gum's best efforts.

"Can you hear me alright?" she said.

I nodded, confused.

"Good, cos I've got an important message for you. Think of it as a directive for future life, if you get me." She grinned, and leaned in closer. "We know about the magazine, and we know about your little police visit this morning. And guess what? We ain't happy, not happy at all. You've pissed me off, and Pops? Pops is livid. Wanted you dead, straight off. Pretty fucking stupid thing you did, I must say, writing that magazine thing. You got a death wish or something?"

For the umpteenth time that day, I tried to explain what had happened, what a perverse accident it all was, and how sorry I felt, my regret. But she wasn't interested, and slapped my face repeatedly until I fell silent.

"Listen! And listen good. You say a word to the police about anything, anything at all, and we really do come and kill you. And when I say kill, it ain't no figure of speech. You understand?"

I told her I did.

"What happens if you forget?" she said.

I assured her that this was hardly likely.

"Well, just in case it does, I'll leave you with a little reminder."

A flash of gold, the crunching noise of impact, and the pain was immense. It felt like boiling water spread across the entire left side of my face. I fell back into the couch, groaning, and tasted blood. She pulled back and examined her finger candy, then reached down to the neck of my T-shirt and brought me back up into a straight-backed position.

"You alright?" she asked, with mock concern.

Then she filled my face with her fist again. I felt every ring, every ridge, as the air was knocked out of me. I saw nothing but swimming figures dancing before my eyes, while a sharp ringing swamped my ears.

She pulled me back up again, her eyes directed into mine.

"No joke," she said, darkly. "Don't forget."

She let go of me and I deflated down into a near horizontal position.

"Be seeing you," she said, the sing-song element now restored.

Then I must have blacked out.

When I came to, Katkin was hovering somewhere above me in the process of placing plaster on wound. Wounds. The antiseptic cream she'd already smeared across my face was what brought me to, and I felt an intense stinging.

"Taxi?" I said, suddenly remembering.

"Shh," she responded. "I've paid the taxi. We're going nowhere tonight."

She busied herself around my face.

"What on earth happened to you?" she said.

I said nothing, merely complained whenever pain rose to the surface, which was often.

Having exhausted the bathroom cabinet of first aid supplies, Katkin made her way into the kitchen and brought back a bottle of whiskey which, she said, would further help to dull the pain.

"Oh, by the way," she said. "Your answer machine is flashing. You've a message. Shall I press play?"

She did, and John Sultan's angry, raised voice filled the room.

"Jake, John Sultan here. Listen, you little fucker. Ever darken the door of my magazine again and it'll be the last thing you do. Thanks to you, I almost spent a night in prison! I thought you said that article was lies, fiction? The fucking police questioned me long into the night because of you! They even threatened the magazine with legal action, and it's all your fault, you bastard! I've cancelled your cheque. You're not getting any money out of me! And that other commission? Forget it. You're fired!"

Katkin poured two very large whiskeys, added some ice, and sat down next to me, pressing a cold flannel to my forehead.

"You have the imprints of at least four rings in your face," she said, matter-of-factly. "There was a lot of blood. The couch is stained, it may be ruined. And you've just lost a job I didn't even know you had. You and I," she said, suddenly sounding like her mother, "have a lot to talk about."

I drank heavily from my glass, wincing as the thick liquid scorched my throat.

*

Some time later, Katkin helped me off with most of my clothes and guided me gently into bed. Then she disappeared into the en suite bathroom and re-emerged a quarter of an hour later in one of my larger T-shirts which came down to her dimpled knees. She slid in and settled by my side, leaned over to give me the very slightest of kisses, and switched out the light. My face felt like a mountain bike range, lots of hills and valleys, but the pain was gradually easing, not least because of the amount of alcohol I'd consumed. I quickly fell into a heavy haze until eventually sleep came and took me away.

I awoke the following morning to blazing sunshine which fell directly onto my face and toasted it. Sleepily, I placed the pillow over my head, intent on returning my semi-conscious state to darkness, but let out a roar of pain upon contact. In my still dazed, hungover state, I had completely forgotten about the events of the night before, although now, thanks to the pillow, I was brought viciously back to all senses. And each of them ached. Easing myself up onto the headrest, I prised open both eyelids and blinked around the room. Contact lenses in my present state were completely out of the question, and so I fished around for my glasses in order to put the world into some kind of focus. I was, it appeared, completely alone. Katkin answered none of my agonizing cries, and from downstairs came nothing but silence. And the silence spooked me. I got up, put on some loose clothes, and went into the bathroom where I came face to face with a bloody monster, its features twisted out of all proportion, a black eye, a bruised cheek, torn flesh, some dried blood, peeling plasters. My hair, meanwhile, stood to alarmed attention, and my eyes were bloodshot. I looked terrible, and fell dejectedly onto the toilet seat when I heard the front door downstairs slam shut. Every muscle tightened as I feared the worst, a repeat performance of last night. Next, there was the sound of running feet on the stairs, and the swish of the bedroom door being pushed open. I held my breath, but could do nothing to stop the furious beating of my racing heart. Then the bathroom door opened and she burst in, a whirlwind of energy despite the hour, smiling encouragingly, despite what she saw.

"Feeling any better?" asked Katkin, as my heartbeat attempted to rediscover its regular rhythm.

"Not really," I said, "no."

"Never mind," she replied, "we'll get you on the mend soon
enough."

Katkin's reaction to all this was surprisingly calm, not least for
someone prone to hyperventilating after a win on Monopoly. Last
night, as the whiskey flowed, I told her everything, feeling it
pointless by this stage to hold back anything. Plus, I felt the need
to unload, to share the extraordinary recent events of my life with
someone. I told her about my legacy, the disastrous farce with
Zeitguy and my similarly hopeless sojourn with Chemical Cosh, and
I then told her about Short Order, the police, and described the girl
who attacked me yesterday, who I guessed must have been Short
Order's pitbull of a granddaughter, an inbred bitch. While her first
reaction was one of shock, she was also unable to stop smiling, the
shape of her mouth - spread wide, revealing a proliferation of
gnashing teeth - making her look slightly unbalanced. She thought
everything incredible, said it all sounded awfully exciting, just like
a movie. I tried to explain to her that this certainly wasn't the case
for me, that excitement didn't even come into it, but she wouldn't

169

have it. She said that it was all quite thrilling, and proclaimed my grandfather absolutely wonderful for leaving me so much cash. She was sure that this thing with Short Order was merely temporary, and that when everything had blown over, I'd live the life of the rich, perhaps confusing my rather moderate lump sum for a figure far greater.

"Do you know," she began, "that if I hadn't come to meet you last night then I'd have been in bed by ten o'clock? This is the most exciting thing that's ever happened to me." She laughed as if she'd been tickled, and helped herself to some more whiskey until there was none left.

She'd risen an hour earlier than I the following morning in order to buy some food for breakfast, but proclaimed upon her return that as it was such a lovely day, we should instead venture outside and find a cafe. No one would care about my appearance, she assured with confidence, but just in case they did, she put a baseball cap on my head, and gently slid a pair of sunglasses over my prescription pair and onto the bridge of my nose. I dared not check out my reflection, as I'd already had enough bad news for one day.

"And if you still are in pain," she said, "I've the perfect remedy."

Up in Notting Hill, we rounded the corner, headed for a small cafe next to the cinema. But as we approached the traffic lights, a tall, wiry white man with a head full of thick dreadlocks and a webbed tattoo on his left cheek stepped out of a doorway and greeted Katkin in thick patois. I understood nothing, but Katkin looked elated, like she just found something she'd been searching ages for. She greeted him back in an identical accent and they knocked knuckles together three times, before slapping one another's outstretched palms. They conversed back and forth, a thick, treacle-like exchange of words that, to my ears at least, were completely impenetrable. She then followed him back into the doorway, and, after a blur of activity in which several things appeared to change hands rapidly, then jumped back out onto the pavement in less than three seconds flat.

"This should take away some of the pain," she said, placing a tiny packet into my hand as we crossed the road.

I looked into her face, which at this moment was curiously unfamiliar to me, and nodded thank you.

Before secreting myself into the cafe's shoebox-sized toilet to snort the contents of the packet up into my nose and send my brain into temporary freefall, we settled down to breakfast. Forsaking my fitness regime in favour of a fry-up, I shovelled sausages, bacon and beans into my mouth, suddenly ravenous. The previous day I'd only eaten peanuts, and later in the evening I'd had all my energy punched out of me; I needed some put back in. It was deliciously fatty. Katkin, meanwhile, delicately set about eating two slices of granary bread and honey, and drinking some camomile tea, while between mouthfuls she told me about conditions back at home, how things between she and her mother had gotten so bad that Jaz was now preparing to move out.

"The tension," he had told her one evening, "does not suit me. I'm sorry, I must go."

She continued to unravel the barbed wire that punctured her heart at some length, resolving to not shed any tears and instead maintain her anger, her resolve. She proclaimed that things had reached a head. Being with me had given her inspiration, she said, to take flight and flee the nest. It was time for the next chapter. A clean break, a new start.

"Which is where I hope you come in," she said, gazing with intent into my hidden eyes. "I'm not sure exactly what your feelings are about me, but I'm really very fond of you." She took another bite of toast, and washed it down with some translucent tea. "What I'm trying to say is..." she paused again, torturously, "...is, can I move in with you?"

My forked sausage hovered in mid-air, and started trembling. I removed the sunglasses and looked at her squarely. But I couldn't speak, my voice shocked into temporary hiding, and so she quickly jumped in and explained once more just how impossible things had become at home. Jaz, she insisted, couldn't move out because her mother relied on his rent money to help with the mortgage. Katkin herself, then, was mere extra baggage for her mother, as she paid absolutely nothing towards any costs.

"It would just be temporary," she said, of her intentions. "Well, temporary if things don't work out, anyway. But maybe they will. Maybe they'll work out wonderfully and we'll get along like a house on fire?"

The sentence ended with an inflexion of pure hope.

I was still unable to find any words. And so I excused myself, squeezed into the minuscule bathroom, and got ridiculously high. When I returned, Katkin was midway through a ferocious crying jag that had her shoulders trembling violently. Tears streamed from her eyes like Niagara, and they burned bright pink. When she saw me, she abruptly stopped, and sniffed hard.

"What's wrong?" I asked.

"Nothing," she said. "Nothing."

*

When we arrived home, some thirty minutes later, my gait unsteady, Detectives Russell and Banks were waiting on the step. They greeted my arrival tersely, and when they saw the state of my face, they became officially suspicious.

"Well, well," chuckled Banks. "What happened there, then? No, let me guess. You walked into a door, right?"

They followed us upstairs, barged into the living room, and sat down on the couch, Russell noticing the dramatic blood stain. Banks suggested coffee again, and while I reluctantly retreated into the kitchen, they spoke with Katkin in low, mumbled voices. When I came back in, Katkin looked mildly flushed, and slightly nervous.

"So," smiled Banks, "it wasn't a domestic, then? Your lady friend here maintains complete innocence in the matter. Didn't lay a finger on you, she says."

"What did happen to you?" asked Russell.

I sat down and told them. I explained how the flat was broken into the previous night, and when I returned unexpected, they proceeded to beat me up. The detectives wanted to know what was stolen. I told them that because I'd walked in on them, they had got away with nothing.

"How many were there?" Banks asked.

"Just one," I replied.

"Just one? You said they."

"No I didn't."

"Yes you did. You said they."

"Well, I meant him."

"Him?"

"Yes."

"Describe him."

I improvised, stuttering.

"I can't be sure exactly," I said in summary, "because it was dark, and it all happened so quickly."

"Even so, sir," said Russell, reading over his notes, "average height, average build, brown hair, trainers, doesn't exactly give us much to go on."

"Well, I'm sorry, but that's all I can remember. I was concussed, after all."

Impatiently, Banks came to the reason for their second visit.

"We've some photographs we'd like you to look over," he said.

"What, again?" I said.

"Again."

A further eight A4-sized black-and-white photographs were spread across the coffee table, this time featuring younger people, both men and women, some black, others white, one Asian. Again, seven of them meant nothing to me, while the eighth was the psychotic girl who had beaten my face into a bloody pulp. Involuntarily, I winced, and Banks instantly zeroed in on her.

"This one?" he said, tapping his finger on her forehead with relish. "You recognize her?"

I swallowed hard.

"No."

"I think you do. Where do you recognize her from?"

"Unless that's Hazel Harper," I said, "who I went to primary school with but haven't seen since, then no, I don't recognize her. She does bear a certain resemblance, though."

Banks was not amused.

"Take a closer look," he said. "But it's not Hazel Harper."

I studied the photograph intently, and managed this time to keep the shiver hidden within. Like her grandfather, or whoever he was exactly, she radiated pure nastiness. Hers was a stare that could prompt complicity in anyone, if only because it was blatantly apparent just what she could do to someone who didn't follow her orders to the very letter. I took one last look, then looked away, hoping that I'd never have to set eyes on her again.

"No, I'm sorry, but I've no idea who she is."

"Well," said Banks, "I wouldn't be surprised if you came into contact with her, sooner or later, as our investigations progress. And if you do, here's our card, give us a call immediately. We strongly recommend you do."

Over black coffee on the blood-stained couch sometime later, I
received another grilling, this time from Katkin.

"That was her, wasn't it?"

I told her it was.

"Just as well you said nothing, then, because if she did this
to you unprompted, then God alone knows what she'd do if you went
running to the police."

She then asked why the police were so insistent that I
recognize at least one of the faces proffered, and I told her that
they were convinced that I knew them, or of them, and had the kind
of inside track on either that could well lead to an arrest and,
ultimately, a concrete conviction. It was clear that both Short Order
and the girl were well known to the police, and it had become
increasingly clear that the former had had dealings with my
grandfather. The police had obviously been after Grandad for years.
Throughout his life, he was clearly adept at remaining a very tidy
criminal, rarely, if ever, leaving a traceable scent. According to my
mother, he'd been imprisoned just once, back in the fifties, for

handling stolen goods. He'd received six months, served just three, and never saw the inside of a prison cell again. Nevertheless, the police knew of his activities, and those of Short Order. They just never had any solid proof. And then I arrive on the scene, writing a feature for public consumption that suggests I have answers for a great many questions. So. The police think I'm an ideal informant, Short Order's convinced I'm a potential grass. One's intent on me opening up, the other will do anything to ensure I keep schtum.

"But you actually know nothing about them at all?"

"Not a thing. He never mentioned their names to me, and if he did, then I certainly don't remember. Trouble is, the police don't believe this, and neither does the old man. So I'm kind of stuck in the middle."

"Oh dear," said Katkin.

"Yes," I said. "Oh dear."

Just then, the telephone rang. I told Katkin that I couldn't face talking to anyone, and wondered whether she'd take a message for me. She walked over to the phone, and picked it up on the fourth ring. I heard her say, no, he's not here, and, I'm his girlfriend, I'll take a message. Then she held the receiver away from

179

her ear as the voice at the other end shouted into it. When the call had ended, she came back over to the couch and sat down.

"It was that man John Sultan. He said that in next month's issue of the magazine there would be a disclaimer, distancing the magazine from your feature in any way. He said, read it and weep, because afterwards you'd be virtually unemployable. Then he slammed the phone down."

A smile hovered, then settled on my face, its presence testament of the only possible reaction to the sudden ground-level turbulence I was experiencing: one of absolute, quizzical disbelief. What next? I wondered to myself. Desperate for levity, I thought I may as well try my chances with Katkin. Since my beating last night, she did seem permanently aroused. I'd certainly nothing else to lose. It was a little after three in the afternoon. I had no commitments, nothing of any pressing importance to deal with. On a deep breath, I asked her if she'd like to follow me upstairs and into bed?

A minute went by, then two, then a further nine months of pregnant pauses, and still I awaited an answer.

Finally she approached, eyes first, took me by the hand, and led the way.

Ten. Fugitive Pieces.

In a plume of post-coital cigarette smoke, the decision was made.

My current abode was now prone to giving me the creeps and,

temporarily at least, I felt I needed some distance from it. Katkin

agreed when she saw me jump involuntarily at the sound of the

phone, the front door, the kettle.

"Just for a few days," she said. "Allow dust to settle."

And so I packed another overnight bag, locked up, and

followed Katkin over to Shepherd's Bush for her to do likewise.

Then we sat back in the taxi, stretched our legs as far as they

would go, and tried to decide on an appropriate location.

"I know," said Katkin, and leaned forward to inform the driver.

*

Sex, in its first flush, is a magnificent life force. This is

something anyone with such experience will vouch for. But sex

when laced with the distinct possibility of outside danger is even

more thrilling. The point of penetration becomes plug and socket, the vital electricity it creates acting as confirmation that you are still alive - alive, kicking, living. For four uninterrupted days we were holed up in an exclusive West London hotel, the kind so discreet that you'd never know it existed at all unless someone with prior knowledge - in this case, Katkin - alerted you to the coveted fact. It was obscenely expensive, but Feng Shui'd to perfection. Our room was bleached white - white walls, white bed linen, white closets, white en suite bathroom - the only colour provided by a constantly-replenished fruit bowl: a bolt yellow banana, a lush green apple, an electric orange tangerine, a fuzzy brown kiwi. Inside the white closet sat a streamlined black television with over one hundred channels and access to Scandinavian porn. We barely left the room at all, ordering everything by phone, paying for everything by credit card. While cocooned safely here, the crippling cost meant nothing to me whatsoever. Like any new couple without a care in the world, Katkin and I became obsessed with each other's bodies, and were fascinated to discover how exactly they fitted together through myriad contortions that often called upon Katkin's basic knowledge of Tai Chi. Sex became acrobatic, intense, profound, and, ultimately, it became a kind of loving. While no such declarations were ever voiced, the stares with which we addressed one another were loaded with enough silent symbolism to leave either of us in little doubt. We'd kiss respective tonsils, feed each other, scrub one another's back, caress ourselves to sleep, and awake wrapped up in a tight embrace. The four days stretched on like infinity, and we were convinced that they'd never end, that outside interference would never puncture our bubble.

Until, of course, it did.

On the fifth morning, I awoke with a crook neck, my head wrapped awkwardly in one of Katkin's arms, my nose to her armpit, both legs tied into a knot with hers. I stirred gently until I managed to wake her, and then we stretched independently, showered together, and ordered breakfast. Over our respective dishes, we tuned into the early morning news as we both secretly anticipated another day of Kama Sutra couplings. The news reader reported on the latest developments in the world in monosyllabic tones, but we paid more attention to each other than to the screen. Moving breakfast to one side, our lips met in a bacon-and eggy kiss, and subsequent stirrings from down below suggested that within moments we'd be horizontal again. I broke off, found the remote control, and was about to silence the television when I saw a blown-up photograph of the girl who'd attacked me staring from the television screen. Quickly turning the sound up, I heard, ...was arrested last night after a brawl with police outside a pub in Deptford. The woman, Treeza Burke, 20, is wanted in connection with several armed robberies in the area. Detective Inspector Roger Banks was the arresting officer. "We came to question the young lady on matters concerning a current inquiry, but, completely without provocation, she blew up in our faces and started attacking me. Look, she's cut my cheek. I'm bleeding." It took four officers to restrain the woman, and she's currently being held at Peckham Police Station, awaiting charges.

The stirrings promptly ceased, and Katkin and I looked at one another, mouths agape. I turned the mobile phone off, just in case.

*

Katkin told the taxi driver to take us to a street somewhere in Acton. She wouldn't tell me where we were going.

185

"It's a surprise," she said. "Let's just say we're going to take the bull by the horns."

Another mad glint in her eye unsettled me further still, because the more I stared into her face, the less I recognized her.

"You will," she said, intruding into my secret thoughts. "Patience." The wallflower I'd known in Shepherd's Bush was becoming a chameleon.

We pulled up alongside a used car lot, and I followed Katkin as she strode up towards the small grey caravan on bricks that constituted the lot office. As she walked through the rows of motionless cars, she looked at each vehicle on her left and right, trailing a finger on occasional roofs and bumpers, checking for rust, for dust.

"We'd like a car, please," she told the dealer, a rotund, red-faced man in his fifties wearing nylon slacks, a tight white T-shirt that struggled to cover his bloated gut, and a faded brown leather jacket.

"Certainly, my dear," he replied, beaming. "What did you have in mind."

She led the way and we followed obediently, stopping before

a gleaming silver machine with no roof and white hubcaps.

"This one," she said, pointing.

The dealer shot me a sideways glance but quickly realized that I was of little consequence here, and transferred his gaze back to Katkin.

"Ah, a woman with taste," he replied. "Would madam like to take it for a test drive?"

Katkin slid into the driver's seat and clicked the door shut quietly.

"No time," she said. "I would, however, like your absolute assurance that this car is fit to drive and worth every penny of this rather over-inflated price?"

"Madam, I wouldn't dream of selling anything less to anyone, much less someone as clearly discerning as you."

"Pleased to hear it. If anything does go wrong, we will of course return immediately. And we'd be far from happy."

The dealer, his expression unflinching, continued to beam. "My word is my bond, madam."

"Lovely. You take Visa, I presume?"

"I take anything that will help pay for my extension," he

replied, chuckling.

She then snapped at me to produce the card, and as we pulled
out of the yard fifteen minutes later with a costly acquisition she
deemed as absolutely necessary to our needs, she kicked her head
back and started to laugh. "You never know when we'll need to
getaway," she said. The laughter grew in volume and strength, and,
as I worried over her fitness to drive in such a hysterical state,
then suddenly changed into great heaving sobs. We pulled over, and
I offered the comfort of open arms. She dived in and soaked my
shirt through with tears.

Later that day, with our classic 1971 Mercedes parked out
front, we huddled together before an unnecessary but nevertheless
romantic fire in a small hotel just outside Oxford. We were making
light work of a bottle of vintage port, and Katkin was earnestly
colouring in the grey bits of her life for me, explaining the reasons
for all the sudden crying fits.

A week ago, the father she hadn't seen or heard from in over
a decade hanged himself in his Hackney bedsit. He and her mother
had never married and, shortly after Katkin's birth, he disappeared
back to his native Germany to reinstate previously severed family

ties, before flying over to America to lend his support to the Vietnam peace protests. From what Katkin gathered via intermittent postcards over the next decade, he had taken the film Easy Rider a little too literally, and had Harvey Davidsoned his way around various states impregnating countless young women en route. By the late eighties, he was facing several paternity suits - having now settled down, and been successfully traced to Nebraska, where he was working as a student adviser - and so felt forced to flee to London where he remained unemployed and, due to what a doctor later confirmed as manic depression, unemployable. He'd contacted his daughter just once after his return, but as their reunion was less than a happy affair, he'd refrained from trying it again. He died destitute, heavily in debt, and naked, and wasn't discovered until the neighbours complained about the smell nine days later.

Then she started in on her highly erratic relationship with her university boyfriend Simon, and the rollercoaster of emotion she continues to experience with her mother.

When she stopped talking, the bottle of port was empty, Katkin in need of instant replenishment.

The next morning, regardless of our hungover state, we drove into town and, at Katkin's instigation, spent more money on clothes than I'd make in six months as a temp. She then booked herself in for a haircut and emerged, an hour later, with a short black spiky crop that took my breath away on sight. Her previously blonde, bubbly definition had been completely eradicated. She now looked mysterious, sexual, her face somehow sharper, more real.

"The perfect therapy," she beamed, crying now only for brief moments.

*

We checked out of the hotel the following day and drove through streets I'd never previously visited until we reached Stoke Newington, somewhere in North East London, a place where the tube doesn't quite reach. This, I was informed, was to be our new location, Katkin revelling in our sudden nomadic nature. We were to stay in a flat belonging to one of her old boarding school friends, a split-level studio on the top floor of a crumbling Victorian house. Although cramped, I instantly took to the anonymity of the locale and naively kidded myself that it brought me safety, made me less exposed to danger. The place was ours for as long as we needed it as the school friend, Tatjana, was on a round-the-world trip with a rich boyfriend.

"She's probably enjoying a love-in somewhere in Goa right now," said Katkin with a sly smile as she retrieved the front door key which Tatjana had sellotaped to the bottom of her dustbin.

The flat was small and chaotically messy, consisting of a small dining table, a sunken sofa, several thirsty cacti, and, up five wooden steps to what constituted the balcony area, a perilously low futon which covered all available flooring. The kitchen, meanwhile, resembled a family box of matches without the contents, and there was no cooker, just a microwave. The fridge, which would probably seem enormous to a four-year-old, lay open. A strange smell emanated from somewhere within, and was possibly lethal.

"Lovely, isn't it?" said Katkin, through rose-tinted spectacles. "Let's tidy it up a bit, make it fit for a fugitive couple."

From under the sink, she unearthed a pair of pink rubber gloves and a cloth.

"You spit, I'll polish."

That night, we watched North By North West, the classic

Hitchcock film in which an innocent man - a victim of mistaken identity - finds himself on the run for his life. Ordinarily a rich advertising executive, Roger Thornhill, played with impeccable charm by Cary Grant, nevertheless manages to handle himself magnificently when his world is suddenly turned upside down and violently shaken from side to side. With barely a hair out of place, he succeeds in outwitting his pursuers at every turn, and even gets the girl at the end. I made a mental note to buy some fixing gel the next day and secretly prepared myself to become a hero, happy at that moment to allow a fancy flight into daydreaming consume me whole.

The following day, I dared switch on my mobile again and found nine VoiceMails awaiting me. With much trepidation, I accessed them, only to discover nine messages - each over a minute long - of absolute silence, with maybe the merest of hints of steady, menacing breathing at the other end.

"Don't worry about it," said Katkin, assuringly. "Mobiles always pick up cross lines, you just happened to pick up nine, that's all."

I turned it off again and followed my breezy girlfriend into the outdoors, towards streaming sunshine, and a picnic in the park.

After an al fresco lunch of French bread, Italian ham, Dutch cheese, English strawberries, a light Australian wine, and some orange juice from Safeway, we lay back into the dry, brittle summer grass and dozed in a state of extreme relaxation, my right hand and her left laced delicately at the fingers.

We awoke some time later tingling all over, fearing at best slight sunburn, at worst sun poisoning. Katkin's face now resembled a cherry tomato, while I felt like a lobster on a grill. On the way home, we made a mercy dash to Boots to purchase several tubes of after sun cream, while at the off license next door, we stocked up on more wine, also to aid the easing of pain.

Back at the flat, I gently lowered myself into the sunken sofa, wine and corkscrew in hand, and switched on the television while Katkin disappeared into the loo. Still hazy from over-exposure to the sun, I found myself illogically mesmerised by the action on Baywatch in which a woman in a micro red bathing costume was administering mouth-to-mouth to a large, nearly-naked man lying prostrate on the golden Californian sand. From the music that welled up around the action, I took it that this man's life was in grave danger unless the blonde lifeguard was able to conjure up a miracle by blowing sweet oxygen into his lungs. Her hair fell over her eyes as she worked, while around her there grew a large, interested crowd.

What happened next took a split second, but seemed to last forever, in extreme slow motion. Katkin, returning from the bathroom, entered the living room at a peculiar angle, head first. A large fist was pulling her by the hair, and I noticed that she was unable to scream due to the small hand towel stuffed into her mouth. Her hands were bound together with rope, and her eyes were bulging out of their sockets. Her face was no longer red, but bright purple. Despite trembling limbs, I managed to find my feet, but was quickly knocked back down again as Katkin then flew through the air and hit me full in the body with hers. The wind was knocked out of me as we both crashed onto the sofa violently. It took a moment to gather my senses and as I opened my eyes I saw a huge fist coming my way, about to make contact with a face still bruised from its last attack. At the point of impact, I felt no pain, just suffered all-consuming blackness.

Time passed, I've no idea how much. My eyes blinked, taking several moments to focus. My hearing took in the closing theme to Baywatch, but not much else. As I tried to sit up straight, I knocked into Katkin's motionless frame and winced as the pain shot through me like lightning. As my eyes gradually righted themselves, I saw a figure towering over my slumped form. It was an elderly man with pug features, newly-shorn white hair, fierce eyes, and spittle-inflected thin lips. A single vein throbbed in his forehead.

I felt a flash of remembrance, his name on the tip of my tongue.

Short Order.

"We meet again, much as I thought we would," he said in his gravelly voice. "Didn't take you long, did it?"

I just looked at him, saying nothing.

He picked up the intact wine bottle from the floor, smashed the neck on the wall, and poured the alcohol over my head. "Perhaps we should celebrate," he said, "you and me meeting up again." He held the half-full bottle over his mouth, tilted, and poured some wine down his throat.

Beside me, Katkin stirred, and issued a low moan. Short Order doused her with some remaining wine and slapped her cheeks gently, almost tenderly, to bring her back to full consciousness. He removed the towel from her mouth and freed her wrists from the rope.

"Sorry about that love," he said, "but needs must."

He cleared a space on the small dining table with a grand sweep, and sat down facing us, his arms resting on thick thighs.

"Now," he said. "Down to business."

The side of my face felt on fire, the pain almost unbearable. I could feel broken bone, and tasted blood. I turned to look at Katkin, and she returned my gaze, her own eyes bloodshot and paralyzed with fear. She too had a bruise on her cheek, and her wrists were pink and raw, less from the sun than the rope. She tried to smile at me, a morsel of empathy, but failed.

"Right," said Short Order, "as I'm sure you're aware, my daughter was arrested recently."

"Daughter?" I asked him, confused, convinced that Treeza Burke must surely be his granddaughter.

"Yes, Treeza, my daughter, the one who paid you a little visit the other day."

"Oh."

"Yes, oh. Now, while she may not have helped matters by attacking that copper cunt, she was eventually let off with a caution, cos they couldn't make anything stick. See, we run a very tidy operation, we do. And the girl takes after her old dad." He leaned in closer. "Interesting thing was, while she was being questioned, they asked about you."

"Me?"

"You. Wanted to know of any connection we may have, said you suggested that you and her were - how did they put it? - acquaintances. Now, I told you they'd come sniffing, and I knew as soon as looked at you that you'd put us in a dangerous position before long. Son, I'm an old man and I'm slowly winding down towards retirement. I intend to see my days out in the Spanish sunshine, not inside some prison cell, and so all my few remaining business deals, shall we say, have to proceed without cock-ups, something which your very presence makes difficult, maybe even impossible. Copshop has started sniffing like pigs, and it's all down to you. I still reckon you know more than you're letting on, and the police very strongly suspect the same. You're a thorn in my side, mate, your very presence annoys me."

He got up and paced the room, kicking aside any object that lay in his path.

"The police could run you in tomorrow, come down heavy on you, give you the full Yellow Pages treatment to the top of the head, and you'd tell 'em everything."

I tried to tell him that I really did know nothing, but discourse was something we weren't about to indulge in.

"As long as I regard you a threat, son, you're a threat," he continued, pointing an accusing finger in my direction. "So I've come to a decision. As I'm a little old to get too much blood on my hands, I'll refrain from cutting your girlfriend's arm off and beating you to death with it. Instead, I'm going to turn the tables and make you a temporary accomplice. I'll smear guilt all over you, so much so that the next time they come visiting, the police won't be there to question you about us, they'll come to lock you up, maybe even throw away the key. That should get them off my back once and for all."

He smiled derangedly. "It's not a bad idea, is it?"

Katkin's leg found mine and pushed hard.

"We'll be in touch," said the old man. "Oh, and tempting as it is, what with your new car and everything, don't be thinking of doing a runner. Because we will find you. And we'll bring the axe with us."

He proceeded to demonstrate his ability to find us - wherever we may stray - by recounting everything we'd done since leaving the flat in Notting Hill. Somehow, he knew about our every step, the West London hotel, the Acton car dealer, the picnic, even the after sun.

As he turned to leave, he reiterated his promise.

"We'll be in touch. Keep the mobile on."

And then I passed out.

*

When I came to some time later, I heard the sound of running water. I attempted to move, but my body felt like a dead weight, bruises blossoming everywhere, my sunburnt skin resembling a mushroom patch. Within a blink, I was under again, then with another, I came woozily to once more, breathing heavily, irregularly. Holding my head to steady my gaze, to level out my equilibrium, I realized that Katkin was standing in front of me, a towel wrapped around her body.

"Come," she said. "I've just had a bath and washed all the blood off. Your turn."

"You - you okay?" I managed to ask.

"Better than you by the looks of it," she replied evenly. "The old bastard was only toying with me. It's you he was serious with."

"But your bruises, the rope..."

"Don't you worry about me. It's you we have to mend. Your face is a mess, and you're missing great chunks from three teeth. I've put them in a saucer in the kitchen. You'll have to see a dentist." She tutted.

I looked up at her, stunned by her resolution. "Look, Katkin, I'm really sorry about this. I don't know how he found us, but I'm..."

She put her index finger to my lips, silencing me.

"Shhh. Don't say anything." Then she found a smile. "In sickness and in health, remember."

That night, the bad dreams began.

I dreamed that Short Order's fist, now gigantic in size, is accelerating through thick fog towards me. I'm unable to move. It makes contact with my eyes, nose, and mouth, and my entire face folds in on itself, allowing the fist access down through my throat and into my stomach, after which it explodes out of my rectum, trailing my bloody innards as it goes. Then I see a wine bottle, its neck broken, pierce my eyes, producing projectile blood which splatters all over his face and barrel chest. He blinks, shakes his head, and my blood dances in the air. I see him taking an axe to Katkin's right arm which, on impact, soars up into the air. Dropping the axe, he catches the severed limb and proceeds to beat me about the head with it. The arm surprises me with its weight - it feels like iron - and the fingers are outstretched, clawing at my flesh until it reveals the white of bone. Blood is pouring everywhere. One moment it's ankle deep, but it keeps flowing and keeps rising until it's up by my waist, my chest, until I'm completely submerged and I'm drowning in my own blood, drinking it down into my lungs, where it instantly coagulates, creating a fantastic pressure that squeezes every last drop of life out of me, until all I see is the colour red, until I see nothing else at all, and wake up drenched in what is thankfully only sweat, hearing Katkin whimpering beside me, both her arms still intact.

The dreams continued night after night, each more vivid than the last. Teeth being pounded by a hammer, Katkin being raped, me bound to a chair, forced to watch. Running down dark alleyways, streetlights flickering and failing, the rumbling sound of heavy footsteps encroaching ever nearer, too scared to turn around and face my nemesis. Being dropped from a great height into thin air, falling at terrific speed towards earth, bracing myself for impact but never arriving, just plummeting endlessly, the wind soaring right through me, my cheeks flapping with the force of my fall. Treeza Burke dragging me by the hair into a stinking public toilet, ripping my clothes off me and forcing me into her, jumping on my lap, banging her head on the ceiling, her fleshy thighs slapping loudly on mine, grunting with drunken passion, until I helplessly shoot my load which instantly travels up her uterus and meets an egg, which it duly impregnates. She gives birth almost immediately to a hideous, bug-eyed red monster who calls me Daddy, jumps into my arms then melts all over my chest like soft and sticky purple-blue glue until there's nothing left but what looks like afterbirth, with eyeballs that stare into mine with a horrific pleading expression: why why why?

And each morning was the same, me waking soaked in a malodorous sweat, Katkin pressing a damp towel to my head telling me everything will be alright, even though she hardly believed this herself.

Approximately a week after we moved back into the flat, the phone call came. It was a little past midnight, and we were stewing in front of the television watching another vintage Hitchcock. The dormant mobile burst into sudden life, glowing green, and tentatively I put it to my ear, its poisonous rays microwaving my brain in an instant.

The voice, familiar by now, ordered me to go to a pub in Deptford, known locally as The Dog's Bollocks, just before closing time tomorrow night.

"Come alone," he said.

That night, the bad dreams began even before I closed my eyes. This time I was a chicken in its little wire mesh prison which was torn apart by a big bad wolf. I pleaded with the wolf not to eat me, to please spare my life. I put my wings together, prayer-style, begging for mercy. He let loose a nasty cackle, opened his jaws wide, and with one bite removed my head from my body. Running around the farmyard headless, my feathers flying, blood spurting in great arcs from my neck, I looked like a surreal drinking fountain careening out of all control.

I needed help, but from where, from whom?

Eleven. Jesus Lives.

The dentist's reception area was disarmingly lavish, far plusher

than any apartment I'd ever come across, including mine. Looking

more like a high-class restaurant than a mere waiting room, with

its luxurious armchairs, its chrome coffee tables, ornate lamps, and

expensive art adorning every sky blue-coloured wall, the resulting

ambience was enough to remove all lingering fear from those who

otherwise harboured a great reluctance for drill work. Classical

music was piped through strategically-placed speakers and the

receptionist greeted every patient's arrival with a smile more

appropriate for the cover of Vogue. I, however, didn't smile back,

acutely aware that my missing teeth made me look about as

attractive as a backwater yokel. I took a seat at the far end of the

room, my buttocks sighing blissfully upon contact with the smooth

leather surface, and buried my head within the pages of a mens'

health magazine. At the stroke of ten am, I was summoned through

to meet my new dentist for the second time, a ridiculously handsome

middle-aged man whose skin was clearly used to a St Tropez sun.

He had jet black hair and a neat silver beard, kind eyes, and a manner which, in harmony with the general atmosphere, immediately put people at ease. He bore absolutely no resemblance to my previous dentist, the one who'd filled my teeth from the years seven through seventeen, but then the distance between Peckham and Mayfair is immeasurable in every way.

Dr. Katz spoke in a low whisper, with a voice reminiscent of both a children's television presenter and a late-night radio host. Having taken imprints of my teeth two days earlier, he was now ready to cap them. At the sight of the needle, I lowered my eyelids and began breathing evenly through my nose, concentrating hard on the classical music which continued to pour into my ear canals. I lay beneath Katz and his predictably beautiful female assistant for some time, vaguely listening to them talk stocks, bonds, and shares, feeling nothing but calm, the former occasionally murmuring soothing platitudes from somewhere up above me, while the latter made sure comfort never strayed from my prostrate position for more than a second at a time.

When, afterwards, I stepped back out into a brilliant early afternoon, several hundred pounds lighter but with my confidence restored, I felt my new teeth with a curled tongue and smiled into the nearest shop window, admiring the reflection. For a few blissfully oblivious moments, positivity was restored and happiness seemed a viable goal. But then remembrance of my eleven o'clock appointment at the pub called The Dog's Bollocks hit me like a concrete block, and the sinking feeling was instantaneously restored.

I decided not to return home just yet, despite Katkin's expectation. It was a beautiful day, and the afternoon was mine. I wandered into Picadilly Circus, towards Eros, my face long, eyes downcast, a frown tattooed onto my forehead, and inadvertently bumped into a young woman with straw-blonde hair, an open face, round glasses, and a battered acoustic guitar around her neck.

She beamed, as if lit from within.

"Hello, friend," she said brightly.

I looked her up and down, slowly, and immediately recoiled. The brightness of her eyes, the smile which played upon her lips, and the position of the head, tilted to one side like an eager puppy's, suggested just one thing. She'd been a victim of major brainwashing. She was, simply, too ebullient for so early in a new millennium, her senses distorted by a pronouncedly evil force. Suspicions were then confirmed as my eyes panned down to her oversized purple jumper which bore a large yellow badge that read: JESUS BELIEVERS.

"Why the miserable face?" she said. "It's sunny! Life is good! Smile."

Helplessly charmed, I smiled, revealing my new teeth.

"There! You have a lovely smile."

At the sound of these words, I was suddenly transported back in time. About a decade earlier, my brother Tom answered a sharp knock on the door one early Saturday morning. My mother was out at work, leaving the two of us to our own devices, which centered mainly around arguing over the television. Tom saw two people in unconventional clothing staring brightly back at him, both grinning, both eager to shake his hand and engage him in conversation. This visit came at a stage in his life when he was experimenting with as many new fads as possible. He'd recently fallen off the vegetarian bandwagon and was back on the veal escalopes, but, he said, the temporary exclusion of meat from his diet was was a valuable experience nonetheless. Then, after a school assembly on the subject, he decided that he would next learn more about world religion, either that or study a foreign language not taught at school. The arrival of these two Hare Krishnas, then, determined that he'd plump for the latter. He believed this to be fate, and was later resistant to any mocking. The woman, dressed in loose-fitting robes, had a shaven head and a large red smeer on her forehead that, when you peered into her big brown eyes below, looked like an irregular exclamation mark. He found her beautiful, a ravishing, unusual creature, and invited her, and her friend, in.

"You have a lovely smile," she remarked.

What exactly they talked about I never learned, as I was promptly banished into the living room with the remote control at my sole disposal. They, meanwhile, disappeared into the kitchen where they spent much time murmuring in what I considered to be a suspicious manner. When they left, Tom's eyes were strangely translucent, and he clutched in his fist several leaflets. In marked departure from his usual lack of solicitude toward me, he then cooked us both a lunch of boiled brown rice and vegetables.

While he of course never converted, the novelty having quickly worn off once he'd actually read the leaflets, his momentary enlightenment both fascinated and disturbed me, and I became vaguely eager to try something similar.

209

The opportunity, however, had never presented itself to me.

Until now.

The girl continued to smile at me, and took me by the hand.

Helplessly, with the beginnings of butterflies in my stomach, I

acquiesced and followed her lead. While we walked, she told me

about herself - homeless, disillusioned, a lost soul; then saved by

the Jesus Believers, re-christened Moon Flower, discovered salvation.

"I became lucky," she said, her gaze now luminous. "Lucky in

life. I found God, which is a very special thing. Believe me, friend,

no problem is insurmountable, no matter how grave it may seem."

She told me that her "job" - the quotemarks hers, made with

the briefest flutterings of two fingers dancing in the air - now

consisted of her meeting young people such as myself, and allowing

them a peak at the light. Should they choose to follow, then the

light becomes all-consuming and a baptism is quickly arranged. The

"job" didn't pay, but then as Jesus provides, what need for money,

anyway?

Despite an underlying scepticism, I decided to unburden myself

to her, and told her everything. While recounting my tale, her smile

floundered, her eyes scrunched up as if suddenly painful, and she

210

kept fondling her Jesus Believers badge nervously. When I finished, she took a deep breath, and clutched at her split ends.

"You must come with me at once," she said, "because this is just too ... too intense for me. You need to see Evening Breeze. He has all the answers. He'll know just what to do."

We walked at brisk pace, she leading, me following. Perhaps, I thought, religion does have its uses after all. A sudden outer-body experience allowed me to see myself in the third person, and I chuckled at the attendant humour of the situation. I knew that Evening Breeze was to prove about as much a salvation for all my problems as my running to the police, but even the act - the charade - of praying my way to a solution somehow had the effect of lifting my spirits. Things could be worse, I reasoned. Instead of being indicted into criminal activity by an old age pensioner - which at least possessed a rumour of glamour - I could be pledging my allegiance to a man by the name of Evening Breeze, then committed to a life of roaming busy city streets in ill-advised woolwear, with a badge that reads Jesus Believers attached to my breast.

If I could survive an audience with this character, then surely I could almost survive anything?

The bus was parked on a small cul-de-sac off Regent Street, its original red colour completely obliterated with garish tones of yellow, orange and purple. In place of the bus number and destination were the words JESUS LIVES: SEE INSIDE FOR DETAILS. Moon Flower was now pulling at my arm like an insistent dog owner, desperate to get me inside the mobile place of worship just as soon as possible. I complied, and prepared to give myself over to the ordained.

Inside it was dark, velvet curtains embossed with Jesus's benign face stapled over every window. Incense sticks were burning from every crevice and ambient music wafted just above my head like the lapping of waves. People, mostly young, and either ugly or facially peculiar, were sitting on seats, their eyes closed, their hands pressed together in prayer. Some were chatting quietly, some clearly fast asleep. Moon Flower went up to a young girl of a similar age who was cross-legged on the floor and whispered in her ear. The girl smiled, looked over at me, her smile increasing in width and scope, and silently pointed either to the upper deck, or to heaven itself.

"Come," said Moon Flower in a tiny voice. "He's upstairs."

We went upstairs, where it was darker still, the lingering smoke created by the incense as thick as fog. On the back seat was a young Indian man shaking a tambourine with a great deal of trepidation. One girl, who looked like a teenage Cher, was crying gently to herself two seats further up, dabbing her tears with her long black hair.

"That's Cinzia," explained Moon Flower. "She's Italian. She arrived here a few days ago after an old boyfriend committed suicide. Sleeping pills." She lowered her voice further and whispered directly into my ear. "We frown upon suicide here. He'll burn in the pit of hell for all eternity for that, but Cinzia here is happy now."

I remarked, noting the waterfall of tears, that she didn't look particularly happy.

"No, she's fine," she insisted. "She's just a little temperamental, that's all. Those tears are cathartic, she's working her way towards ultimate happiness. She's a recent addition to our

213

family, you see. We're going to call her China, because she's so delicate."

On the periphery of my vision, several rows up from the weeping Italian, I was aware of a figure hunched over what appeared to be a large book. There were several young women around him, all humming in tuneless unison.

"Evening Breeze," said Moon Flower triumphantly, aware I'd seen him. "Come."

As we approached, the women drew back, smiling shyly at me, and made their way downstairs, suggesting that my audience with this hirsute young man was to be exclusive. Moon Flower crouched down beside him and the pair spoke sotto voce for several minutes. Then she stood up, touched my shoulder, and walked away.

I looked into the man's eyes, shrouded behind a pair of gold-rimmed round glasses much like mine before I discovered lenses, and attempted to suss him out. He had a pleasant face, the lower half of which was entirely covered in a bushy brown beard. His eyes were blue and were surrounded by fine lines which either indicated premature aging or a sense of humour that caused him to laugh a lot. His nose was home to several broken veins, both blue and red, looking like a miniature map of the London Underground. He was wearing what looked like a kaftan, a shapeless piece of cloth dyed purple and black, and so expansive that underneath he could either have been hideously large or dangerously thin, with no one any the wiser. Somehow, it suited him. Eventually, he raised an upward-turned palm towards me, then brought it back down to his lap: an invitation to take the seat opposite him. I did.

He studied my face with as much interest as I did his. Occasionally, he would nod or frown, close his eyes then open them wide. All the while, the long fingers of his left hand explored the hidden areas of his wild beard. From time to time, he'd remove something from it and flick it away without any apparent irritation. Meanwhile, I fidgeted in the seat and attempted to hold his stare, which for some reason made me a little uncomfortable.

Eventually, he spoke.

"You appear troubled. Your life has taken an unexpected turn. I can feel it."

"Moon Flower told you as much, so I'm not surprised you can feel it," I replied, mildly defensive.

"Moon Flower told me nothing," he replied, smiling evenly. "She merely told me you needed guidance. And here you are, for guidance." He breathed deeply, appearing to count to ten. "Tell me. Are you willing?"

"Willing for what?"

"For guidance. From Jesus?"

The truthful answer was of course no. I opted to lie.

"Yes, I suppose I am."

"Tell me, then. Tell me of this unexpected turn."

I told him exactly what I'd told his disciple, but unlike her, his reaction was minimal. He fixed me with his stare, and didn't move, didn't even blink.

When I finished, he asked whether I spoke the truth or whether my tongue was tainted by poisoned lies. I told him that it was all true, why else would I be here?

"Then you are indeed in need of guidance."

He told me to remove my clothes.

"What? All of them?"

He nodded, still smiling.

Antagonism rose inside of me, my left eyelid twitching.

"To even begin to help purify the soul," he explained, "one

must remove any defensive layers. Clothes are defensive layers foisted upon us by The Man. Were it not illegal, then we'd never dress at all." He blinked slowly at me.

English reserve permitted me only to undress down to my underpants which, rather fortunately, were clean, new, and rather fashionable. Evening Breeze noticed the designer label and turned his nose up in undisguised scorn, but kept spoken criticism to himself.

He leaned towards me, he on the edge of his seat, me on mine, and placed both hands on my bare thighs. I began to think this a huge mistake and desperately wanted to flee. Instead, I stayed where I was, alert to his slightest movement, ready to attack should his fingers reach for my groin. (I wondered whether Tom had enjoyed such treatment with his Krishnas.) But his hands didn't move, they just pressed down firmly, and he began a quiet incantation, spoken more to himself than to me. This went on for several minutes, his lips moving, his eyes closed, while mine remained wide open, attempting to prepare myself for any hidden eventuality.

Frustration mounted until I could take it no longer.

217

"Look," I said, interrupting his flow. "What I need is some advice, not a lot of meaningless mumbling."

Evening Breeze blinked his eyes open, his eyebrows pointing down like arrows. Keenly aware that the Italian girl and the tambourine-shaking Indian were still in their respective positions at the back of the bus, he leaned in close to me so as not to be overheard. His breath smelled of apples - cider, perhaps.

"Look, friend," he began, "and this is off the record, alright?" I nodded. "You've got yourself into some pretty heavy shit here. I wouldn't even begin to know how to help you out, and you're a fruitcake if you think a few wise words from me are going to make any difference. What I can do, however, is help purify your soul which, if successful, should see you through this particular hurdle in life."

"What about tonight, though? My appointment with the old man?"

"With respect, friend, you're on your own on that one. I'll be praying for you, and I believe that Jesus will be watching over you. The purification should help ensure that you deserve His guidance."

With that, he stood up and squeezed into the free seat next to me until he was facing my back. Twisting slightly, I saw him remove his kaftan, revealing a pale, thin, entirely naked body, then press himself up against my spine. His hands came down around my neck and onto my ribcage, both palms hot against my chest. The incantation resumed, and this time I stared ahead without question, attempting to free myself of all thought in the fanciful hope that a deity I didn't even believe in would show me the way, grant me redemption.

Twelve. Sleeping With The Enemy.

After Jesus's very subtle purification of my soul - which Evening Breeze was convinced had taken place mere moments after the incantations had ceased - I returned home to find Katkin naked but for underwear and balancing precariously on the balls of her feet. Utterly immersed in concentration, she then pounced forward, both arms thrust out in front of her. She made no acknowledgment of my appearance and so I stood to one side and watched. She retreated back into her original position, then repeated this move several more times, only with greater force and alacrity. Next, in one incredibly fluid movement that saw her negotiating the living room's furniture with ease, she swung, leapt, kicked, plunged, pirouetted, and bent herself double before straightening back up again, as erect as a skyscraper.

Her eyes swivelled in her head one hundred and eighty degrees and found mine.

"Hello," I said. "That was impressive."

She thanked me.

"My old boyfriend," she said. "A black belt in karate. I'm a bit rusty actually, haven't done it for ages, but thought I'd better polish up just in case."

She asked where I'd been.

"Trying to save my soul," I told her.

"Never mind your soul," she replied. "Just concentrate on saving your skin for the time being. Your soul is something we can work on later."

At nine o'clock that evening, we got into the car and started to drive, Katkin insisting that she accompany me regardless of orders to the contrary. She told me to drive via an address in White City where she had some business to conduct. I glanced over at her, she still looking a virtual stranger since the radical hair redesign and swift change in character, and asked her to elaborate, but she remained silent, emitting an aura that gave off clear signals that she wasn't about to elucidate either, no matter how insistent I grew. En route, we stopped off at a cash machine where she demanded my credit card and pin number. Again, I complied.

We then drove through a series of dark estates, almost every streetlight burned out, until we came to a small, four-storey block.

"Stop here," she instructed me. "And wait patiently."

She returned a quarter of an hour later - during which time I'd managed to smoke four cigarettes, each of which had a diminishing effect on my nerves. Katkin was now clutching a brown envelope, the look of determination thawing into one of satisfaction. I started the engine, pulled away from the curb, and pointed the car south. Katkin stopped the music I was listening to, removed from my mouth the fifth cigarette, stubbed it out, and put on a CD that featured the strangely tranquil sounds of dolphins mating.

"Take the quietest roads you can," she instructed. "Because I want you to try and clear your mind of all thoughts."

"The cigarettes help," I told her, but she ignored this, deeming it unworthy of a reply.

"Unfortunately, you're not able to do this properly, because you really should be crossing your legs, but never mind. Try to breathe from your diaphragm and then, once you've got a rhythm going, begin to om. You can use any sounds you choose, but I find that om works really well."

Taking my eyes off the road momentarily, I watched as Katkin assumed the position of a yogi in the small passenger seat and om herself into a trance.

"Whenever I feel that things are getting too much for me, or that I can no longer cope for whatever reason and in any situation, I do this."

Her eyes were tight shut, her lips drawn together in a thin pout. She appeared to be vibrating from her stomach upwards, looking faintly possessed.

"Don't mock," she warned. "This has seen me through three relationship break ups, countless exams, and the death of my father. It may work for you."

Ten minutes later, we'd exchanged positions in the car and it was me who was now affecting the pose of a yogi, albeit a rather stiff one, muttering under breath a succession of whispered oms. Meanwhile, the dolphins continued to simulate the sounds of an arcane video game around my head, and Deptford drew ever nearer.

Eventually, I asked her what was in the package.

"Another alternative," she said. "But meantime, continue meditating."

Any effect, however, was conspicuous by its absence.

When we arrived, a good thirty minutes later, she showed me the gun.

"Where did you get it?" I wondered aloud.

"You saw where I got it from."

I expressed surprise that she knew people who could sell her a gun, but again she decided to remain mysterious.

"I got us some drugs as well," she added, "but perhaps you should remain lucid tonight. It's up to you."

In the end, I opted for any lucidity I may still have possessed.

Ten thirty. Half an hour to go. I was sitting in the car, with the engine off, opposite The Dog's Bollocks in Deptford. Katkin was by my side, the small package in her lap, trying to get me to do what we'd practiced earlier. Right now, however, it wasn't working. She'd already filled my head with myriad ways in which to deal with this impending situation, and I had some alternative methods of my own. I could either call upon the good will of Jesus, or I could sit still and, as Katkin had previously showed me, meditate, or I could stuff the small gun into my jacket pocket, its reassuring weight offering me all the confidence I'd ever need. I felt pulled in every direction, but found a solution in none. Instead, I breathed deeply and evenly, almost savouring the nervousness that made my heart beat irregularly. Then I opened the car door, got out, and walked across the road and in through the door marked Saloon.

Inside, the pub was dank, fetid, and full of bodies, the smell of stale ale entwining with the spent smoke from a million cigarettes to form a series of heavily pregnant, cancerous clouds. Underfoot, my feet squelched on the sodden carpet and I strained to see where I was going. At the sound of the clanging bell which signaled last orders, everyone surged forward towards the already crammed bar, shouting their orders at lifeless staff. My eyes roamed the area in front of me, both left and right. The pub's clientele appeared exclusively primitive male, and I felt about as home here as a cow would in an abattoir. Each time I found myself in the way of someone, or happened to intrude upon their personal space, I was forcibly jostled aside, and afforded a stare that suggested I shouldn't stray into their path again. On either side of the U-shaped bar, there was a dartboard, a threadbare pool table, and two television screens, each showing a programme from a satellite channel in which the female contestants had to complete an assault course dressed only in loose-fitting bikinis. Eventually, after some effort, I finally managed to spot Short Order, seated at a large round corner table with his daughter on one side, and two younger men, with arms like adverts for tattoo parlours, on the other. The table was cluttered with empty glasses, but as I approached, a full pint of ale found its way from the bar, through the crowds, and onto his coaster without any apparent effort or request on his part. When I finally reached him, I cleared my throat and waited for him to look up.

This took longer than anticipated.

After what felt like an age, Short Order finally looked up, and greeted me with the kind of smile that oozed poisonous malice. His two male companions followed his gaze and snorted when they saw me, while Treeza Burke started applauding my very presence. I felt myself redden, but was determined to stand my ground.

"You wanted to see me," I said.

"Lads, Treeza, if you'll excuse me. I've got a little business with my friend here."

The old man led me through a door beside the bar and down a thickly carpeted corridor until we reached a room at the end. He opened the door into a chamber that consisted of a large desk, two chairs on either side, and an old fashioned leather sofa that faced an unlit fireplace. Above the mantelpiece was a large mirror that seemed to distort images. My head appeared to have shrunk, its features blurry, while his grew to the size of a bull, his eyes now bulbous, his nose a ripe red pepper.

"Have a seat," he said.

I sat on the smaller of the two chairs, while he took the larger one behind the desk. He leaned forward to examine me closer, again affecting a stare designed to make the recipient cower.

"Glad you thought it wise to show up tonight," he said. "Save any of the unnecessaries, that way."

I nodded.

"He was a good man, your Grandad. I ever tell you that before?"

I then fielded several minutes of misty-eyed recollections, all yellowed and curling around the edges like old paper, before he finally got onto the business at hand.

"Right, as I'm sure you're aware, one of my many concerns is collecting. This weekend, I've got something I want collecting, and I want you to get it for me."

Inwardly, I felt every muscle relax. All he required of me was collecting, nothing more. I'd been fearing the worst, of course - a bank job, a kidnapping, murder - convinced that he regarded me capable of whatever it was he and my grandfather had collaborated on in the years previous. But collecting? No problem. I was out of the woods, back up into the clear. Were I among friendlier company, I'd have smiled.

"It'll be this weekend. Treeza will come along, show you the ropes, keep an eye on you. After that, we'll assess the situation, then think what to do next."

Next?

I looked at him, mouth agape. "What do you mean, next?"

"What I mean is," he said, his tone becoming serious, "next. I'm working you up, sunshine, working you up slowly. You can't just jump into guilt. You've got to earn it."

"And what if I refuse?" I said.

"Oh, you won't refuse." His words were like lead - they weighed heavily upon me. I heard his teeth clamp together, the sound like bones splintering.

I considered challenging this further, attempting to make clear to him that I wanted to find my own way in life and to follow no footsteps but my own, but instead went back out into the pub where, to my considerable horror, I found Katkin seated at the table with Treeza, both women sniffing and laughing hysterically.

My surprise was matched only by Short Order's, who's eyes appeared to burst into flames.

*

By the time we'd arrived home, Katkin was still buzzing, and sniffing deliriously. She wanted some shooting practice with the gun, which she waved carelessly in her hand, and wondered aloud whether we had any empty drink cans for targets, but I managed to wrestle it free from her grip and hide it while she crawled, on all fours, into the kitchen for some water.

"Thirsty. Want drink."

Worried that I was taking perhaps too long back in pub, she'd come to find me, her resolve emboldened having snorted some cocaine back in the Mercedes. There, she introduced herself to Treeza and in a veritable feat of instantaneous female bonding, the pair were hoovering up lines together and whooping loudly, while the heavy male contingent watched on, clearly aroused.

She knew exactly what Short Order had in store for me, Treeza having filled her in on everything while winking conspiratorially. What's more, she had a surprise of her own, which she retrieved from her sleeve and whacked across my face without forewarning.

"I'm coming along for the ride," she said, laughing. "But Short Order no know. Shhh, say nothing. Ung."

She fell back onto the sofa, then rolled onto the floor, and started snoring.

I left her there and went to bed, alone, and stared at the ceiling, wide awake.

By four am, at her endless insistence, we were driving around London's deserted streets, the windows open in attempt to clear Katkin's head and restore its equilibrium. She was no longer feeling high, and instead a mawkish depression had set in. We drove through a neon-lit Queensway, round by Paddington's illicit backstreets, upon which the skin trade was brisk, along the empty Marylebone Road with its succession of green traffic lights, and up into Camden, which was in the process of being cleaned by the kind of people you'd never see during daylight hours. We decided to park the car in Primrose Hill, possibly London's most illustrious neighbourhood, where the truly rich rubbed shoulders with their nouveau counterparts in what, at least on the surface, looked like total harmony. Katkin needed to stretch her legs, suck down some clean oxygen in her lungs, and so we decided that we'd make our way up to the top of the hill and watch a cloaked London slowly begin to light up and grind into motion, ready for the onslaught of another day.

As we reached the park's gates, the big chrome padlock alerted us to the fact that they would remain closed for several hours to come, thereby thwarting our plans.

"We'll have to climb over," I said.

Katkin shook her head, explaining that she was in no fit state to scale any fence whatsoever. She looked completely deflated, and about to cry. I told her to resume oming. As we pondered our next move, we noticed a tall, rugged man walking towards us, his leather trousers squeaking with every stride, his cowboy boots scuffing along the pavement, and his bleached blonde corkscrew curls bouncing around the shoulders of his unbuttoned white silk shirt like mini springs. His face bore the kind of suntan that one can only successfully acquire from a bottle, and he was smiling knowingly, his seen-it-all-before eyes sparkling brightly.

"You want in?" he inquired of us.

Katkin told him we did.

"Then walk around the corner, and follow the fence until you're about halfway down. You'll find a little gap between the bars. Your friend may find it a tight squeeze, but you, darling, will fit through no problem."

Katkin's thanks were profuse.

"Going to watch the sun rise?" he asked.

We nodded.

"Well, enjoy."

As he scuffed his way across the road and towards the bridge, Katkin sighed heavily.

"He was gorgeous," she said. "Restores my attraction in older men completely."

"That," I said, a pillar of information, "was Robert Plant."

Katkin looked quizzical, uncomprehending.

"Led Zeppelin," I said.

"What, like the balloon?" she said blankly, her head floating around cotton wool clouds of her own imagining.

*

The orange yolk of the sun slid, against gravity, up from the horizon, relieving the capital of its monochrome pallor and flooding it with a little colour. We sat huddled together on a bench, smoking a cigarette each, watching in silent awe. The Post Office tower began to glisten like a phallic Christmas decoration, fresh light bouncing from its glass front and onto the city streets below. Gradually, the roads filled up with cars, buses, and taxis, and the grizzled hum of a million engines filled the air like a distant murmur at the back of the throat.

Katkin put her hand to my cheek, and let it settle.

"Just think of it as a little life experience," she said. "You'll probably adapt to it like a fish to water, you'll see. It's in the genes, after all, or at least in your grandfather's."

I shrugged.

"It'll only be temporary anyway," she continued. "He just

wants to make sure you're not about to run to the police, that you're no longer a threat. His methods may be a little extreme, but this way, in the long run, we'll be safe from him just as soon as he feels safe from you. So just go with it."

"I don't seem to have much option," I said.

"And don't forget, I'll be with you," she said, attempting reassurance. "You'll be safe with me."

It was like a scene from a corny film, the helpless damsel desperately not wanting to part with the chiseled hero on his daring mission. But in reality my damsel was in fact a femme fatale, whose very presence come Saturday could only bring me shame, and public emasculation.

Suddenly ravenous, we headed back down to Camden and the nearest kebab shop.

*

A slow-motion blink of an eye, and Saturday was upon us.

It was a dazzlingly bright morning, the sun streaming down in great waves of heat. London was taking its clothes off, preparing to roast like sausages, before drinking the night away in a haze of alcoholic revelry, a toast to British summertime.

Over a breakfast of bran flakes, I told Katkin I'd rather she not come. Katkin, however, was in a world of her own. She didn't sleep at all the night before, choosing instead to prepare herself mentally and physically for the morning's requirements. At first, I suspected drug use, but gradually came to realize that what Katkin was emitting here was excitement, pure and sheer. Her life had turned a corner; she liked what she found. Why bother with the routine drudgery of office work and ordinariness, when she could teeter on the edge instead?

At a previously appointed time and place, we pulled up outside the bus stop in Deptford, Treeza Burke dressed in the garish lime green shellsuit and impatiently awaiting us. She climbed into the back, and we sped off. The two women exchanged brief hellos, but otherwise there was silence, interrupted only by the sound of tobacco burning from continuously deep inhalation.

I still had no idea exactly what this collection job entailed, although I did fear it wouldn't be exactly pleasant, enjoyable. Sporadically, Treeza would bark directions from behind my right ear, and we ended up in a council estate in Brixton. When I parked, and disengaged the engine, she finally explained exactly what was expected of us.

It transpired that one of her father's many sidelines was local loan shark, the associated interest rates he'd glean high enough to keep him in gold for the rest of his natural. While the business prides itself on smooth running, she explained, there are inevitably occasional hiccups when clients fall back on repayments. Methods employed to keep this occurrence to a minimum inevitably involve, initially, the threat of violence, then violence itself.

Leeroy St. Coke was someone who would often rely on Short Order's loans to help supplement his gambling and drug habit. His surprisingly enduring luck with the former meant that he was almost always able to pay back any monies owed, but his dependency on the latter ensured that any winnings gained were also very quickly frittered away. Recently, he'd fallen a few rungs down on luck's ladder. Thanks to his habit, now unignorable and spiralling out of all control, he'd lost his job as a mechanic, and had owed Short Order œ500 for over four weeks now. It was hardly a vast sum of money, but Short Order ensured his ship remained a tight one by chasing up every loose end without delay, and often without mercy.

Plus, he wanted the money returned before St. Coke's very probable

OD, clearly imminent according to those who knew him.

We were here this morning to collect the outstanding sum,

along with a further œ250, the fixed fee for a home visit. Leeroy St.

Coke wasn't expecting us, and therefore our wits had to be primed,

our senses alert.

From her attitude, I gleaned that Treeza was far from happy

with having to take me, a stranger, along for the ride. While she

doubtless understood her father's reasoning, she also doubtless took

me for an idiot, someone so wet behind the ears - a leaking font of

inexperience - that I'd probably turn out to be more of a hindrance

than a help. Due to what was at stake for me here, I was determined

to convince her otherwise, but had to bide my time. Frustratingly,

she seemed far more taken with Katkin, impressed by her karate

skills and her infectious character. They may have inhabited

opposite ends of the social scale, but a bond quickly emerged

between the two women. Their smiles were like pieces of a jigsaw

that fit effortlessly together. I envied Katkin's ease with new people,

and resolved to make brisk amends.

We walked through the estate, every labyrinthine alleyway foul-smelling and steaming from fresh piss, our gaze passing over walls that had graffiti scrawled over graffiti, a new technicoloured coating every day. As we rounded a corner, we happened upon an elderly woman, her back hunched, her frail hands clutching her handbag, shuffling at a snail's pace. When she saw us, she immediately began to tremble, raise her arms, and whine repeatedly, "I've no money, no money, let me be!" Treeza chuckled at this, and told the woman that today was her lucky day, she could proceed in peace. In the lift, we stood side by side, again in silence, disrupted only when Treeza cleared her nasal passages of all phlegm, then spat a large deposit on the corrugated metal wall, and watched with satisfaction as it stuck fast, quivering ever so slightly. When we arrived at the second floor, we got out, turned left, and walked up to the appropriate door.

With her large fist, each finger heavy with cheap gold, she banged loudly, then took a step back, Katkin and I flanking her at either side. As she was about to knock once again, the door opened, a long silver chain pulling taut between it and the wall.

"Yeah?" came a voice from within.

"Leeroy?" Treeza said calmly.

"Who wants to know?"

Treeza lifted her right leg until her knee drew level with her chin. Then, with all the force she could generate, she thrust her leg forward, foot flat, against the door. It offered little resistance to the kick and flew open, the chain sailing into the air, Leeroy falling back into the hallway, and landing with a heavy thud. He quickly scrambled to his feet, still winded, screaming, "What the fuck?" When he saw Treeza, who now stood before him with her arms crossed against her chest, a look of resignation fell across his face.

"Oh," he said, "it's you. You'd better come through."

Before he turned and led the way into the living room, he looked over at us, his eyebrows raised.

"Meet the muscle," said Treeza with a smirk.

Leeroy sucked air through his teeth, then spat it back out again.

The living room was small and cluttered, consisting of the remains of a sofa, a couple of easy chairs, a large wall rug depicting the smiling face of Bob Marley smoking a fat one, a gigantic hi-fi system along with state-of-the-art TV and video, a large fishtank containing some rainbow-coloured fish, and a small table upon which sat a tidy mountain of powder narcotics and associated implements, including several needles, some of which had clearly been used. In one corner, in front of some plastic building blocks, sat a small child the colour of caramel dressed only in a soiled nappy. Dried snot grew around its nostrils like fungus, and when it saw us, it smiled, making goo-goo noises.

"You know why we're here, Leeroy. So don't make it difficult."

Treeza held out an open palm expectantly.

"Listen, yeah, Treeza, I know I'm a little behind, yeah, but you know I'm good for it," he said, looking panicked. "Just give me a bit more time, yeah?"

"Seven hundred and fifty quid, Leeroy. Now."

"Seven fifty? No, man, you're mistaken. I owe you four -" he looked up at her, then stuttered, "- five hundred. Five, not seven, yeah? Look, I'll get it. I just need a couple more days, yeah?"

"Leeroy, it's seven fifty, an extra two-and-a-half compensation. If you're lucky, the muscle here won't lose their temper. If not..."

All the windows were closed in the flat, and the heat was intense, hot enough to make chicken skin crackle. The baby was watching us intently, its eyes hopping from one face to another. The smile on its face didn't know whether it should be there or not.

"Leeroy, son, you've got two minutes. Don't push it."

Seemingly realizing the futility of his situation, he made placatory noises and disappeared into the bedroom, from which we could hear the sound of rustling, then no sound at all. Moments past, suspended in anticipation. The baby went goo goo.

Then Leeroy went ga ga.

He came back into the living room at great speed screaming demonically, swinging a baseball bat over his head. He lunged at Treeza, who jumped to one side and watched with clear pleasure as the bat crashed down into the fishtank which exploded into a hundred thousand pieces, water gushing everywhere, the rainbow-coloured fish flapping and suffocating on oxygen, seemingly aware that they'd now landed into the metaphorical frying pan. The baby started screaming as loud as her father, crawling on fours towards the fish. Treeza made a counter lunge towards Leeroy but went headfirst into the still-swinging bat. She went down like a building being demolished. Then he came for me. Suddenly seeing a violent red, from where I don't know, I dived for his legs and knocked him backwards. He kept a tight hold of the bat while falling, and began hitting me repeatedly on the back with it. Eyes clamped shut, I started punching with flailing fists, crawling up his body until my punches rained down all over him. From somewhere behind me I could hear the baby's wails becoming louder, more insistent, more confused. Then, quite suddenly, I felt Leeroy's body being whisked out from under me, leaving me on top of nothing but shattered glass. I looked up and saw Katkin thrust him against a wall, then take a few steps back, before administering a lethal karate kick to his chest. The wind knocked out of him as ribs cracked, and Leeroy collapsed, slumped, gasping. Katkin then jumped onto his horizontal form, her bottom positioned squarely on his broken chest, removed the gun from her back pocket, and forced it into Leeroy's mouth. Everything went quiet. Even the baby fell temporarily silent, watching in awe as the fish flapped less and less, slowly asphyxiating.

With one free hand, Katkin brushed some hair from her eyes.

"You are about to die from swallowing a speeding bullet," she told him. "Blink if you understand."

Leeroy blinked a thousand times.

"Now, where's the money?"

He made a strange, strangulated noise.

"Where, Leeroy, is the money?" She pushed the gun deeper into his mouth until it kissed the back of his throat, forcing him to wretch.

He made another painful noise, and Katkin gradually drew back the gun, placing it instead on top of his left eye.

"A-all ... all the m-money I got," he said through rushed breaths, "is over there. B-biscuit tin."

Treeza, a large red bruise on the side of her forehead and cuts on her hands, stood shakily to her feet, and went over to the biscuit tin. I, meanwhile, also got to my feet, examining the cuts to my arms and, through soft denim, my legs. My back, too, was swelling, the pain expanding and contracting. She pulled out a wad of notes, counted them quickly, and demanded the rest.

"There's n-no more. On my kid's life, I swear. I ain't got no more m-money. I need more time, yeah?"

Treeza retrieved the baseball bat from the floor and, while Katkin remained in her position on his chest, brought it down with terrific might onto his left kneecap, then his right. He roared in agony, thrashing so much that Katkin was flung to one side. The baby screamed in more confusion, then grew fascinated at the blood which began to trickle from its open palm.

Over the cacophony, Treeza told him that he may never walk again. If he fails in producing the rest of the money before the following night, she said, he'd stop breathing, too. Then we left, taking the stairs this time, and trying not to pay any attention to the baby's increasingly air-starved sobs, which seemed to follow us down.

Back outside, the sun was now even hotter, and we melted back into everyday regular life as if nothing had happened, the coast clear.

*

When we arrived back at the pub in Deptford, having given Leeroy St. Coke a beating he wouldn't quickly forget, Treeza told us to wait in the car while she went inside. And so Katkin and I sat obediently in the front seats, exchanging uncomfortable silent looks, until I turned on the radio to break the suffocating atmosphere. A sports talk show was on, where callers phoned in to disagree with the host on any given subject, although usually football, in loud, irascible tones. Neither of us focused in on any particular conversation, but it did its job and disguised our awkwardness. Fifteen minutes went by before Treeza reemerged. She walked across the road and towards us, now holding a damp cloth to her bruised forehead, and bent at the open window.

"Okay, you's can go now. We'll be in touch."

She thrust five bunched-up ten pound notes into Katkin's hand, then turned and walked back to the pub. I pulled away from the curb, turned left and merged back in with the Saturday traffic as a brutal condemnation of Manchester United from a caller in Highbury flooded from the speakers.

Katkin carefully unfolded the money, flattened each note out on her thigh, and counted them.

"Not bad," she said.

I looked over at her, my left eyebrow several centimetres higher than the right.

"Fifty pounds," she said. "We've been paid! I suppose we can take that to mean a job well done, no? Let's go into town and spend it, celebrate."

Thirteen. Card Trick.

Tom hadn't shaved for days, and the pronounced five o'clock shadow
didn't suit him. Where, on some men, a face full of whiskers looks
mannish, affording the wearer the appealing look of a rogue in full
possession of a very healthy libido, on others it simply looks a
mess, an ugly sprawl of charcoal grey on white canvas. His tie was
askew, his pale blue shirt stale with sweat, and his jacket had gone
missing, presumably still awaiting collection from the last bar he'd
frequented. His hair was matted to one side and his expression
looked stricken. I'd seen him like this just once before, years
earlier, when his only true love had broken his heart. Tom had
never fully recovered from Melanie, a girl he'd met at 18 and lost
at 21. Even I thought her the sweetest girl in the world, and one
of the prettiest, while my mother was convinced that here stood her
future daughter-in-law. But three years at the hands of an
arrogance like his reaped predictable results, and eventually she
left him, exhausted, for someone nicer, kinder. That was what
initially prompted his descent into drugs, an addiction which lasted
until he'd developed a cloak of stoic cynicism capable of protecting

him from all the world's future right hooks. He wielded something resembling total control ever since, possessing the air of a man to whom things happen, but only with his consent and full cooperation.

"I need to talk," he said, the words spilling from the side of his mouth like lava.

I stepped aside and let him into the empty flat, Katkin having left earlier with my credit card in her hand, pin number scrawled on palm, muttering excitedly about wardrobe enhancement.

"I'd offer you a drink," I said, "but it looks like you've pre-empted me on that one."

"Jack Daniels," he responded. "No ice."

This was all most unusual. Control-freak Tom was virtually at the top of his tree, career-wise, something he'd never fail to remind anyone he ever met. He was making money hand-over-fist, and his future was bathed in bright spotlights, like a runway. Perhaps justifiably, he was immensely proud of his achievements, as would anyone in such a coveted position, but his incessant boasting was boorish, intolerable. The smile that played about his lips dripped pure smarm, and so self-reverential was he that he found it impossible to believe that anyone wouldn't be as interested in his progress as he was himself. To see him like this, then, prickled my curiosity like a gas flame under boiling water, but I decided to approach this slowly, like a Christmas present, unwrapping one layer at a time.

"Nice day at the office?" I asked.

He emitted a low murmur, a rumble made from sandpaper, and knocked back his drink in one, then poured another.

It was late one Thursday afternoon, several days after the collection job for Short Order. I'd spent most of my time since then re-living the events, coming to terms with them, and treating my body for its bruising. Katkin, however, was like electricity, buzzing with bright energy, as if a whole new - hitherto hidden - persona had suddenly blossomed from nowhere. Her reaction confused me, as did my own to the new her. Part of me was repulsed and bewildered, wondering just where these character extremes had come from and what she might be capable of next, while another part was so consumed by lust, I could hardly think straight. If I'd previously felt rather fond of her, now I was magnetized by her mystery. I coveted her in every way, and sexually she delivered, each time more rampant than the last. But I still felt ultimately insecure, as if

I somehow knew that things could suddenly spiral out of all control, and I could lose her, along with everything else, from just one phone call, one sudden action. She'd taken an unhealthy interest in my credit card, which I nevertheless allowed her free reign over, feeling it my only true bargaining power.

So I had more than enough of my own problems. Turning attentions to Tom' gave me a pleasing, if temporary, distraction.

"Right," I began, "what's up?"

He looked at me with saucer eyes. Sweat dotted his upper lip. His left eyelid twitched.

"Look," he said, "I know we've never been close, but you're all I have right now. I need you, I need your help." He shifted in his seat, looking awkward, uncomfortable. "I'm in twenty kinds of trouble. I don't know what to do."

You and me both, I thought.

I poured us both some whiskey. Double measures.

"Go on," I said.

"Well, I'm..." he stuttered, then floundered, and gulped down his drink, "... it looks like I'm going to lose the flat. I'm three months behind on mortgage repayments."

Tom lived in the Docklands, in a huge, New York-style loft apartment that appeared as long and as wide as a football pitch. It was decked out with zen minimalism, alongside the very latest in entertainment equipment, a selection of leather armchairs and mahogany furniture, and a games corner featuring a pinball and an antique Space Invaders machine. The kitchen was from Conran, the art from Africa, and the cleaner, who came once a week, from Poland. It was the kind of place owned by a tremendously flash fool with more money than sense. I'd been there once and hated it.

"How? You're loaded, surely?"

"And there's trouble at work," he continued, ignoring my question. "I've been ... my attention has been wandering, I've not been as thorough as I should have been. I've messed up programmes, I've been late eleven times this month alone, I've been selling embargoed information to the competition to help with my debts, and this morning I've been found out. I'm facing suspension, and very probably the sack. It could even go further."

I looked at him aghast, stunned, fascinated. The scales were tipping.

"Does our mother know all this?" I asked.

"I'm having an affair as well," he continued, rubbing a hand over his ashen face, then corrected himself. "Several affairs actually. And I'm back on the coke, I'm gambling everything I earn. More. I was arrested last week for being in the wrong whorehouse at the wrong time, pending charges. And I'm to be married in a couple of months, all being well."

Like freshly baked bread, I allowed all this information to rise, to settle and cool down, before approaching, fingers outstretched, to prod tentatively. Tom had been living a big lie, a colossal fabrication. I'd previously thought him on top of his game, on top of the pile, control clasped in his vice-like grip like a squash racket, while I perennially flailed. But it turned out he was human after all, as vulnerable as everybody else, and just as fallible.

"What?" I said. "Surely you're not serious?"

There are some facial expressions more eloquent than a thousand words, a simple lip tremor, repetitive blinking, or a flinch of the eye, each worthy in itself of a dissertation on agony. Tom pulled one such expression and remained silent.

"Christ," I said, attempting empathy. Then, after draining another glass free of its contents, puzzlement rained down on me from above.

"You said you needed my help," I said. "How, exactly?"

Tom redirected his gaze from the bottom of the glass onto mine, his lids creasing slightly.

He opened his mouth to say something, but nothing came out, not a word, not a sound. Just stale air. Then he slowly shrugged his shoulders.

"I don't know, exactly," he said eventually. "Blood is thicker than water, I suppose. And I can hardly go to Mum."

We sat facing each other for some time, saying nothing, just pouring and drinking.

"Anyway," he said at one point resignedly. "What's up with you? What went right all of a sudden?"

I told him that I went right, that things just clicked after months, years, of concerted practice. He nodded uninterestedly, looking hurt, and thoroughly pathetic.

Several hours later, the coffee table now cluttered with the remains of a sticky Chinese takeaway, we sat stewing in front of satellite TV, conversation temporarily suspended, when Katkin breezed in through the door, two armfulls of designer-label shopping bags at her side.

"Ah!" she said upon sight of Tom, before focusing properly. "The older brother. Come for a visit?"

She then saw the state of us, clocking the half empty cartons and the empty whiskey bottle, and snorted derisively.

"Oh dear," she mocked, disappearing up the stairs and into the bedroom.

When she came down, she called out to me.

"Here," she said, and carefully tossed my gold credit card toward me. It rose, arced, and made its descent, carving the air between Tom and myself, landing squarely on the table, a perfect throw. Tom noted the colour of the card, its familiarity to him, what it suggested about the holder, and then looked up at me and the space where Katkin was standing before she ran upstairs again, his face contorted into confusion and suspicion. He sat up straight.

"Can I stay here tonight?" he asked.

This was my big mistake, perhaps the very point where I inadvertently pulled him in alongside me for the ride of his - our - life. I should have been more aware, more alert, wiser. I should have shaken my head. But I knew, secretly, that whatever his current state, I now needed him around.

So instead of outright refusal, I shrugged my shoulders, and said yes.

*

Stress is a predominantly new disease. Its victims are, essentially, everyone. Like cancer, it isn't fussy who it preys upon. It'll attack anyone. It is not necessarily caused by drinking, or smoking, or unfitness, or a poor diet, unsafe sex, addiction to daytime TV, homosexuality. But then again, it is. It's caused by all these things and more. Overwork, constant pressure, a lack of sleep, the inability to relax, addiction to drink, drugs, sex even. Competition in the workplace doesn't help, neither, bizarrely, does a fat pay packet, because those who earn a fat pay packet are only too aware that there are countless other people out there just waiting to steal their position at a moment's indiscretion. Sufferers experience stress at many different levels. There are those who appear completely immune to it until they awake one morning to discover they can't move any part of their body below their neck. Others get stomach ulcers, coldsores, migraines, RSI, ME, permanent indigestion, grey hair, hypochondria. Some heed its warnings early and recover, others ignore it until it's far too late. And these people, like Tom, suddenly collapse like a deck of cards, stress's killer punch having dealt the ultimate body blow, relishing in its punishment of the ignorant.

Disregarding every telltale sign that came his way, Tom foolishly believed himself indestructible, entirely resistant to any weakness. He was, but only up to a point. Still two years shy of thirty, here he was now, crumpled concertina-like on the sofa, crying into his drink and worrying out loud that the baliffs' arrival was imminent. The surround-sound TV would be taken under his very eyes, so too the sumptuous Harrods sofa, the pinball machine, the candle chandelier. The bank would assume control of the flat and sell it to begin paying off his debts, and the company would begin their investigations. The frequenting of the brothel charge would probably come to nothing, a mere fine if he were lucky (though how to pay it?), and the affairs would have to be truncated. And the marriage? Who knows?

Despite his drunkenness, it took long into the night before Tom asked me the question I knew he'd inevitably arrive at. Humbled,

but resigned, he said it as if wondering aloud. "...Thought perhaps,

maybe, you could shout me some cash? Just a little to float with? I'd

... I'd pay you back, of course?"

"How, exactly?"

He sighed heavily, and began to whimper into his hands, which

were poised and ready when his head collapsed into them. He then

pulled himself together, and fished around inside his trouser pocket,

retrieving a small wrap and a credit card identical to mine. He

arranged the white powder into four neat lines on a small space on

the coffee table, then from another pocket pulled out a small steal

snorter.

"I'll split this with you," he said, in a tone of voice usually

reserved for fake Father Christmases promising young children their

presents of choice.

I watched him hoover up the first two lines greedily before

passing the snorter to me. I noticed the sweat begin to trickle from

his hairline, and waved my hand at the gift.

"I'll pass," I told him and lit a cigarette instead.

Deciding against insistence, he dove back down to the table

and breathed deeply through both nostrils, snorting like a fattened pig.

*

In the past six months, Tom had been frequenting a casino near Knightsbridge, located in the basement of a plush high-rise hotel. His relationship with a girl called Susannah was beginning to bore him. They'd been together, on and off, for going on a year, and Susannah was allegedly pressing for commitment. Commitment, for Tom, was the only C-word that sent shivers down his spine, a predicament he quickly remedied by diving into a succession of barely concealed affairs with a succession of younger, more attractive women, leaving many a telltale sign for Susannah to discover. Suddenly, his pockets would be full of condoms, he'd have lipstick on his collar, a telephone number inside a book of matches, and at the point of orgasm, he'd cry out another's name. The ridiculous level of cliche mattered little here; the message was nevertheless conveyed loud and clear. Surprising him with her measured acceptance of defeat, Susannah quietly packed her bags and moved out, leaving Tom in exactly the position he'd craved for so long. Single again. However, again with crushing predictability, the loneliness of the serial one-night-stander began to haunt both his waking and sleeping hours. Drugs reared their ugly head again, which simultaneously staved off encroaching loneliness - along with every other emotion - and afforded him the confidence, and balls, to bet, and lose, an awful lot of money at the roulette wheel. Meanwhile, the atmosphere at work had suddenly turned grave with the arrival of another boss - this one, somewhat radically, female - who refused to view Tom with as much enthusiasm as her predecessor, and suddenly he was forced to work harder, and for less immediate riches. Tom promptly turned Judas and, over a power lunch one day, struck a profitable friendship with someone of seniority from his company's main competitor. But insider trading at this level was myriad, and his indiscretions soon found their way back to his new superior, who placed him under immediate suspension.

"I think it's the mid-life crisis," he said between sobs.

I reminded him his age.

"Then it's come early," he said. "I've spent a lot of time alone recently, and I've come to a dreadful conclusion."

He waited for me to press him for an answer, but I just sat back in my chair and allowed my head to be swallowed up in a fug of nicotine smoke.

"I hate myself," he whined. "I'm not fishing for sympathy here, either. It's just a realization that came to me last week. I'm like some relic from the Eighties, living this Me Me Me indulgence, caring about nobody but myself. I've been a bastard to girlfriends, to family, to you, to poor Grandad, to everyone. I've been motivated solely by money, by greed. And now look at me. Ruined, washed out at thirty."

"Twenty eight," I corrected.

"Near enough," he said. "I've lived a total sham of a life."

"Oh no," I said, "you're not going to tell me that you've found God are you?"

"No, no. Nothing like that. I've not become a religious zealot overnight, not yet anyway. I've just done a lot of self-assessment, and I've realized I need to change if I'm to, you know, save my soul."

Clearly, this was merely his panic talking. My eyes moulded

themselves into an expression of scepticism.

"Think what you like," he said. "If you're not careful, judging what's going on with you right now - whatever the hell it is, anyway - then you'll be in my position too, in a few years."

What did he mean? How much did he know?

"I've already made it up to Susannah," he continued. "At least I've begun to. She seems to have faith in me, or at least faith that I can change. I proposed, and she accepted - on certain conditions."

Somewhere off on the horizon, the sun was slowly creeping up, so I made my excuses, and told him he could have the couch for tonight. His gratitude was muted, slightly shame-faced.

As I was getting undressed in the bedroom, Katkin sleeping soundly, Tom climbed upstairs and opened the bedroom door, about to ask something further of me. Instead, he stopped dead in his tracks and watched silently as I obliviously continued to remove my T-shirt, revealing my badly bruised back.

"What the-?" he began, his voice raised in shock.

"Shh, not now," I whispered, and closed the door in his face.

My explanation could wait.

*

I awoke last the following morning and when I got downstairs, I saw that Tom, hangover aside, remained his uncharacteristic new self. He had made breakfast, and upon the table sat several varieties of cereal, a steaming coffee pot, some tea, and a selection of croissants and marmalade. Katkin was seated opposite him, and they were engaged in what looked like friendly discourse. Swallowing a yawn, I went and joined them.

"Tom has been telling me why he stopped shaving," said Katkin with a smile. "And we thought we had problems, eh Jake?"

Tom shot me another glance dripping with suspicion, but was unable to commence interrogation as Katkin took hold of the conversation and directed it accordingly.

"I know!" she said brightly, as if a lightbulb had suddenly appeared above her head. "Let's all go to the gym. Tom, you like swimming? Because there's a wonderful pool there. Or you can just sit and bubble in the jacuzzi, or have a go on the treadmill. Forget hair of the dog, what you need is an assault on your fitness. Come, let's go."

In swift, fluid movements, she guided us through the door, down the stairs, into the car, and drove us all directly to the club, where she presented the receptionist with my membership card and two guest passes, already filled out with hers and Tom's name. Once she'd gotten us here, however, self-obsession quickly stole her away. Upon receiving her towels, she immediately swanned into the changing room, into her swimming costume, and dived into the lagoon-like pool while my brother and I watched from the balcony above. As she began doing her lengths, her breast stroke as effective as her karate chop, Tom and I bought coffee and sat at a table in the bar. Tom's current state suggested that were he to come into contact with any water deeper than bath level, he'd promptly drown, while I decided that my battered and bruised upper body should be kept shrouded from prying eyes.

"So," he began, with purpose resumed, "what on earth is the deal with her?" He pointed towards the swimming pool. "She's scary, like she's possessed or something." He lowered his voice and leant in towards my ear. "And what the fuck has happened to you? Your back, the gold credit card, the flat? Come on, we're brothers. Confide, open up."

While we were not quite Kane And Abel throughout adolescence, there were nevertheless distinct similarities. The term sibling rivalry is understatement personified when attempting to describe the relationship between thirteen-year-old Tom and ten-year-old Jake. If he was chalk, then I was the unwilling blackboard upon which he'd scrawl all his pubescent antagonisms. With an absent father and a wayward mother, Tom was unofficially appointed my guardian, a job he believed he excelled in, but which I took great pains to suggest otherwise. We argued over everything, from which television programme to watch to whether we should buy plain pork pies for lunch or ones with powdered eggs in them. Mutual ridicule turned to fist fights until Tom began sprouting in every direction, leaving little doubt who was emphatically the boss. But within a couple of years I was virtually fending for myself anyway as his social life began to take off and keep him out until all hours of the night and the morning after. The contact we had later, during our early twenties, was minimal and always fraught with difficulty. We were effectively strangers, two very different people linked only by shared genes. If, during such contact, politeness reigned, then it did so because we were both on our best behaviour, normally to please an attendant mother who had orchestrated this come-together in the first place. Otherwise, we just let one another get on with the other's life, with virtually no interference at all. Were we ever truly to bond, to gel in the way fiction tells us that siblings should, then something significant needed to happen first. We would have to meet on a suddenly-formed neutral ground. The scales would have to be tipped not quite in my exclusive favour, but certainly in that direction. Tom's supremacy needed to be eradicated, taken down a peg or two, so we could meet somewhere in the middle. Until very recently, however, this was nothing but a fanciful long shot.

But then all this happened, to both he and me. Simultaneously. Sat over another necessary bolt of caffeine, mid-morning on this otherwise regular Friday, Tom and I were, to all intents and purposes, now equal. He even looked different - his shoulders slumped, a tiredness around the eyes, his irises rheumy - like someone who needed sympathy, my sympathy. Perhaps we were now both in a mutual position, one where I could help him and he me? All this didn't come to me as a conclusion, but rather as a mere notion, a vague possibility. We looked at each other across the table.

He smiled, revealing crows' feet at either eye. I smiled back, with equal openness.

Then I started talking.

Tom's mouth hung open, a perfect O. If I'd had a camera, I'd have started snapping. This was an expression wholly unused to sitting on a face as accustomed to confidence as his. In it, I read bemusement, puzzlement, shock, jealousy, muted rage. I'd been the favoured grandson and it clearly rankled. The sudden action my life was now experiencing caused envy in him - and immediate incessant craving. Questions were proffered, the answers to which prompted yet further queries, alongside regular gasps of incredulity, his eyebrows making like caterpillars on an already-frowning forehead.

When explanation had all but expired, I took out my cheque book, without particular ceremony, and wrote him a cheque large enough to cover all his immediate debts. While money may well be at the root of all evil, it is nevertheless pretty handy to have around. It makes everything so easy. Recently, both myself and Katkin had been spending considerable amounts of it with as much carelessness as rice is thrown outside churches. I made a mental note to learn my current balance, and perhaps become more frugal in the future, to pace myself. Tom accepted the cheque with gratitude in his wide eyes and a sudden reddening in his cheeks, but no appreciative words dribbled from his lips. Then he got to his feet, shook my hand - something I think we'd never previously done; it was clammy - and left. As I watched him disappear behind the automatic doors, I felt a belated tweak of conscience, realizing I'd just given a coke fiend several thousand pounds. Fool! But then I reasoned that he wasn't that far gone just yet, and that self-respect was more important to him than any drug. He loved that pinball machine.

"Where's your brother?" asked Katkin, thirty minutes later, her rosy cheeks radiating health.

"He had to go. Much stuff to do."

She sat opposite me, slipped off her trainers, and placed her talcumed feet in my lap.

"Knead me," she said, lips thinning to reveal bright white teeth.

Fourteen. Love Bites.

"Ah, if it's not the ladies man. Come." Fingers jerked in the air,
pointing over his shoulder. "Come on through."

Resignedly, I followed Short Order's thick neck down the
carpeted corridor and into the room at the end where we assumed
the same positions as we did a couple of weeks earlier, him towering
above me on a tilting chair, a large desk separating us. This time
I avoided eye contact with the mirror altogether, feeling inwardly
already quite distorted enough.

Now that we were alone, his grinning disposition was replaced
by one of severity. He began methodically to crack each knuckle,
revealing, on the third of his left hand, a faded small blue tattoo of
a skull-and-crossbones. Then his fingers went to his teeth, using
the long nail of his pinkie to extricate white meat from between
several molars. A clearly confused spot, the kind which normally
honed in on teenagers, had somehow found its way onto his face,
and was beginning to blossom bright yellow on one side of his
cauliflower nose. Try as I did to avoid staring, my eyes were drawn
to its lunar-like landscape like they would to a car crash. By now

the game was already disappointingly familiar. I'd be brought into his inner sanctum and viewed for several silent minutes by grey eyes with pupils no bigger than pinheads, the purpose to make me squirm in dreaded anticipation. Desperate to get this whole business behind me and not dwell on it in any way - lest Katkin acquire a genuine taste - I helplessly played my part and squirmed accordingly.

"Bit of a ladies man, then, are we?" he reiterated inexplicably.

I waited for him to expound, and eventually, with much unnecessary elaboration, he did.

Short Order had heard, via his daughter, that we were accompanied to Brixton by another young woman, by the name of Katkin, who appeared to be a friend of mine. When he'd initially spoken of his requirements of me, he'd not mentioned that the invitation extended to anyone else, much less a helpless young woman. He presumed all this was quite clear, if not completely obvious. Again thanks to Treeza, however, he'd since learned that Katkin was of much use that Saturday morning, and were it not for her presence, then it would be likely that his daughter would be nursing much more than a mere bash to the head right now.

Nonetheless, this didn't particularly endear me to him, and he expressed much mock surprise that I failed to prove as handy as his dearly departed former colleague. "Weak genes," he grunted. The money paid to us was more for Katkin than for me, a show of gratitude, he called it, and he'd hoped it was spent on her, not me. I assured him this was indeed the case, that I could show him the receipts if required, and he smiled widely, his teeth still liberally flecked with bits of white meat, wriggling like worms.

"You realize, I hope, that you are going to go through with this," he said. "It's not a question of choice. You will earn your guilt, and you'll earn it good and proper, until the risk you pose to me and my setup has been completely diminished. At which point we should be able to happily go our separate ways, no questions, no comeback. But before you're ready, you've got to prove to me that your ready."

He got up from his chair and as he walked around the desk, I was reminded again of his physical power, a power that someone of his advanced age shouldn't even be able to remember, much less continue to possess. He sat on the edge of the desk, his cotton trousers stretched tight over thunder thighs, and leaned towards me, with now no more than twelve inches separating our faces. I could smell him - eau de rancid OAP - and was able to judge that the spot would be ready to burst by tomorrow morning, lunchtime at the latest. Not a proximity I particularly enjoyed.

"I've got another collection I want doing," he said. "Only this time, you'll do it on your own. No assistance. This one's another down-and-out loser. Lost his job, wife and kid left him, the whole spiral of shit."

From his breast pocket, he retrieved a piece of paper, folded several times over, and handed it to me.

"That's the who when where," he said. "I think you may even enjoy this one. To give a bloke what's coming to him can be very cathartic, son. Do this, do it good, and you'll learn the many redeeming qualities of violence." He patted the side of my face paternally, the father I never had. Then, in place of the word goodbye, the lowlife philosopher said, "Don't fuck up this time. I'll be watching."

By the time I left the pub, night had fallen and the South East London sky was as black as licorice. I got into the car, which was parked opposite the pub, and drummed fingers on the steering

wheel, blowing air through pursed lips. But as I started the engine,
I had immediate cause to switch it off again. I'd seen something that
prompted in me no little shock, and I wanted to investigate further.

Under the limp glow of an ailing streetlight, I saw the figure
of a man in his late thirties, dressed somehow uncomfortably, as if
he were in fancy dress, in blue T-shirt, faded blue jeans with an
elasticated waist, scuffed trainers, and a worn brown leather jacket.
His hands were thrust deeply into the jacket's pockets, and
everything about him spelled furtive. I recognized the face, although
not the dress sense. Just before a hand went up onto the pub door,
which would swing open and swallow him whole, he looked over his
shoulder once more, first left, then right, and seemed to focus in on
me, although I'm sure he saw only a parked car. It was only once
he'd disappeared, that I managed to place him. It was Detective
Banks, the officer who'd gotten his bad cop routine straight from
the kind of lame American police show they used to make in the
seventies.

I turned off the engine, and waited.

Time passed like treacle, and I sat there in my driving seat,
my head surrounded by cigarette smoke, feeling like I had

inadvertently given myself a cameo role in that lame American police show. All I was lacking was black coffee, sugared donuts, and a girth the size of a beer barrel.

Maybe an hour later, possibly slightly less, Banks reemerged, his pace hurried, his features still anxious. This time, he headed my way, and for several moments I froze, breath trapped, convinced he was coming straight for me. Instead, he walked right past, and on up the road. I started the car and slowly three-point-turned, keeping the lights off, and silently praising Mercedes for making cars with such quiet engines. I watched him get into a large Ford, an old model, the kind that takes up far too much space in motorway lanes and whose back passenger windows are always obscured by grey blazers which hang from a hook and sway. He got in and closed the door, then turned the in-car light on, his figure clearly hunched over. I eased into first gear, and slowly approached. Lights still off, the engine barely purring, I crept up on him as if invisible, and as I passed, I looked in on Banks and saw, quite clearly, him counting a great wad of money that spilled from a brown envelope.

From there I quickly shifted from second to third gear, turned a corner, then eased into forth and up into fifth, the needle

climbing up the neon green speedometer, my head reeling in wonder.

Detectives Russell and Banks were now presumably part of my

past.

*

My refusal to believe in God - any god, either thin and crucified

or fat and balding - also precludes me from believing in the

devil. But nevertheless I began harbouring distinct suspicions

about Short Order, whose entire being appeared to personify

everything demonic. It seemed that nothing could happen without

his prior consent or, at the very least, his full knowledge. His was

a guiding hand that pushed anything he wanted into required

positions and directions, his power all-consuming. Although a rather

unexpected surprise did lie in store for him - one that would

eradicate prescience from his vision for the remainder of his days

on Deptford's green and peasant land - this was still a little way off

in the future. For now he was a veritable totem of self-

empowerment, and I feared him greatly.

His all-seeing eye had found for me another collection job, one that could practically be described as personal. The unsuspecting victim from whom I was to extricate an overdue repayment of œ150, plus œ250 for the home visit, was Terry Flanagan, a twenty-five year old man who, a decade previously, had made my life hell at school until expulsion thankfully eliminated him completely from my then miserable universe.

When I unfolded the piece of paper Short Order had given me and saw this name, with the address underneath, a freezing shiver chased an imaginary mouse down my spine, then back up again. Butterflies started flapping manically in my stomach, and blood began to throb in my temples. Suddenly, I found myself wanting to scream, but instead managed to keep this passion pent up inside of me, storing it for a later, more appropriate time.

*

Around the same time that I realized the passing infatuations I had for girls were, in fact, the beginnings of an obsession that would never recede, I became friendly with someone called Carol.

275

This was my first embryonic friendship with a fledgling woman. It was exquisite; it was horrific. She was fifteen, several months and inches taller than me, and her radiant beauty belied a natural timidity that extended to everyone bar a select few close friends. We'd shared the same class at school for three years, but had yet to exchange any greeting other the indiscernible raising of eyebrows which effectively constituted whole conversations: hello, goodbye, how are you, this exam's tough, etc. One cold November morning, I missed the bus and was late for school and, consequently, locked out of assembly. I was directed to stand in the hall by a passing teacher and await the bell before making my way to the first lesson. After five minutes' hopping on either freezing foot, a very flustered Carol arrived, her cheeks pink and her hair celebrating the fact that it had yet to come under instructions from the morning brush by standing to erratic attention. When she too was told to stand alongside me, her eyes fell to the floor in tortured embarrassment.

"Oops," was the very first word she'd ever uttered in my direction, one sweet syllable that I took to mean that she too had overslept, missed breakfast, and failed in catching the bus. Her shirt was slightly untucked, her tie loose, and her thick woolen

tights needed a good hoisting up. It was at this moment I felt the
fist of love as it landed in my stomach and uncurled, extending
spidery fingers into my soft, sensitive guts. I didn't expel air for
almost a minute.

Gradually, an awkward conversation was established, and it
emitted a delirious warmth like cashmere. I told her about my
reasons for being late, exaggerating every calamity, and this had
her giggling almost uncontrollably, a reaction that made me, in turn,
feel omnipotent. From that day on, a faltering friendship grew
between us, one that remained chaste but quite perfect, unsullied
by the ravages of teenage lust.

But as Carol grew prettier, seemingly with each passing day,
her figure developing into a shape that resembled the soft curves
of a number eight, so she reaped the attention of every boy in our
year, albeit unwittingly. It became every straight-thinking male's
sole objective to procure her for himself, each reeling with a level
of public testosterone that I could only ever exhibit in private.
Terry Flanagan, one of the year's more athletic males, beat such a
convincing path to her door that he knocked anyone else who dared
follow in his wake with the kind of force his father doubtless

exerted on him. And Carol, clearly confused in a rush of bewildering adolescence, fell temporarily smitten.

A stake was therefore instantly driven between us, our friendship now reverting back to covert smiles and the odd complicitous note. While the innocent rapport refused to wilt irreconcilably, her new-found sexual identity nevertheless rendered her a galloping mare compared to my seaside donkey, and she was soon off and running, a male teenage thug by her side, incredulous at his stroke of luck, gurning like an idiot.

And then one day, the heavens opened and the sun started to shine - all especially for me. Carol arrived at school one ordinary morning, her newly-applied black makeup creating spiderwebs down her cheeks, the tears rolling freely - sad, fat drops. She snuffled through the first three lessons, and was the first out the door at the sound of the lunchtime bell. Terry, meanwhile, was nowhere to be seen. Like a bee with the scent of nectar, nothing stood in my path. I forewent the dubious pleasure of a canteen lunch and rushed directly out into the playground, intent on offering my female friend a shoulder upon which to sob. Eventually I found her, seated alone on one of the few benches with any slats left, and perched myself awkwardly at the end, suddenly unsure of whether she'd welcome my intrusion.

She did.

They'd had an argument. Several, in fact, the kind which to me at least confirmed every suspicion. They simply were not suited to one another.

"I hate him," she spat, soaked in the agony of wasted adoration, looking utterly exquisite. "But the trouble is, I love him too." A sudden spear through my heart, the lump in my throat the size of an apple. "Can you understand that, Jake?"

Jake, putting the feelings of the woman he cherished over his own, told her that of course he could understand. Love, he explained, is equal parts pleasure and pain - a nugget of pointless information he'd read on the back of a matchbox once. Further platitudes spilled from his mouth, well-meaning but ultimately hollow, for now Jake was outside himself looking in, desperately wanting to reveal his true feelings, to steal this young woman away from such an ignorant caveman but tragically aware that her feelings for him were virtually insignificant compared to the ones she continued to harbour for someone who clearly didn't deserve her. It was all Jake could do not to crumble before her, to become dust before her eyes; eyes that may as well have been blind for all the truth they could see.

Then she embraced me, called me such a great friend, and I dissolved into her outstretched arms like aspirin in water. She smelled of lavender, of washing powder, and felt delicate, in need of protection.

"Thank you," she whispered in my ear. "Thank you."

When we parted and looked up, our heartbeats suddenly stopped, then resumed beating, only faster. Terry was now standing before us, the expression on his face not one of happiness, nor understanding. Like a deranged lion, he began to roar.

And that was how it began. If ever I faced him on the football pitch after that, his studs would become a US heat-seeking missile to the Iraq of my thighs. They'd make regular contact whether I had the ball or not, boring holes into my legs like mini drills, until I'd so many black bruises I looked like a Dalmatian. In the canteen at lunchtime, he'd upend my plate in my lap, baked beans drowning in my groin. Or running down the corridor, his outstretched hand would make contact with my face, the sting as sharp as a wasp's, the handprint it left as red as blood, leaving what looked like a fifty percent blush. A whispering campaign began, scurrilous, incorrect rumours and lies, and regular taunting whenever possible. My bag would go missing, its contents stolen, never to return, ditto the money in my pocket.

All of which was very exact, precise, carefully contrived. Terry could easily have filled my face with his fist and I'd have been unable to reply similarly. He was bigger than me, and far stronger. He could kick me senseless any time he desired. But that was too easy, and not fulfilling enough. Via my close friendship with his girlfriend, I'd dealt him the most painful body blow of all. His manly pride was completely deflated, Carol and I having indulged in social intercourse. Thus, his bullying of me was required to be less obvious, more surreptitious, and ultimately more devastating. Today, I almost feel like applauding him - it's certainly the most intelligent, thought-out thing he's ever done. But back then it was agony. He continued to employ cunning wherever possible, and he contrived that it was always possible. Once, when I did dare answer him back - foolishly before several of his friends - my head was flushed down a toilet in the girls' WC and I was left on the floor to recover at the very point the bell went off. Two dozen girls flooding the bathroom a moment later to find me sprawled beneath them like a corpse did little for my social standing, and probably even less for my health - my mouth tasted of bleach.

And Carol?

Carol now kept a distance the size of the Atlantic between us. If our eyes ever did meet, then it was by accident, hers quickly flitting back again while her features took on an expression of either shame, regret or pity, I could never quite discern which. Perhaps all. To my agonizing incredulity, she continued to see Terry. If anything, they became closer still, leaving me in a perpetual state of gloom that my mother put down to drawn-out teenage turbulence.

Shortly afterwards, Terry and friends discovered canned lager, and an off license that didn't care about the age of those they sold the stuff to. He'd arrive in school increasingly inebriated, ignoring all cautions, and two suspensions. Then, one morning, I was late again and took my place in the hall awaiting the end of assembly. This time, however, I wasn't joined by Carol, but by Terry and two of his friends sharing a six-pack between them. Upon sight, his face lit up like torch paper and the cackle he emitted haunts me still.

"Right, boys," was all he had to say for them to all fall in with perfect synchronicity. One grabbed my left leg, another the right, while Terry took both arms, and I was transported to the girls' toilet where I was stripped completely and hung from one of the cubicles. Both hands were tied together onto the top of the door frame with the kind of knot a scout master usually awards prizes for, my white shirt doubling effectively for rope. My knee-length socks secured either leg, and my pants were put on my head, with my nose poking out of the Y front. When they'd finished, they admired their handiwork, and, laughing drunkenly, gave one another high-fives. Then the bell went, and they hit the cold floor running. I couldn't make a sound, all oxygen having left me, yet my heartbeat careened out of all control, my absolute panic mounting. Suddenly, I heard a familiar female voice - the history teacher's, an elderly woman whose teaching methods remained rooted in the past - cry out Terry Flanagan's name in vain. Seconds later, she rushed in to see what damage he and his associates had wreaked, and she found me, now whimpering pathetically.

"Oh my," she gasped, catching her breath.

I could just see her through the narrow slit of the Y. She looked utterly mortified.

"You poor, poor boy."

She rushed back to the door of the toilets and I heard her command a passing girl to stand guard and under no circumstances whatsoever should she allow anyone in. Then she came back to me and began untying the knots, crouching at my ankles, her face mere centimetres away from the small embarrassment dangling pinkly between my legs. When she stood to free my wrists, she pulled the pants from my head with tweezer-like fingers, a grimace bearing down on her features. It was then that I heard the furtive giggles. Turning my head toward the door, I saw several girls all pressed tightly together and peaking at me, each one with a hand clasped to their mouths to stifle screams of laughter.

Ms Dawes shrieked. "Girls! Get out!"

Terry Flanagan was expelled the next day and I didn't see him again. At the end of the school year, Carol also disappeared from my life, never to return.

*

A lifetime later - a curiously static one, at that - and Terry now lived in the same area he'd grown up in, Lewisham, on a labyrinthine estate where crime of every sort was a daily occurrence. He clearly hadn't made a success of himself in the interim, the environs told me that much, and from this I gleaned much satisfaction. I truly hoped him miserable, his existence wretched; forgiveness being something I would never grant somebody like him. On the drive over, I'd replayed the events of that school year over and over in my head, feeling increasingly sick with every mental snapshot, my grip tightening on the steering wheel until I practically left my imprint.

Revenge has never been particularly high on my list of ambitions, chiefly because I had little to seek revenge on. Whenever the image of Terry Flanagan flooded my memory, as occasionally it would over the years, I felt sadness more than anything. But tonight was different. Tonight, bolstered by Short Order's speech about the many redeeming qualities of violence, I felt determined to inflict damage, either mental or physical. Terry was now in a most humbling position. The tables, gloriously, had turned. And if I had

my way, I was going to ram the table down his throat and watch
him choke.

*

I arrived at a little after ten in the evening, parked the Merc
under the direct glare of a streetlamp in the hope that such
limelight would afford it safety from the neighbourhood's joyriders,
locked it, set its alarm, and walked carefully, my wits alert, through
the estate, up the piss-stinking lift to the ninth floor, and banged
loudly on his door after the bell failed to work. A lock slid to the
left and, slowly, it opened. A pair of blurred eyes peered out.
Clearly several hours into his day's drinking, Terry looked at me
without comprehension. It was the first time we'd seen each other
in almost a decade. I remembered him as big and strong, assertive
and ominous. But the intervening years hadn't been as kind to him
as they had to me, and I could hardly contain my glee. Meanwhile,
he studied me blankly. Gradually, his brow creased, and I sensed he
was on the verge of pinpointing the vague memory, but instead he
shook his head and simply said, What? I told him who I was, then

reminded him further of our shared history. His eyes widened, and the penny dropped.

"Jake!" he said, laughing, and pumped my hand enthusiastically, much as one would a former fond friend. "Come in, come in." Eager for the company, he ushered me into the kitchen and offered me a can of lager which I declined. We sat at a small table, a single can of Fosters between us, the lame candles flickering in the breeze that the cracked window pane couldn't quite keep out, casting us both in shadow. "Electricity's on the blink," he said, in faltering tones so heavy with squirming embarrassment that even a fool could work out he'd been cut off. As he went to the fridge for another beer, I lit up a cigarette, and allowed the ash to spill to the floor.

"So," he said, growing confused as to my presence.

I explained to him why I was there. Upon hearing Short Order's name, he groaned and shook his head, but expressed no visible surprise that I was working for him. Instead, he took a long swig on his beer and started to bemoan his predicament, claiming himself an innocent victim of circumstance. "I need to get back on my feet, but, you know, it's a little hard when every fucker's against you. I've had a run of bad luck, mate." He shrugged his shoulders and looked beseechingly at me, still oblivious to any tension there may have remained between us. I asked him about Carol, and the floodgates opened. He told me all about her, their marriage, the child, the unemployment, her affair, the separation, the loneliness. I listened, nodded, then told him about the career, the money, the gym, the girls, the Merc. I showed him my palm-top, my threads, my muscle definition. I rubbed his nose in the role-reversal, a long time coming, and I gloated good. Before launching myself upon him and exacting a little physical revenge, I first needed him riled up. I didn't want to hit an apathetic face, I wanted to hit a furious one. Insult was the natural way forward, the only way.

I waited until his bottom lip stopped trembling. He looked up at me with those pathetic eyes, jealousy oozing from his stare, and I grinned back loudly. This was the moment. I leaned forward. Pointing to the photograph of Carol he had sellotaped to the fridge - an older Carol than I remembered, sagging, weathered, spent - I told him that he was best rid of her, that she was probably past her best anyway. "Fuck her," I told him, adding, "I speak metaphorically, of course. Especially as she's not here anymore. And anyway, you never really deserved her in the first place, did you?"

That seemed to do it. His face contorted into pure purple rage, and he jumped up and lunged at me, tattooed fists outstretched. But with the grace of Barishnikov, I side-stepped him, brought my palms together, fingers entwined, and brought them down with great force upon his bent back. He thudded to the floor, sprawled out like human birdshit. As I considered whether or not to make a hasty exit, he scrambled ungainly to his feet, grabbed a chair, brought it up over his head and attempted to bring it down on top of me. Again, I thwarted his efforts, jumped back on the balls of my feet, before propelling myself forward through the air, as aerodynamic as Concorde, my right foot outstretched, my leather brogue pointing forward, and made perfect contact with his nose. The crunch was satisfyingly loud, and seemed to echo about the kitchen. He let out a cry and slumped to the floor, straddling the broken chair. Next, I administered a deft rabbit punch to his left temple, grabbed his hair, raised his head and brought it down hard on the kitchen floor once, twice, three times, until a pool of claret spread out, framing his cranium in a red halo. He made no noise, no movement. I then

289

removed the photograph of Carol from the fridge, set it alight with my Zippo and dropped it to the floor ceremoniously, stepping over it, him, out of the kitchen, out the front door.

The Merc was waiting faithfully for me downstairs, bathed in a glorious yellow glow. I clicked off the alarm, clicked open the door, and fired her up. As I sped away from the curb, I activated the in-car CD system, swamping the enclosed space with music at ear-splitting volume. I then swerved onto the main road and made my way west, towards Notting Hill Gate, home.

This has got to stop, I thought to myself as I pushed the speedometer up past sixty mph. This has really got to stop.

*

It was only as I neared home, paying as much attention to my swelling fist as the twisting road in front of me, that I realized the glaring omission. I'd completely forgotten to retrieve the money owed. Shit! I could hardly go back now, that wouldn't do at all. I'd be a laughing stock back in Deptford. But it had been a strange evening, in which nothing went quite as I'd imagined, even the beating itself. And how, exactly, had I left him? In my head, I saw the flash of fist, an explosion of red, an echoing silence.

I pulled over. Within the car seat, I felt myself sinking, while reality loomed large. I held up both fists and examined them. The right pulsed methodically.

I had killed him, killed him with my bare hands.

Me, a murderer.

After I was done, I just wanted to get out of there fast; the money went clean out of my mind. So, a few miles before home, I pulled up at the nearest cash machine, found my Visa - the Switch card still presumably in Katkin's possession - and took out four hundred pounds, which covered it. Short Order need never know. The money didn't matter, not to me, and I could still well afford it, anyway. While tapping away, I decided belatedly to check my balance, fearing I'd spent perhaps as much as ten, fifteen thousand pounds in the last few weeks, leaving me with - what? - just over one two seven. Ish. But then, of course, I had to take into account Katkin's spending sprees, and the fat chunk I'd loaned Tom. That'd be another what - forty five, fifty? More? Christ. In electric green neon, my new balance emerged on screen and glowed before my eyes. It was a completely incorrect amount, far, far less than I'd anticipated, and absolutely impossible. So I tapped in a few more instructions, and was fed a mini statement, which contained similarly foolish information.

According to this worthless bit of paper, I'd been taking five hundred pounds cash out of the account - the maximum allowed - every day for the past six weeks. That's twenty one thousand! On top of that Katkin herself had spent a colossal amount, approximately ten big ones in various shopping emporia, which, when added to all my other various expenses, left me with a new total of just over fifty thousand pounds. Down almost a hundred grand on the original sum in just a few weeks. Jesus Christ!

Suddenly, Notting Hill was hit by an earthquake. I almost fell to the ground as everything beneath me shook, shifting my feet on the tarmac, before sending tremors up my legs and into my spine, then erupting within my skull. My eyeballs felt like they were about to pop out and bounce off down the convulsing pavement. I turned quickly, determined to get back into the car, convinced of greater personal safety within its supposedly indestructible shell. But as I got in, I realized that Notting Hill wasn't suffering an earthquake at all.

I was.

Twenty one ping pong balls darted about inside my head, each one as heavy as lead. My stomach began inflating and deflating rapidly, and my right knee started trembling furiously against the steering wheel. I was sweating profusely. My tongue turned to sand.

Three cups of coffee from the nearest petrol station later, and I began to gradually pull myself together, to reorganize a steady breathing pattern. I located my mobile phone and punched in a series of digits. Tom picked up on the fourth ring. The other day, he needed me. Once again, positions were reversed and I now needed him - badly.

"You'd better come over," he said.

I drove fast.

Fifteen. Betrayal.

A revision. Money doesn't make things easier as all. It fucks everything up royally. It turns friends into parasites, can bring family out of the woodwork with their hands outstretched, it causes suspicion, greed and scheming, and can turn girlfriends into petty thieves.

Not that there's anything particularly petty about twenty one thousand pounds.

"Look, let's take this slowly. Let's examine the evidence, or at least the suggestion of evidence."

Tom was taking all of this in his stride, confidence now restored since paying off most of the debts - as well as having recently revisited his dealer if the sporadic sniffing was anything to go by. He poured a couple of stiff drinks, handed one to me, and sank opposite into a plush leather armchair, the kind which moulds itself around the body in consummate accommodation. He was wearing T-shirt and sweatpants where usually he'd still be loafing around in the day's suit. Clearly still under suspension, he nevertheless appeared completely at ease with this temporary unemployment.

"Cheers," he said, and raised his glass.

A icepack, recently retrieved from the giant refrigerator, was wrapped around my fist, each knuckle now the colour of a winter's day and as sensitive as a poet's disposition. The chill helped calm the pain down a little, but it still felt like I had much of Terry's face ingrained into my hand, every tendon and fibre on fire. While explaining just how I'd gotten in this state - although I decided against telling him just how fatal my punches had proved - Tom beamed with a brotherly pride as if I'd just told him I passed my driving test with flying colours. Like Katkin, he seemed excited by violence, both the prospect of and the execution, and complained aloud that there were many people he'd like to make bleed, but punching was frowned upon at the office and in the computer business in general. He shrugged. Then I told him about the financial situation, and my subsequent suspicions, which were swimming around my head like fish.

"I never did trust her," he said after the expletives died down.

He'd only ever met her once.

"Twice," he corrected. "The funeral. Anyway, I'm a very good judge of character. She's not to be trusted, she's shifty. Believe me, it takes one to know one." He grinned. "I am; she is."

It is true that she not only had easy access to my card, along with the pin number, but ample time in which to plunder into my account without my knowledge. She'd disappear on me several times a day, to where I never quite found out. I originally thought she'd merely gone shopping, courtesy of me and my funds, and to be honest, I was happy to help out, convinced that it made me almost as content as it did her. And she was certainly grateful upon arriving home, several new outfits stuffed into bags which she clasped in each hand, and a red kiss on her mouth coming my way. I was giving her happiness. What was wrong with that? Now, however, I just felt colossally stupid, embarrassed at my own staggering naivety.

"Well then," said Tom, underlining every tortured suspicion I had with a thick marker pen. "That proves it."

"It proves nothing," I countered, desperate to believe her innocent. "Maybe somebody else has gotten to it. It does happen, you know."

"Not with that kind of account," said Tom knowingly. "The

bank values our sort of customer far too highly for that. Those kind of crimes only ever happen to ordinary card holders. Once you've gone gold, security is paramount. Believe me, it's her. It has to be."

I still refused to let myself be convinced. She couldn't have, surely? Not Katkin. Why would she need to - we were together after all, what was mine hers and hers mine? No, until I came to any conclusion, I needed proof.

"Fine," my brother said, "let's go get some."

*

It was after midnight when we arrived back at my place, and the flat was dark. I walked up the stairs with Tom tiptoeing beside me, his heartbeat considerably slower than my own. I slipped the key into the door and it swung open silently. A small light crept from a crack somewhere upstairs. I closed the door and waved a firm index finger in front of Tom's face. He nodded, and I went on up. He stayed where he was.

Katkin was in bed with Jackie Collins, utterly engrossed. When she saw me, she tossed the book aside, and crawled across the

297

duvet to hug me.

"Where were you?" she said. "I was so worried! I've been calling you for ages, but I kept getting VoiceMail."

As we embraced, I noticed that my credit card was sitting under the bedside lamp, twinkling bright gold.

"Sorry," I told her, "the battery died."

She pulled away and looked deep into my eyes.

"How are you? How did it go?"

For the second time that evening, I explained what happened between myself and Terry Flanagan - again not divulging every detail - and showed Katkin my swollen knuckles. She listened rapt throughout, and although I searched her expression for even the slightest evidence of foul play, I failed. As far as it seemed to me, Katkin was, and remained, loyalty incarnate. She made every appropriate placatory noise, hugged me, stroked my hair, and applied butterfly-light kisses to each of my four mushroom-like bruises.

"I'll go and get us a drink," she said. "Something thick and sweet and painkilling."

I tried to object, but this proved wholly unsuccessful and

Katkin was quickly out the door, taking the stairs two at a time. I sat tight, fingers crossed, praying Tom would have enough sense to hide himself inventively. Hugging my drawn-up knees for support, I braced myself for the sound of a sudden scream and dropped crystal, ice scattering across the linoleum in the kitchen, and voices raised.

It didn't come.

Katkin arrived back with two glasses of Southern Comfort on the rocks, one in each hand, a wide smile between the two. We drank them while resuming horizontal positions, Katkin assuring me that this would all be over soon enough. In my eyes, her innocence was promptly, undoubtedly, returned, and I felt the stabbing pain of guilt that I'd ever suspected her in the first place.

From downstairs came a sudden thud. Katkin sprang into a seated position and shook me by the shoulder.

"What was that? Wait there," she said, getting out of bed.

This time I was quicker.

"No, let me," I insisted, racing to the door and pulling on a T-shirt.

"Maybe it's Terry Flanagan?" she said.

"Maybe," I agreed, avoiding eye contact. "Stay there. Under no circumstances come downstairs. I'll deal with this."

"Be careful."

I went downstairs and switched on a lamp, expecting to see Tom standing there, explanation and apology at the ready. But he wasn't anywhere to be seen. As quietly as possible, but with as much venom as I could muster, I whispered his name, in sharp italics. Tom! Nothing. I tried it again, but still nothing, and gave up, suddenly feeling really very tired indeed. I went back upstairs and slid under the cover, assuring Katkin that it was nothing, that no one was there.

"Must have been the neighbours," I said.

My plan was to wait until I heard a steady breathing coming from her nostrils, then creep downstairs to see what, if anything, my brother had found in the way of incriminating evidence. But as soon as I was prostrate, I felt a huge pulling, and before I knew it the lights went out in my head, unconsciousness all-enveloping.

I only awoke when I realized it wasn't a dream, that in fact I did have a hand pressing hard down onto my mouth and nose, momentarily suffocating me. I began to wriggle until I blinked and saw Tom above me, eyebrows like daggers. Slowly, he lifted his hand and beckoned me to follow him. It was still the dead of night. Silently, I slipped out of bed and walked on eggshells, allowing myself finally to breathe out only when we were both huddled into a corner in the kitchen, the glow of the moon transforming us both into alabaster mummies.

I looked expectantly into his face, nervous with anticipation.

"Nothing," he said.

Relief swamped me, and I relaxed.

"I've looked everywhere, in every drawer. I even managed a quick root in her handbag."

Her handbag?

"I found it inside her bedside table, which I was convinced meant she was hiding something. But I found nothing. Your credit card is next to the lamp, though."

"I know, Inspector Clouseau."

He shrugged helplessly.

"She's in the clear then," I suggested.

"Rubbish," he responded. "Not yet she's not. I'll have to find out tomorrow."

"Tomorrow?"

This was ridiculous.

*

The next day, at Tom's continued insistence, we were walking along Kensington High Street, approximately one hundred feet behind Katkin. We were following her, tracing her every move. So far, she'd been into several shops and had purchased at least one outfit. By lunchtime, I was visibly waning, desperate for this to stop. But Tom was adamant that we continue.

Earlier, she and I had enjoyed a perfectly civil breakfast at home, after which she explained that she had to visit her mother today in a bridge-building exercise.

"I've left it far too long," she said in earnest.

We made arrangements to meet later back here, before possibly going out again to one of the many local restaurants for a romantic evening meal. She kissed my cheek, left me the washing up, and offered a last quick wave as she disappeared behind the front door. Immediately, I raced upstairs praying for at least one expectation to be confounded. But the bedside table was clear, my credit card vanished.

"See?" said Tom, almost gloating as he rolled out from under the desk in the study. "What did I tell you?"

Within seconds, we were hot on her trail, he insisting I keep up.

As it later transpired, Tom was right all along. Moments before she took an outside table at a swank Kensington restaurant, where she met her former boyfriend Simon and planted a loving kiss upon him that went much further than the lips - to the extent that I feared she'd ever get her tongue back again - she made a visit to the cash machine. Wasting no time, Tom assumed a position that gave him full view of her imminent transaction while I held back, now unable to watch. She retrieved, he reported, a fat bundle of notes which were quickly swallowed up into her svelte black handbag, then made a beeline to the restaurant where the waitress greeted her like a regular.

I felt sick.

Katkin ordered a moussaka along with a side salad, while Simon - looking dapper in a blue linen suit and tortoise-shell Ray Bans -

had a golden poussin with a sprig of parsley. A bottle of fresh white wine sat between them, perspiring gently. Whenever their respective dishes allowed, they'd eat with just forks, thus enabling them to hold hands, while their legs were entwined beneath the table like vine. For desert, she ordered a light fruit salad while he, boldly, went for blackcurrant cheesecake. They both had coffee, and he a pregnant glass of brandy. When they'd paid for the meal, Katkin slipping two instantly recognizable crisp fifty pound notes onto the small silver tray that contained the bill along with four pellet-sized mints, they brought their chairs closer together and it was then I witnessed the ultimate killer blow. Dipping a dainty hand into her purse, she retrieved the tidy wad, peeled off a few notes for herself, then handed the bulk of it over to Simon who promptly placed it into his inside jacket pocket in one quick, easy movement. Then, after kissing some more, they stood to leave, hand in hand.

Words, gasps, strangled cries, roars of agony. All refused to leave my throat, and they gathered together in my thorax, a palpable lump, feeling like cancer. I stormed off in the opposite direction, crossing the road and completely ignoring the blaring horns of taxis and buses.

*

I arrived back home sometime around six, exhausted in every way.
Katkin was waiting for me, looking crushingly beautiful in her
new outfit and appearing very pleased to see me. My credit card
was on the coffee table, looking completely innocent despite its
heinous complicity with the enemy.

"Hi baby," she cooed, approaching and draping elegant arms
around my taut neck. Kisses fluttered across my cheeks and she
pressed her breasts tight up against me. But before she could
mount me completely, the telephone rang. I made a lunge for it.

It was Short Order, requesting an audience.

"When?" she asked me when I'd replaced the receiver.

"Tomorrow evening."

I looked, or so I imagined, furious, full of awkward, unspoken
consternation. And I was. I still had no idea how to deal with her,
despite Tom's many murderous suggestions. Katkin took this
expression as a result of my brief telephone conversation. She
joined me on the sofa, offering sympathy like a nurse.

"It'll all be over soon enough," she assured. "I'm sure of it. He's probably aware of how well you dealt with Flanagan, so maybe the big one is imminent." She slipped her hand into the space between my arm and chest, as if we were walking down the aisle together. "After that, it'll be just you and me, living the life of luxury."

I turned to face her. Her betrayal continued to incense me. Stealing from under my very nose, with almost bizarre recklessness. Did she not think I check my balance from time to time? Evidently not.

"Money's important to you, isn't it?" I said.

"How do you mean?" she responded blankly.

"Just that. You like money."

"Of course I do. Don't you?"

"Not with as much determination as you."

"Determination?"

"Yes, determination. You seem completely determined to live, as you've said, a life of luxury."

"Well, I was unfortunate enough to grow up with never very much of the stuff, while all my friends at school had loads. Do you have any idea what that feels like? I never fitted in, I always felt left out, neglected. Now we've got it, why on earth not enjoy it?"

I reminded her that, at just under one hundred and fifty thousand, it was hardly lap-of-luxury stuff. In fact, it was barely five numbers plus the bonus ball.

"True, but it's what you do with it when you've got it that counts."

"What do you mean?"

"You've got to make it work for you."

"Really?"

"Yes. Simon, my ex, was always very good at making money work for him."

I wanted to drill a hole on either side of my head; anything to relieve the colossal, mounting pressure.

"But the money isn't working for us at all," I said. "It's just sitting in a building society."

Without even the merest hesitation, she said, "Ah, but it will, it will. When all this is behind us, we'll have it working for us. I'll double it in no time, then treble it. You'd be surprised."

"Oh, I don't doubt that."

Her eyes asked the question: what?

"That you'll surprise me," I explained. "I'm sure your quite capable of that."

She offered me her most attractive smile, and winked with her right eye.

Later, in bed, I wanted to remove the pillow from under my head and place it over her sleeping face until she stopped wriggling and ceased breathing altogether. But if I did that, I wouldn't be able to retrieve what she'd stolen from me.

And I very much wanted to retrieve it.

Sixteen. Complicity.

Again exerting the kind of resistance I proved incapable of

thwarting, Katkin insisted she come along for the ride the

following evening. It'd be good PR, she wagered, and also she

wanted, at long last, a proper face-to-face with Short Order.

"After all," she said, "I saved his daughter's life, practically.

He'd probably be very happy to see me."

We arrived at the pub in Deptford a little after ten thirty in

the evening, and the place was busy even for a Friday. Like

sardines in a rusting tin, the place smelt of the possibility of

quickie sex, if only by virtue of the situation. Everyone was pressed

so tightly up against everybody else, that all anyone needed to do

was lower a trouser zip for there to be an immediate orgy. Disco

music from at least three decades earlier blared from crumbling

speakers, over which the gathered men attempted to shout their

barely secret messages of lust into the pale, gold-studded ears of

women. There was very little available oxygen, the only tangible air

stale and heavy with the odour of nicotine. I lead the way,

reluctantly allowing Katkin a hold of my hand, and I squeezed through the throng like a fat bubble through a straw, until we reached the appropriate table.

"They've both got great big cunts on 'em!"

Short Order was seated in the corner, leaning back, clapping his thick hands together and roaring with laughter at a joke a middle-aged man to his left had just delivered in broad cockney tones. His face was the colour of beetroot after boiling, and sweat dotted the invisible line where hair used to grow. The laughter became a coughing fit which climaxed with a colossal clearing of mucus from his nasal passage, which he then spat on the floor between his legs, the fruit of the deposit looking as heavy as lead, as green as grass. The joker, similarly, was rocking back and forth on his chair, his own laughter the sound of rapid machine gun fire. This man was maybe a decade younger than Short Order, and stockier still. He appeared to have been carved out of the base of a tree trunk, with a thick solid torso, tattoed arms like meat cleavers, and a skull like a bowling ball, completely bald, but with, at closer inspection, lumps, bumps, rivets, and old scars. His eyes were the colour of death, his insane grin the shape of purified evil.

Both sets of eyes looked up at us, but passed over me

completely in favour of a visual appraisal of the girl at my side. Katkin had dressed provocatively in an outfit that suggested her figure was worthy of applause. Her skirt was as short as her red top was tight, her bright white teeth caught the light and appeared to sparkle. Short Order immediately became a gentleman and pulled out a seat for her, while the joker watched silently as she folded her feminine wiles into the chair and crossed one leg over the other, right over left, revealing thigh, revealing meat. I sat down beside her and waited patiently while they introduced one another, spittle on the mens' lips, a pointed tongue on Katkin's.

The joker's name, explained Short Order, was Joaquin Mullard. He pronounced the christian name Joe-a-kin, as if chewing tobacco.

"His mother was Spanish," he explained. "Not that he ever learned the lingo. East End born and bred, this one. We call him Joe."

Joe was very pleased to meet Katkin.

"Charmed," he said in his sandpaper voice, looking less the result of Latin genes than a Borstal upbringing in South London.

Introductions dispensed with, Short Order leaned across Katkin to get to me, using her knee to rest an arm upon.

311

"Don't you have something for me?" he asked.

From my trouser pocket I retrieved the four hundred pounds and placed it in his outstretched hand, his fingers instantly curling into a tight fist upon receipt. Leaning back, he began counting the notes with supple fingers that had clearly spent a lifetime collecting monies owed. Once finished, he nodded and allowed a brief smile.

"Heard you took my advice?" he said.

I nodded yes, though remained unsure what, exactly, he was referring to.

"And it made you feel good, right?"

I told him yes.

"Nothing's sweeter than revenge," he said, patting Katkin's thigh, an oily smile spreading across his chops. "Well, almost nothing." He showed teeth. "Anyway, good job, son. You're getting closer."

Awkwardly, nerves mounting, I asked him, sotto voce, for a quiet word. After considerable pleading, I managed to get him into a corner, where I huddled up close.

"So ... so you saw the, um, the body, did you?" I asked him.

Short Order removed the cigar he'd been chewing on from the

corner of his mouth, and squinted.

"The body? What you talking about, son?"

I explained, my voice a low whisper.

The old man looked at me with incredulity, then rocked back
on his heels and let out a coarse laugh.

"He's not dead, you idiot!" he chuckled.

I became dizzy. "Well, he looked pretty dead when I left him,"
I vouched. "The blood, and stuff."

Short Order laughed some more, and placed a heavy hand on
my shoulder.

"Our friend," he began, "has a rather nasty headache. And his
nose snapped in two, hence the red stuff. He may not quite see
things now as he did yesterday, but he'll live, don't you worry
about that. You're not quite the killer you think you are." A
condescending chuckle dribbled out the side of his mouth.

When we arrived back at the table, everyone looked up at us,
expectant.

"Prick thought he killed that bloke," he told them loudly.

Dirty cackles swamped the table. Katkin looked up at me with
alarm, then joined in with the laughter. I took my seat, a little

unsteadily, and waited for the drunken merriment to recede.

The rest of the evening began to swim in a haze of cigarettes and alcohol, and I watched with barely disguised amazement at Katkin's ability to charm anyone she came into contact with. Within minutes, she had both men eating from the palm of her hand as if proffering peanuts to monkeys. Furthermore, she retained full control, always pulling back when the flirtation became borderline pornographic, and deflecting the relentless come-ons with a diplomacy that could well land her a job with Unicef. At some point, possibly coinciding with the arrival of yet another tray of drinks, Treeza Burke came sat down accompanied by a man maybe half a dozen years her senior. He was tall, but looked compressed, as if his beefy frame ideally needed seven feet for optimum comfort, but instead had to make do with a mere five feet ten inches. His stomach was looser than his chest and, spread tightly under a tucked-in white T-shirt, looked like the moon setting beneath the horizon of his black jeans. His face was red and bulbous, and he resembled a younger, uglier, version of Joe. His son, maybe? He had a full head of brown hair, triumphantly unkempt, and his forehead was dotted with as much sweat as that which gathered beneath his armpits. A second chin was beginning to form underneath the first. Upon sight of Katkin, he too fell under spell.

At this point, Joe spoke.

"My son Xavier," he said, pronouncing it Hex-avi-yer. "Another Latin lover, like his old dad."

Xavier smiled idiotically at Katkin, revealing the absence of middle tooth, lower jaw.

"We call him Dave," said Joe, "his middle name." He ruffled his son's hair until it stood up with static.

While I tried to ascertain exactly what was going on here, Treeza regaled the table with a recount of our visit to Leeroy St. Coke, specifically how Katkin came heroically to the rescue with the insertion of a gun down his throat. She peeled back the blue plaster from the side of her head to reveal a large bruise, still electric red and clearly sore, in the middle of which sat four delicate, slightly crooked stitches. Of these she seemed inordinately proud. War wounds. Talk then turned to me and my own expert handling of Terry Flanagan, before the two older men began reminisces of my grandfather, without whom this evening wouldn't have been possible, as well as their various spells in prison. In between stories, they roared with laughter, drunken saliva flying between them like tiny acrobats, and they'd regularly hit the table with an open palm to hammer home a particular punchline. The liberating qualities of drink helped peel away inhibition, and I too laughed along with them in as convincing a display of shared bonhomie as I could muster. Dave's tongue, meanwhile, was all over Katkin's lobe, his right hand holding onto her right shoulder while he positioned his mouth close to her left ear, into which he delivered a succession of drink-fuelled words, she nodding and laughing as required. Occasionally, she'd turn my way and pull the kind of face that suggested she'd just swallowed poison. As for Treeza, she had temporarily fallen silent, allotting all her attention on the creation and rolling of a rather large joint.

Sometime long after midnight, the conversation appeared to at last wind down, and I breathed a huge sigh of relief, anticipating a merciful conclusion to tonight's proceedings. I'd handed over the money, surely I could leave now? In the interim, I realized I'd smoked far too much, and had contorted my face into an expression of joviality to such excess that every muscle now ached. My ears were ringing, my eyes stinging. I felt drunk, queasy. Katkin was

316

now facing me, seemingly intent on giving Dave the cold shoulder.

"I've a terrible headache," she whispered to me, and I nodded back, before shrugging helplessly.

My attention was then drawn back to Short Order who sat back in his chair, arms crossed purposefully. If either he or Joe were as drunk as I felt, then they certainly didn't appear it. The latter's son, meanwhile, was stupidly drunk, and, along with the former's daughter, three-quarters stoned. They sat quietly, amazed at the blinking of one another's eyelids.

"Well," said Short Order to Joe. "What do you think?" He nodded fractionally in our direction.

Joe rubbed his chin with a cupped hand, then moved the hand back and forth over his bald pate. This, clearly, was the art of concentration in motion. He made a low murmur, perhaps unconsciously, a meditative hmmm, his eyes bouncing between mine and Katkin's. At this, I felt increasingly uncomfortable, desperate to learn what exactly he was appraising. Presently, he turned back to Short Order, and the two men leaned into one another. Some unintelligible mumbling went on, a collection of unheard questions, indiscernible answers.

Eventually, Joe nodded his head, and accompanied it with a satisfied yeah.

"Good, then," said Short Order. "Let's take ourselves into the back room." He clapped his hands together. "Come."

*

Once in the now-familiar room, Short Order wheeled his chair around the desk until it faced opposite the leather sofa, then sat down, Joe on the other chair by his side, the pair looking like interrogators. The remaining four of us, consequently, had only the two-seater in which to squeeze. Dave collapsed down first, immediately conquering fifty percent of cow hide with his expansive behind. Katkin sat beside him, attempting to make space for Treeza, but she decided to sit on the floor, while I took the sofa's arm, attempting to look comfortable, feeling anything but.

The mood had noticeably changed, from drunken to sober. Short Order had purpose now etched into every crevice on his elderly face, while Joe remained more passive, clearly the more mysterious of the two. There was something about him that seemed immovable, indomitable, that if there was anyone to truly fear here, then it was he. His son, meanwhile, just looked like an idiot, all brawn, no brain. Katkin, I noticed, sat back, legs crossed, a look of eager determination about her.

"Right," Short Order began, directing his words at Katkin and myself. "You've both proved yourselves, your worth, so to speak, and you've both behaved impressively enough for me to invest a little trust in you. So it's time. Now, son, you can do your grandfather proud and earn your guilt." He lit a cigar. "We want you back here, the pair of you, a week on Saturday, noon. You're going to be upgraded from collection to aiding and abetting. Joe here, his son Dave and my daughter Treeza have agreed to allow you both to come with. They'll monitor you at all times. You're to follow instructions, do as your told. It's nothing complicated, not for you two, anyway, just a job that requires the presence of at least five people. A little violence may be necessary, but it's unlikely, and anyway, you've both proved yourselves capable in that department, so there shouldn't be any problems. Just listen, watch, and obey at all times."

"What, exactly, will we be required to do?" asked Katkin, a

slight tenseness in her throat.

At that point, both Short Order and Dave spoke simultaneously. The old man replied, "Just do as I say, that's all," while Dave blurted out, "We're going to do a jewellers." A look of awe crossed Katkin's face, a rising anger attacked Short Order at the temples. Treeza chuckled to herself, shaking her head, and Dave made placatory noises that suggested apology.

"Now, as I was saying," continued Short Order. "It's your presence that's required more than anything. No heorics, unless strictly necessary."

"Will you be coming with us?" Katkin asked.

"I don't get my hands dirty no more," he said. "But don't worry, love, Joe'll look after you."

Joe himself then leaned forward, his voice a low murmur, yet utterly indefatigable.

"But if there's even a suggestion of you fucking everything up," he said, "then I'll fuck you up good and final. Right there, no question." Then he looked at me. "Son, I don't care who your grandfather was, and," turning to Katkin, "that goes for you too, darling. If either of you put any of us in any kind of danger whatsoever, then you'll suddenly be as insignificant to me as a security guard." He fashioned his fingers into a gun, cocked it, then shot. "Pop."

"We'll put you in no danger whatsoever," said Katkin. "I can assure you of that."

A barely perceptible smile played upon Joe's mouth. He eased back into his chair.

"Meantime," said Short Order, "you carry on your week as usual. Anything out of the ordinary, and you can rest assured I'll hear of it, so behave yourselves. Tell no one, and don't even think of doing a runner. The moment you leave Zone Two I'll come bearing down upon you like a ton of bricks. And I won't be lenient. And Jake, don't go writing no articles about it."

Wordlessly, Dave struggled to his feet and left the room, clutching at his groin and no doubt toilet-bound, the two older men watching him go without expression. Treeza began to make another joint, while Katkin made noises to leave.

"Next week," said Joe, as we left the room.

In the hall that led back to the bar, I was aware of Short Order's presence right behind me, a footstep away. A firm hand on the shoulder stopped me in my tracks. He told Katkin to go wait for me in the car, while he led me into another, smaller room. Save for a few empty beer barrels, and an old, broken arcade game, the room was empty. Just four white walls, bare floorboards, one lightbulb, no chairs. We stood.

"If you do fuck up," he warned me, "and we don't get to you first - we will, of course, but let's just say we don't - then there'll be enough shit on you to put you inside for a fifteen year stretch. And if there's any talk of deals with our friendly boys in blue, information that'll reduce your time, then rest assured I'll get to you on the inside. There'll be no bars that'll stop me getting to you, one way or another. I just want you to understand that, alright?" He held my face between his iron fingers, squeezing my lips into an unemployable kiss.

I nodded as much as he'd allow within his grip.

"But if it goes smoothly, then you and your girl can walk away, you can both leave town, the country, whatever," he said, letting go. "That'll be the end of it. We need never meet again. So make sure you don't fuck up. Make very sure."

I had just one question.

"What about the two police officers?" I asked. "They've already been sniffing around me quite a bit. What if they come back next week?"

"I can assure you that won't happen," he said.

"I think I saw one of them, Banks, coming in here last week," I added, curious to gauge his response.

Short Order pointed an index finger at me, waved it in my face, then brought it to his lips. Shh.

"You talk too much," he said. "Now go on, piss off."

*

Home, sometime later.

She slapped me hard across the face, then the tears cascaded down her cheeks, a complete facial downpour. But these weren't tears of helplessness. There was blind rage behind them. She flounced into the kitchen, swung open the fridge, and grabbed a bottle of whiskey by the neck. She spun the top off, tossed it into the sink, and with two glasses in her other hand, came marching back into the living room, her footsteps as loud as a drum solo.

"Sit," she commanded.

It must have been around three in the morning by now, maybe later, and the argument, which had begun the moment we left the pub, was stretching into its second hour. Our heated exchange had led to some erratic driving on her part, and she raced through empty streets towards an imaginary finishing line which we didn't cross until we reached home, mercifully without interruption from the police. She parked carelessly, two wheels up on the curb - a crime punishable by the clamp I found clinging to the back wheel the following morning - and stormed upstairs, slamming the door in my face. Initially, I was actually heartened by this response, proving to me that she was indeed human and not merely a cold, calculating harlot. Somewhere around fifty five miles per hour on the Old Kent Road, I'd called her a scheming bitch, then a sick fuck. I was referring to the eagerness she displayed over our pending aiding and abetting. She responded, sharply, by telling me in a completely serious voice that she had a plan, to which I laughed until I choked.

"No, I'm serious," she said. "We could completely turn this around in our favour."

324

I shot her a look over arched eyebrows, at that point convinced she was mad. I even teetered on the edge of revelation, desperate to tell her that I knew all about she and Simon. But I pulled back, firstly because I remembered my brother's insistence to pace ourselves, that the only way we'd ever get back on top of the situation was by choosing our moment (he being, of course, a sudden expert in the matter), and secondly, because I found myself - perhaps shamefully - afraid, scared of just what Katkin was capable of. My brain became swamped with worst-case scenarios, that her scheming, this plan, was at my expense, leaving me to face the music Short Order would doubtless conduct in her absence, while she took off with the former boyfriend to pastures new.

She sat next to me now on the sofa, a crazed look in her eye, and poured the drink.

"I'm serious," she repeated. "Look, this could change everything. This is our big chance." She got up and ran over to one of the side cabinets, from which she retrieved the gun. Then she came back over and sat down. "Once we've got the job out of the way - which, let's face it, is robbery by any other name - and we're driving back, that's when I produce this."

I looked at her, wary for signs of a joke. Perhaps the way she dealt with Leeroy St. Coke had gone to her head, for suddenly she genuinely believed herself capable of taking on somebody like Joaquin Mullard. His idiot son, Xavier, was one thing. Maybe she could even overpower Treeza, but Joaquin Mullard was something else entirely, a formidable entity not easily overcome by anyone, least of all us. I tried to put this to her as clearly as I could, yet again.

"What you fail to realize," she said when I'd finished, "is that there's still so much you don't know about me. You have no idea of my capabilities. You may think you know me, Jake, but believe me, you don't. You don't at all." She dropped the gun into her lap, and stroked it absently.

This proved most intriguing.

"Well, go on then. Tell me all about yourself."

It was now her who looked flustered, unsure what to say next, how much to divulge.

"Look, all I'm trying to say is that I'm not in any hurry to obtain my two-point-four children. I want so much more than that. If you let me, I could turn this terrible experience into a life-

326

changing one. Short Order's an old man, practically decrepit, living off memories. Joe, or Joaquin, or whatever his name is, isn't much better. He's just a lech with delusions of grandeur. They've both been in prison, so they're hardly infallible, are they? Dave is a fool, anyone could deal with him, and even Treeza is all front. As long as we're quick about it - quick, determined and ruthless - it'll all be over within a minute. They will have already done all the hard work, the actual stealing. All we'll be required to do is then relieve it from them. Simple, really."

"Simple, is it?"

"Yes. Yes, it really is. Look, this kind of opportunity doesn't present itself every day, and now that I've tasted it, there's absolutely no way I'm going back to the pathetic life I lived."

"You mean back when you were with Simon?"

Her eyes shot up to mine, focused, then quickly pulled away.

"No, not specifically," she said, no trace of guilt, "just the drudgery of everyday life. My mother, by the time she'd reached my age, had quickly turned into her own mother, old before her time, stuck in a job she hated, and in a rut where misery was basically a way of life for her. I'm not going to fall into the same trap. I'm going to enjoy my life. And taking advantage of an opportunity like next Saturday will help enormously."

"What if we screw it all up? We'll be in big trouble then."

"We won't screw anything up. I won't screw anything up." Cool, calm, precise words.

I changed tack.

"I thought you were happy with what we've got. Only yesterday you were saying that the trick was to play with the money. Invest, gamble."

"You can never have enough. If it comes along, then take it. We're going to take it."

"What then?"

"What do you mean?"

"Well, we will have successfully gotten away with Short Order's haul. What then? We can't stay here, that's for sure."

"Why would we want to stay here? Once we've got it, we're off, away to anywhere we choose."

"And you think we'll have no trouble unloading stolen goods."

"Oh, we'll have no trouble there," she replied, smiling with satisfaction. "I know someone who knows someone."

"Who?"

"You wouldn't know them."

"How can I trust you? You keep telling me how I don't know you, after all. So how do I know that once we've done it, you won't just up and leave me?"

She looked shocked, insulted. "Me? Why would I leave you? Without you, I wouldn't even be in this position." She moved closer, and put both empty glasses on the floor. Her face was now centimetres away from mine. "I owe you everything, and I plan to repay you, in all manner of ways, for a long time to come."

"Oh. Right."

"Jake, you know me enough to know that you can trust me."

"Do I?"

Her lips parted and found mine, her tongue slithered snake-like into my mouth. She tasted of whiskey. But consummation never happened. After raising my body temperature and prompting in me a ready consent that I was secretly ashamed of, she pulled free from my embrace and disappeared into the bathroom, the gun still in her hand. My curiosity rose, and silently I tiptoed over to the bathroom door and crouched down until my eye came level with the keyhole.

I peered in, and immediately wished I hadn't. As the gun took bullets instead of batteries, she had to do all the vibrating herself, but this clearly hampered her little. Within minutes, her back arched, her eyes rolled in their sockets, and she let out a sigh infused with more sensual satisfaction than she'd ever received from me.

I closed my eyes, slumped down onto the floor, and thought of Tom. I needed to get in touch with Tom.

*

Curiously, we spent the rest of the weekend locked together, lounging around the flat in front of digital television and a thousand channels. Katkin made no telephone calls and no attempt to leave my side. We called out for food, for videos, and the only time I had to get dressed was when the de-clamping unit arrived to free the car. Otherwise, we basked in our underwear, enjoying the heat, until Monday morning, when everything changed. Until then, I'd made a concerted effort to enjoy our time together, a regular supply of drink allowing me to blot out all thoughts of deception, of evil, of impending violence. Our own high noon was still a week away, and there were at least forty eight hours until Tom re-entered my universe with all manner of advice and directives, he now appearing every bit as wired as Katkin. My own immediate requirement was simple relaxation, minimal distraction. I needed equilibrium, even if it proved merely temporary. So, it seemed, did Katkin. I looked at her snuggled up on the sofa, her slender frame surrounded by bright yellow cushions, and found myself thinking, In other circumstances, she and me, we could be..., but quickly banished such fruitlessly romantic notions from my head, and concentrated instead on a bunch of classic movies from the sixties and seventies, countless inane quiz shows, and, best of all, several brand new episodes of The Simpsons, which was a little like opening Christmas presents a day early.

Seventeen. Drum Roll.

At a little before two fifteen on the following Tuesday afternoon, four people, all dressed immaculately in suits whose price tags were as steep as small mountains, walked on soft carpeting into a board room, and closed the door behind them. They sat at a round table, and one poured four glasses of fizzy water. There were two women and two men, three of whom held executive positions within the company. They'd long thought that the fourth would also soon hold a similar position, but recent actions now made that appear impossible, at least for the foreseeable future. The atmosphere was cold and clinical. Someone cleared their throat and the sound hung in the air like a grey cloud. Then, a briefcase was opened, some papers removed, and the meeting commenced. They began by expressing dismay and disappointment that Tom had acted so out of character in his leaking of information to a rival company. This point was laboured in professional, though hardly succinct, fashion, and for its entire duration, Tom refused to make eye contact, staring instead at his hands - which held onto one another for support. In particular,

he was looking at the gold friendship ring on the third finger of
his right hand, and tried to remember which former girlfriend
had given it to him and, more pertinently, neglected to ask for it
back. The three executives took turn to berate him, but conceded
that pressures of work coupled with personal problems - the kind
which didn't necessarily need to be voiced to be easily discerned -
had probably prompted an overload of stress which, as everybody
now knows, can no longer go ignored in the modern-day workplace.
Perhaps he needed some time off, they suggested. A little personal
space to re-group himself, work out any relationship issues he may
be experiencing. They added, before he'd had an opportunity to
respond, that they normally wouldn't offer a second chance to
someone in a similar situation, that this was indeed highly irregular
and strictly against company policy, but reiterated that this was no
ordinary case. Tom was highly thought of around here, his future
impossibly bright, and so naturally they were reluctant to let him
go. Or, for that matter, lose him. In summary, then, their conclusion
was to give him a holiday, a few weeks off until this whole thing
has blown over, then he could return and continue with his fine
work, this little blip, this uncomfortable hiccup, put down to a

moment's indiscretion and quickly glossed over, forgotten.

It was all Tom could have hoped for, and more. He'd gambled everything, but had lost nothing. Miraculous.

And so what he did next was not just a little surprising.

While the job was certainly well-paid, Unikam were not exactly known for their everyday generosity. Two years ago, after Tom had come up with a programme that would help save Unikam over half a million pounds a year, they awarded him not with a financial bonus, or shares, but a company tie usually reserved for executive board members. The tie was green with bright yellow stripes and a tiny Latin inscription stitched in red cotton that no one knew the exact meaning of. Tom was wearing it now, initially to impress, but then used it instead to add a little drama to his ensuing theatrics.

He stood, pushing his chairs back, and, while loosening and removing the tie, told the trio that they could stuff their job, that he didn't need them, and would instead now sit back and watch subsequent offers roll in, perhaps even one from the company with whom he had covertly liaised. He threw the tie down onto the table, picked up the glass of water, and started to pour. When the tie was completely soaked, he picked it up, and felt its new weight in cupped hands.

"There, I've drowned the fucker," he said, smiling. "You can have it back now."

He threw it down on the table, spun on his heel, and strode out the door.

*

"You stupid, stupid idiot! What's gotten into you? Are you mad?"

I was amazed, couldn't believe my ears. What was he doing? While I ranted and raved, pacing the room back and forth, Tom just sat back on my sofa, arms outstretched, legs unfurled before him, and smiled. Unless distorted imagination had gotten the better of me, he appeared almost incandescent, as if glowing from within. Tieless, but still suited and booted, he looked completely relaxed, the three undone buttons on his untucked shirt suggesting that the more conformity he shook off, the better he felt.

"Don't you understand?" he said. "This is what I want. What the fuck do I want to stare at a computer screen for the rest of my life? I'm sick of it, anyway. Bored, bored to tears. The job was killing me, Jake, grinding me down. I felt so constricted, like I was slowly suffocating. I think I've always hated it, but the money kept me there. And, of course, the money kept me in girls, so it was easy to convince myself that I was, if not quite happy, then certainly perfectly content. But I realize now that that's all bullshit. I was just kidding myself." He gave a short snort. "I've seen the light!"

He seemed possessed by an almost religious fervour. It worried me.

"Have you ever come across the Jesus Believers brigade?" I asked him.

He looked back at me, confused.

"Doesn't matter," I said, shaking my head, "I was just wondering aloud."

Perhaps, I thought sometime later, this isn't so unusual after all. Whenever anyone depresses the fast-forward button in adult life, everything reaches them far too quickly, at increased speed. By the age of twenty-two, Tom was already earning what he previously couldn't even have dreamt about for thirty-two. He'd scaled the ladder two rungs at a time, was on his second mortgage, had got engaged on at least three separate occasions, and now he had indeed hit the midlife crisis. Over a lunchtime drink in a local pub, he told me that he was going to sell the flat, which would help pay off most of his still-existing debts, break off his engagement, and change everything in his life. Re-evaluate, do new stuff. He also said, just like Katkin had, that the recent events in my life had given him the encouragement he'd previously lacked. So, his immediate future now lay inextricably linked within mine. Blood, he noted again, was thicker than water, thicker even than this pint of Guinness. Plus, a little collaboration would be just the thing to bring us together, hopefully for a mutual benefit.

"I'm along for the ride," he said, although to me it distinctly felt the other way round.

He went back to his drink, then hunted in his pocket for the notebook he'd been keeping on Katkin's movements, and filled me in.

*

When I'd awoken the previous morning, I saw Katkin crouching by my bedside table, her long, elegant fingers searching my wallet for the Switch card I'd hidden the night before. I said nothing, and decided merely to watch silently and see what she'd do. Her face looked flustered, in a state of some irritation. There was little money in there, maybe a single twenty pound note, but Katkin wanted far more than that. Eventually, as it seemed like she'd reluctantly settle on taking my Visa card (credit instead of debit), her eyes darted up to mine to check whether they were still closed. She gave a little gasp of shock when she saw them wide open.

"Oh, oh."

Quickly, her face eased into a familiar smile. "Morning, darling. Sleep well?"

"What are you looking for?" I asked her, pushing myself into a seated position, using the pillow as support for my back.

"What? Oh, your wallet, you mean?"

I nodded.

"Um, I needed a little cash. I seem to have run out."

"So why do you have my Visa card? There's a twenty pound note in there."

She blinked several times. "Well, I needed a little more, so I thought I'd take your card. You don't mind, do you?"

"Normally I wouldn't," I replied. "But I'll be needing it myself today. Sorry."

I could see her twitch, almost imperceptibly. She was desperate to ask the question, but also wary. In the end, she just couldn't help herself.

"What about your Switch card? You could take that, I'll use this. Or vice versa." She reddened slightly. "Where is your Switch? I can't seem to find it in here."

"I was going to ask you the same question," I said.

She looked at me with searching eyes, and for the briefest of moments, I felt like I held a power over her. It was a strange, unusual sensation. She shrugged, took the twenty, and kissed me on the cheek.

"I'm off to see my mother," she said.

"What, again?"

Oddly enough, however, this proved to be quite true. After leaving me, she took the Merc to Shepherd's Bush, Tom following three cars behind. She spent little under an hour there, and before leaving, embraced her mother warmly on the doorstep, as if saying the kind of final goodbye that wrenched the hearts of loved ones.

From there, it was a brisk ten minute drive to a place just behind the Charing Cross hospital, where she parked in front of a large semi-detached house. She rang on the bell once, the door immediately swung open, and she disappeared inside.

The house was located on the kind of street inhabited by people who wanted you to know of their wealth. Opulence could be freely viewed through every window, each of which made little use of their curtains, which hung, uselessly underemployed, at either side. Televisions were as large as the crystal chandeliers. The grand piano was carved from the same old oak as the children's rocking horse. Kitchens were either farmhouse large or bijou and crafted entirely out of sparkling stainless steel. Staircases were wide and broad, or narrow and winding. And the cars parked out front were four-wheel drive and diesel - dark blue, chrome silver, jet black.

Simon's house was well-kept and well-preserved, proud. The front window allowed viewing access into the living room and beyond into the kitchen and back garden. It was very open plan, and tastefully decorated. He and Katkin sat at the broad kitchen table, coffee mugs between them, deep in conversation. It was a bright day, and the sun's rays bounced shards of light off the window making it difficult to see inside without intense concentration. Tom sat in his car, parked opposite, crouched and low, and trained a pair of cheap theatre binoculars on the pair and attempted, unsuccessfully, to lip-read. Whatever they were saying, the tone was grave, serious, emphatic. Although they seemed in agreement, a tension was palpable, even from across the street.

A sharp knock on the car's windscreen brought Tom immediately back to his senses, and flustered him so much that he dropped the binoculars and hit his forehead on the door frame. Trembling, he lowered the window and saw a black uniform, silver buttons up to the neck. With a weary sigh, the uniform lowered towards the ground until a face came into Tom's view, a weather-beaten middle-aged face, bespectacled, hairy, and frowning.

"You want park here, then you want buy a permit," said the face.

Tom relaxed, then groaned.

"The machine over there." He pointed. "You not buy, you fined."

As the traffic warden proceeded down the street, looking for other victims on whom to pounce, Tom resumed his previous position,

341

and lowered himself down on his seat until he became level with the steering wheel. Then he placed the binoculars back up to his eyes and squinted. Katkin and Simon were now locked in an embrace, he stroking her hair, she clutching to his midriff tightly. Then she nodded, parted, and disappeared upstairs. Simon walked over to the fridge, opened it, and studied the contents, motionless, for some time. A quarter of an hour later, the front door opened and they both walked outside. At the gate, they stopped to kiss again, with longing. Katkin then got into the car and drove off, while Simon walked in the other direction. Tom followed Simon.

*

While the rest of the week proved a veritable hive of activity for Katkin, as well as for the man on her tail, for me it was frustratingly empty. I suddenly found myself with nothing to do, except wait. Daytime television had produced in me the desired effect, and by the third afternoon, my brain was boiled cabbage and I became allergic to any programme that featured audience participation, real people. Spurred on by Katkin's efforts at a pleasant mother-child exchange, I decided that I too would pay a visit to mine. Not only would it afford me the warm glow of making her happy - we'd not seen each other in what seemed like ages - but it would also kill time, something I desperately craved.

My mother now lived somewhere on the outskirts of Croydon, a crushingly anonymous London suburb seemingly created, like Milton Keynes, exclusively out of grey concrete, and dotted with small patches of green that constituted parks. Outside of a few local shops, Croydon itself seemed to be one big hypermarket where anything - from lightbulbs to cheap Swedish furnishing to garden conservatories - could be purchased under one gigantic roof. Unless you've a relative who, for reasons unclear, has chosen to actually live here, these hypermarkets are the only reason anyone would dare be seen in such a miserable environment.

She lived, with the mild-mannered Duncan, in a newly-built semi on a newly-built estate in which every house looked like its next-door counterpart. Where the folk in Simon's neighbourhood liked to keep their curtains wide open, whatever the hour, the people of Croydon were all sticklers for keeping them drawn at all times, for privacy. Thus, every house bore four windows decorated in pretty lace, and every front door was either red or blue. The small car park was filled with white, four-door saloons, and each one flashed its little red alarm in perfect synchronicity with the other. It was like visiting the set of a pastel Disney film, and no sooner had I arrived than I longed for the taxi ride home.

I'd only visited her here once before, but remained patently incapable of remembering which door my mother resided behind. Red or blue? And to me, one pair of lace curtains looks pretty much like the next, so there were no clues to be gleaned from those. It was a late Thursday afternoon. I'd arrived here on a whim, fairly sure she'd be home because she always was. Duncan worked for an accountancy firm in the heart of Croydon - which sounds like an contradiction in terms, but curiously isn't - and wasn't due home until six, with supper on the table at twenty past. After walking around the circular footpath several times, I gave up my search and called her on the mobile.

She was very happy to see me, possibly too happy. I walked into the living room, the horror upon first seeing it months earlier instantly flooding back to me, and sat between plump cushions on the flower-embroidered sofa. She was watching a programme in which cute but sick puppies are taken to a bearded vet who usually cures them of any ail shortly after end of part one. She made me tea, still oblivious to the fact that I prefer coffee, but wouldn't allow a conversation to commence until she was sure that the latest puppy would bravely pull through. When this show finished, it was quickly followed by a Scottish soap opera I'd never seen before. My mother immediately set the video and muted the sound, but kept the set on, training one eye on her son, the other on the silent screen. She asked me how I was and beamed a new set of teeth at me. She's only fifty five, though lives like she's far older.

I looked around the room, desperate to shake my head in dismay. Although the megastore down the road had had an advertising campaign recently that urged people like my mother to chuck out the chintz, the message had clearly yet to register within these four walls. A totem of cleanliness and order, everything here had its place and everything smelled of lavender and patchouli and Glade. The small colour television sat on a picturesque table with wheels, and the video recorder was festooned with little nick-nacks, tragically including a torreodor, a gondola, and the kind of guard whose job it was to stand outside Buckingham Palace and ignore the tourists. On the small dining table there lay a half completed jigsaw puzzle, while an in-progress chess game took pride of place on the coffee table. One of Duncan's weekend hobbies was the collection, and the subsequent displaying, of matchstick ships in fat glass bottles, and these were neatly stacked across a wall unit. The carpet was soft and deep, the kind that tickles the bare feet and promotes instant relaxation; my mother's pride and joy. She had a short-haired cat, aged eighteen, whose chief priority in life was to sleep its way into the record books, and it was curled up today in its fake fur-lined cat bed which lay at the foot of my mother's favourite reclining chair, into which she herself was now snuggling while slurping at her sugary tea.

She asked whether my diet still consisted of pork pies and Scotch eggs, and I made excuses to leave the confines of this suffocating room by clutching my bladder. The downstairs toilet was a miniature paradise of pure kitsch. So small you'd have to step outside to sneeze, it consisted of one toilet, complete with furry, lilac-coloured seat warmer, and, opposite, a small sink that shone and sparkled as if the bulb were a spotlight under which it was expected to perform a song or magic trick. The mirror covered the wall immediately above, and in each corner was a stencil of pretty flowers. This tiny space - bijou, as my mother described it - smelled like Selfridges' perfume department, and was hideously intoxicating.

I stood with both legs astride, my behind resting gently on the sink, while I pointed my flow directly into the bowl below, petrified that I may pee on the rim or, even worse, the lilac rug underneath. After shaking gently, and dabbing myself dry with colour-coordinated toilet paper, I zipped up and rinsed my hands, then dried every available surface with the small towel. As I closed the door behind me and walked down the cramped hall, another smell assaulted my nose, one that I instantly recognized as steak and kidney pie, complimented with a side order of carrots, perhaps my least favourite meal while growing up. I braced myself, and walked on through.

The early evening news was now murmuring softly from the television, and the dining table had been cleared of its puzzle and was now set for three.

"You'll stay for supper, won't you?" my mother asked.

*

Duncan appeared alarmed to find me sat at the table, a knife and fork in either hand. This patently wasn't part of Thursday's schedule, and his strict routine now lay in tatters around him. He grunted hello in my direction, and appraised me wearily, as if unsure of my exact motives. Meanwhile, my mother, happy to have more than one person to fuss over, made a great ceremony in serving up both food and conversation. At her insistence, Duncan described his working day for me (drudgery, lunchtime, drudgery), my mother suggesting that perhaps I could get some work experience there seeing as I'd yet to embark upon a career myself. After my choking noises had died down, and I'd wiped the tears from my eyes, she asked about the flat and Katkin, and whether I'd heard from my brother recently. I'd been there less than ninety minutes, but already it felt like I'd never be able to escape. Considering my immediate future, perhaps this should have proved a source of comfort for me. If I was to find safety anywhere, then surely it was here? But I felt stifled, horribly constricted, and for the first time I truly began to appreciate what Katkin meant when she said she didn't want to become her mother. Neither did I,

348

and Duncan certainly didn't fulfill any requirements of paternal role model for me either. I watched him eat with slow, methodical rhythm, his neat newly-grown moustache occasionally flecked with flakes of golden pastry until my mother clearing her throat alerted him to the fact and he quickly buried his face into an iron-pressed napkin. For some time, the only sound was of cutlery against china, followed by concerted mastication, then swallowing. On my right sat my mother, my left her partner, in the middle a treasured son, but we had absolutely nothing to say to each other, no real news to impart, no common ground at all. What alarmed me most was that neither did they between themselves. After several minutes of this, my mother said that we should catch up on the local news, and suddenly the room was mercifully flooded with a kind of life again. So this is living? I thought. Before me lay my own possible future in all its cosy security: the doting partner, the regimented lifestyle, the array of hobbies, a balanced diet.

Ever since I can remember, I've had an aversion to wool. Whenever it comes into contact with my skin, I instantly begin to tingle, as if my blood has suddenly launched into an epileptic dance inside me. It's like an itch, only much deeper, and cannot be cured by hurried scratching alone. The only possible course of action is to remove the offending article of clothing immediately, rip it off my body and toss it far away from me. This can, and has, proved a little awkward in the past, not least when I was once sent, aged around six, to school in my first pair of rough woolen shorts which caused me such irritation that I was propelled to whip them off right there in the middle of a class, tears of agony pouring down my face. I've avoided wool, wherever possible, ever since. But right now, at supper with the folks, a similar sensation accosted me all over again. I began to feel hot, bothered, my blood prickling beneath my skin. I attempted to loosen my clothing, to regulate my breathing in attempt to promote a certain calm, but it was all in vain. My face started twitching, and I shifted uncomfortably in my seat. I needed to get out of here immediately, this very second. My mother now had a similar effect on me as wool - what a tragedy.

With as much conviction as I could muster, I exclaimed loudly, slapped an open palm on my watch, and took the Lord's name in vain, which made Duncan frown. I wiped my mouth, threw the now-stained napkin onto my empty plate, and made flustered excuses.

"Sorry, Mum, but I've just remembered something. I've got to go."

"What, now? We've not even had desert yet," she said, crushed.

"Sorry. Another time, promise."

"But it's custard, your favourite."

I've never liked custard.

"Really, I can't. I'll phone soon."

In the taxi, spread out as far as I could along the back seat,
my physical aversion waned and quickly disappeared. I opened the
window, breathing a deep sigh of relief, and lit a cigarette.

"No smoking," said the driver.

When I got back home, Katkin still not returned from wherever
she may have been, I called Tom.

"Look," I told him, "let's make sure we do this right on
Saturday. I've just had a meal with Mum. There's so much at stake
here."

I explained further and Tom chuckled, as if I'd only just
realized something he'd known all along.

"Oh, we'll do it right," he said, defiance incarnate.

Eighteen.   Gold, Frankenstein, And More.

(i)

Had I not lain in bed for hours, staring at the unmoving ceiling above and watching the night's blanket recede, then the alarm clock would have awoken me in a heart-stopping instant. It seemed louder this morning than it ever had previously, a sense of piercing urgency that I had no doubt only imagined. I rolled over and hit the sleep button, then turned to see if Katkin had stirred yet. But the space where I'd expected to see her body was empty, her half of the covers pulled back. I sat bolt up, about to jump from the bed, when I caught sight of her. She was seated, cross-legged, in the far corner of the room, naked but for bra and knickers, an upturned palm on each bare knee, her eyes closed, her face relaxed. It was then that I could make out a barely discernible om coming from her thin lips.

"How long have you been there?" I asked groggily.

One eye, the right, blinked open and looked my way. She seemed irritated that I'd interrupted her flow.

"Ages," she said.

"Not possible," I replied. "I've been awake hours. I would have heard."

"I'm very quiet," she said, closing the eye again and recommencing her mumbled mantra.

I got up, went into the bathroom, washed, then went downstairs and applied total concentration to the ingestion of a bowl of Cornflakes. Presently, Katkin, now wearing a Japanese silk bathrobe, came to join me but declined the offer of the cereal box in favour of some camomile tea. She appeared disarmingly calm, utterly focused, and not in any way open to an informal conversation. Which, ultimately, suited me fine, as I was convinced that I wouldn't be able to find an appropriate tone, anyway. We dressed silently, and I watched as she concealed the gun about her person so expertly that even a thorough frisk wouldn't find it. Before the bathroom mirror, she tied her hair back into the beginnings of a dwarfish ponytail, and added only the merest touch of makeup. She was wearing a pair of old blue leggings, and a light white top; a self-consciously unremarkable appearance for one capable of so much more. I wore a loose T-shirt, baggy cargo trousers, and the most aerodynamic pair of trainers I could find, in case I was suddenly required to run very fast indeed.

"Ready?" she asked.

"Just about," I replied, then, suddenly agitated, added, "Look, are we going to talk about this? Run through exactly what we're going to do?"

She looked at me blankly. "Yes. Yes we are."

"When, exactly?"

"In the car."

Two bags, containing only the barest essentials, sat by the front door. As we were about to leave the flat for, as far as we were concerned, the last time, our eyes lingered on the delectable living room, offering it a silent farewell

"You've remembered your passport, haven't you?" I asked her.

"Yes," she replied.

"Want me to look after it?"

"No, it's already in here," she said, patting her bag, "under loads of clothes."

En route, we stopped off at Paddington Station where we placed our luggage in a locker. After I'd deposited the required coins, a small piece of paper was produced, containing the combination number for reclamation.

"Do you want to put this somewhere safe?" I suggested.

"No, you look after it," she replied, smiling at me.

(ii)

Tom had been up ages. In fact, he hadn't gone to bed the night before at all. He was far too jumpy, he later explained, too anxious with anticipation, raring to go. Only dope could calm him down, and he chain-smoked a succession of roll-ups while sitting outside Simon's Fulham flat. Simon had already gone out once that morning, dressed in jogging gear, to buy a newspaper and a pint of skimmed milk, then returned to breakfast alone. After he'd done the washing up, he stood in the centre of the front room and, with eyes closed, began to work his way through a Tai Chi form, looking as graceful as a flamingo in courtship ritual. While Tom watched on, he switched on the radio for comfort and, finding a station he was happy with, began dancing with his fingers which moved across the steering wheel like snowflakes falling on grass.

Two days earlier, Tom had contacted an estate agents with a view to put his Docklands apartment on the market. The agent could barely contain her glee. The Docklands, she told him, were no longer tainted with the ignominy of being unfashionable; indeed, in the last few months, the turnaround had been tremendous. Tom'd heard all this before, of course: the Docklands were forever shaking off the shackles of the past and becoming London's latest hot neighbourhood, but this time, the estate agent, insisted, it was true. Upmarket glossy magazines now deigned it the new Notting Hill, with wine bars and select Italian and French restaurants popping up on an almost weekly basis. And the recently-opened Jubilee Line made access no longer the problem it once was. She'd be able to sell it without even breaking into perspiration, she said, clapping her hands in celebration. Tom explained that he'd already sold all the furniture as he was about to move overseas, so the place was empty, keenly awaiting its new owners. Then he left her the keys, and gave her an international mobile phone number along with a PO Box address for future contact. From there, he took his BMW down to a dealership and left with an envelope full of cash, then hired in its place an anonymous four-door saloon that may as well have belonged to our stepfather. He telephoned his fianc,e and explained that he needed time to think and was going away for a while. He'd contact her when he'd sorted himself out, but knew as well as she surely did that they'd never speak or see each other again. He booked himself into a small West London hotel, and existed on a diet of takeaways and marijuana-loaded cigarettes. We communicated with one another through VoiceMail only, keeping direct contact now to an absolute minimum.

After he'd finished his form, Simon then went upstairs and returned, five minutes later, with two bags, one large enough for a two-week holiday, the other smaller but somehow weightier still. Part of the money Katkin had stolen from my account? He placed both on the floor by the sofa, then made a telephone call. Moments later, the front door opened and he emerged, still dressed in T-shirt, shorts, and running shoes. Wherever he was going, Tom thought, he'd be back before long. As soon as Simon had jogged on up the road before disappearing around the first left turn, Tom stepped out of the car, locked it, and walked up to the front door.

We hit the traffic jam at the same time that the heavens opened. Typical. It hadn't rained in weeks, and the long dry spell had had the weather forecasters proclaiming this our best summer since discovery of the hole in the ozone. Suntan lotion had been flying out of the shops for weeks. But no one was applying the stuff to skin today. For while the sun still shone bravely from a far-off corner of the sky, much of the deep blue had been overrun by a gloomy grey, and the rain fell in sheets. We still had an hour to get there, but Katkin was keen to reach Deptford as early as possible, and I was equally keen to keep an eye on her.

While we sat in traffic, watching the windscreen wipers whoosh from side to side, Katkin kept quiet, staring straight ahead, slight stress lines boring down on her forehead. Eventually, she could contain herself no longer and ordered that I find a short-cut, even if it ultimately proved a longer route. The priority here was that we continue an onward motion without pause. Sat festering on an ugly road like this only encouraged bad karma. And today the karma needed to be exclusively good, continuous. And so I negotiated

South East London's backstreets as if on an infinite treasure hunt,

weaving left and right, working my way down one-way streets in

the wrong direction, regularly reversing, and performing several

three-point turns until we eventually found ourselves in the quiet

street that sat at the back of the pub.

"Good," said Katkin, visibly relaxing. She checked her watch.

"We can talk now."

*

It was a virtuoso performance, and I had to physically restrain

myself from applauding once she'd done. With the kind of level-

headed determination and subtle bravado exerted more by stars of

the silver screen than their three-dimensional counterparts,

Katkin basically said that I should follow her lead, that she knew

exactly what the situation required, and just how to achieve it -

largely solo. I didn't doubt it, and it surprised me little that I

myself had merely a supporting role here, because that's all I

ever had in Katkin's big plan. If nothing else, then to watch her in action this afternoon, I thought, should prove fascinating.

When we walked into the pub, the barman, immediately recognizing us, nodded and motioned us to follow him round the back. He pointed to the room at the end of the corridor, and then returned to the bar. Short Order and Joe were seated side by side, oblivious to our arrival, their glassy eyes focusing intently upon a large television screen that resided in the middle of an expansive drinks cabinet. They were laughing uproariously, and swearing loudly. Katkin glanced up at the screen and immediately recoiled. The two old men were watching a pornographic film set in a farmyard somewhere on mainland Europe. Judging by the few clothes the actors were wearing, it must have been filmed at least twenty-five, thirty years ago, a time when psychedelia had yet to be overthrown by punk. The tape was of a poor quality, but the action immediately discernible nevertheless. As we watched on, in abject horror, the scenes seemed to overlap until they became a colourful blur. Cows were taken from behind by randy farmers, a Shetland pony assaulted by three naked women, a pig lay prostrate while a woman serviced him as if ravenously hungry, and a dog paraded on back legs, what looked like scarlet lipstick protruding from his fur and aiming at a succession of subservient Lolitas. A sudden fantasy swamped my mind, one where I took the gun from Katkin and shot the faces off both men, rendering them as another kind of pornographer's dream: dead, mutilated in the throes of ecstasy.

Short Order saw us first and, still smiling, muted the television. In doing so, he somehow reminded me of my mother and her similar televisual actions, and I shuddered. He swung around to face us, encouraging Joe - who was now making animal noises at the screen - to do the same.

"Our friends have arrived," he said.

Joe's eyeballs reappraised Katkin's body, and he winked, motioning over his shoulder to the activities on the screen, and made a guttural noise that sounded like eh? eh? As we sat down on the sofa, Joe's son Dave entered the room looking huge, dressed in black boots, black combat trousers and T-shirt, his hair gelled back, his face more square than I remembered. Give him a couple of bolts on either side of his neck, and he'd resemble the grotesque Mary Shelley monster. He, too, grinned lasciviously at the screen, then peered more intently.

"Seen this one," he sneered, then sat alongside Katkin, thereby pushing me to the far side of the sofa, and patted her knee.

When Short Order's daughter finally arrived, dressed in a metallic maroon shellsuit, the tone changed and the two men got serious as they reiterated the run of events. If anything, Katkin's and my requirements were relatively easy. We were all to wear boilersuits and masks upon arrival, and while the three of them were all to carry guns and shout orders, Katkin and I were merely to brandish long black truncheons which we would probably be required to use as scare tactics.

A sense of the unreal drenched me, I couldn't quite believe what was going on, what was about to happen, and how on earth I had come to find myself here. Joe, now standing, arms folded, legs apart, in a posture as broad as a bull's, was talking about the importance of timing, brevity, control.

"One other thing," he began, but I no longer cared to listen and lowered the volume inside my head until I heard nothing but a continuous nonsensical mumble, his lips flapping like fish.

(iv)

Fortunately for him, Simon hadn't bothered with the dead lock, and Tom was able to gain access with the use of his flexible friend within a matter of seconds. He soon located the living room and was quickly on his knees, unzipping the smaller of the two bags. When the bag was opened, he had to catch his breath. Underneath a layer of T-shirts, there was a great bundle of money, our grandfather's - and, latterly, my - money. He plunged his entire arm in and brought out a fistful of notes and kissed them, some of which spilled onto the floor around him. He smiled deliriously. Couldn't be any easier, he thought to himself. He then lay the larger suitcase flat and opened it. As expected, it was full of clothes, his and hers, all neatly packed and recently laundered. Tom breathed in deeply and was suddenly transported into a meadow of fragrant flowers and endless rolling hills. On top of the clothes were two passports bound together with a single elastic band, his and Katkin's. Thinking quickly, Tom carefully tore out each page that contained their photographs and stuffed these into his shirt pocket. He then replaced the passports, and closed the suitcase. Then, he started gathering up the spilt money and thrust it, along with the T-shirts, back inside, before zipping it up. Now all he had to do was grab the bag and get out of there.

Which would have been so much easier had Simon not returned home at that very moment.

(v)

We travelled to wherever it was we were going in the back of a transit van, Joe driving, Treeza sitting beside him, while Dave sat opposite Katkin and I in the back, all three of us balancing precariously on old, worn tyres. Every time the van rounded a corner, we three went flying into one another, Dave usually making sure he had his arms open wide to catch an in-flight Katkin while I crashed against the side, kissing the black oil that seemed to smear every available surface. In his idiotic, simplistic tones, he endeavoured to chat her up, and had I not known her better, then I'd have been convinced that she was totally charmed by his efforts. She giggled in all the right places, and came on as strongly to him as he to her. At Dave's feet lay an open Adidas bag, and the constant movement of the van made the guns, truncheons, and various other weaponry inside jiggle around like live eels. The windows at the back had been blacked out, and from the front window all I could see was traffic and unrecognizable stretches of road, so I had little idea of where we were. Fortunately, the downpour had eased off, and it was now merely spitting tiny droplets of rain. Upfront, an eager Treeza cracked crude jokes.

After maybe half an hour, we finally reached our destination. I wondered whether Tom had followed us as planned, and hoped that upon opening the door, I'd see him hunched over the steering wheel across the street.

I could make out that we were at the trade entrance of a row of shops. From the front window I could see a succession of doors and gates, loading bays, empty crates, and parked cars and trucks. No people, though. From the bag came five balaclavas with the eyes cut out, but no opening for the nose to poke through, and five black boilersuits. Joe barked instructions at us again, and I watched excitement transform Treeza into something resembling a caged animal about to be freed. She and the father-son duo all claimed their weapons, the former holding a large handgun, while the latter pair had what I guessed were sawn-off shotguns. Katkin and I were presented with our truncheons, and she immediately whipped hers through the air, making a sharp cracking noise. She looked at me and smiled, hungrily.

"Right!" said Joe, checking his watch, and we all pulled our balaclavas over our head, fed ourselves into the boilersuits, and jumped out of the van. Briefly, I looked for Tom, but saw nothing before being propelled onward. As we ran towards a large closed door, it magically opened, and a young man emerged. He stood complacently aside as first Joe, then Treeza filed in, then nodded to Dave, and hurriedly pushed Katkin and I in last, closing it quickly behind us.

We were in the back room of a fairly large high street jewellers, and from the sound of voices, business was brisk. It was a little after one o'clock in the afternoon. We all stopped dead at the raising of Joe's right fist, and assumed positions as we watched him stride through the connecting door and out into the front of the shop, gun drawn, his arm fully extended. He marched around the counter without a word, pushing anyone who stepped in his way quickly aside, flipped the lock on the front door and snapped shut its small venetian blind. Then he rotated on his heel and directed the gun straight at an assistant whose hand was nervously reaching for the alarm button.

"You've got a very simple choice, son," he said calmly. "Push it, and I'll shoot your hand clean off. Then I'll come over there and kick the fucking life out of you, then kill everyone else in here as further punishment. Or you can leave it the fuck alone and I'll maybe spare you." There were eight people in the shop, three employees, five customers. The assistant immediately withdrew his hand and placed both of them in the air without further prompting.

"Good boy," he said. "Right, everyone, all of yous, get round the back now. Quick!" Herding them like cattle, he ushered each of them through into the back room until they faced their balaclava'd assailants, the blood drained from every face.

My own face, meanwhile, began to prickle and burn, the headgear I had on evidently made from wool. I gulped, willed myself to ignore it, and approached the tallest man. I came up only to his shoulder, and noticed that they were as broad as he was tall. I drew the truncheon back sharply and brought it down hard onto his right ear. It made a dull crack, and the man went down like a sack of potatoes, groaning.

"Anyone else who gives us trouble," said Joe, pointing to each one in turn, "and we'll beat you so hard you'll never stop hurting. Understand?"

Their collective pallor suggested that he wouldn't need to reiterate himself.

"Right," he said. "To work."

(vi)

And then Tom started running.

Very quickly.

(vii)

Joe grabbed one of the assistants by the hair, a pretty blonde girl who couldn't have been much over eighteen, and dragged her back out into the shop where he instructed her to empty every tray, each heavy with sparkling jewellry, into the black cotton bag he held wide open in front of him. In the moment before she was forced out front, she looked pleadingly at the manager, a wan-faced man in his late-thirties, who nodded solemnly. It seemed that she was doing everything she could to prevent herself from crying hysterically, her lower lip trembling like jelly. Meanwhile, Treeza cleared out the till.

The man I'd truncheoned was now sitting hunched against a wall, putting a finger gingerly to his ear then bringing it into his field of vision. The sight of blood made him wince, and he complained that he couldn't hear properly anymore. Dave walked over to him, and leaned into the ear.

"I'll make it easy for you then," he whispered, before erupting with noise. "SHUT THE FUCK UP!" The man cowered, and raised both hands protectively over his head.

Then Dave directed the six remaining hostages up against the wall, and ordered them to strip. When the male assistant who'd previously threatened to press the alarm button refused, Katkin was dispatched to crack him over the head with her truncheon. Like the first man, he too went down easily and rolled about the floor in agony. Everyone else quickly undressed to their underwear, and trembled despite the heat. There were three men, four women - five including the girl out in the shop with Joe. They ranged in age from twenty- to fiftysomething. Two were couples, one rather fat, the other slim. The horror of the robbery was then compounded by them having to face us nearly naked. They looked at us with the kind of expressions that fed nightmares. I found that I couldn't meet any of their eyes, Katkin too. Dave, however, laughed lecherously, approached one of the prettier women, and started fingering her bra strap. She began to cry. Unaware that I was going to speak until I did, I shouted his name and told him to stop. In a movement so fluid it seemed choreographed, Dave spun to face me and before I knew it, his gun was resting on the bridge of my nose.

"Use my name again," he whispered into my ear, "and I'll shoot your fucking face off."

I apologized, arms raised.

"Silly cunt."

From over his shoulder, there came another blur of action. The alarm button assistant, dressed now in nothing but tight black Calvin Klein's, made a sudden lunge for Dave, both arms outstretched, a savage look on his face. Again, Dave swung around in a liquid movement, and knocked the assistant flying as the gun made contact with the side of his face. As soon as he landed, Katkin attacked him with her weapon, concentrating on repeated blows to the stomach, until the man started coughing blood. Joe came rushing back, the girl's hair still entwined in his fingers, her body trailing fast, to discover the source of the commotion. When Dave had explained, Joe congratulated Katkin, calling her a good girl, and kicked the doubled-over assistant square in the face before returning out front. Several of the man's teeth scattered across the concrete floor like dropped mints. The young female assistant, meanwhile, was on the floor in tears.

With all the jewellry now bagged, along with the money from the till and each hostage's wallet and watch, we bound all eight up with masking tape, ankle to ankle, wrist to wrist, then brought ankle and wrist together behind their backs, leaving them all resting on their stomach and chests, rocking in an almost perversely comical fashion. Then we taped up their mouths, both eyes, and spun them around like human spinning tops, much to the amusement of Dave and Treeza, who high-fived one another. Before we left, Joe opened the back door and beckoned to the young man who had allowed us initial access. Quickly and silently, he undressed down to his underpants, and Joe carefully taped him up like the others, ruffled his hair and whispered later into his ear.

We were back out in the van and into the afternoon traffic within ten minutes of our arrival, boilersuits and balaclavas off, the full bag of swag the only confirmation of what had just happened.

"Fucking yes!" exclaimed Treeza.

There were whoops, hollers, exclamations, and the congratulations spread even to Katkin and I, although Dave shot me a look that said he hadn't finished with me yet. I looked deep into Katkin's face. She was radiant.

Then she sprung.

In her head, she then counted to three, whipped out her own gun, jumped on Dave, and thrust it into his wide open mouth so quickly neither he nor anyone else had a chance to retaliate.

"Right, everybody do as I say, or fatboy here swallows lead," she said loudly.

Swallows lead?

Dave's eyes bulged with utter confusion, then fear as she cocked the trigger.

With her free hand, Katkin threw the bag of guns over to me for safe keeping, and, suddenly, the ball was in our court.

Tom scrambled upstairs as lightly as he could, found what he guessed was the spare room, and forced himself under the single bed. His heart was again beating so loudly against his ribcage that he momentarily mistook the noise as the sound of footsteps crashing up the stairs in hot pursuit. He began to hold his breath, but if anything, this made the heart beat even louder, albeit slower, and so he attempted to regulate his breathing by sucking in air slowly through his nose and out through his mouth in measured doses. As he struggled to find a comfortable position, he found that he was grinning like an idiot.

From downstairs, he could hear unhurried movement, a single cough, and then some nondescript humming. So as not to alert Simon to the break-in, Tom had left both bags sitting in the front room where he'd found them. This was clever only to a point. If Simon left now, then he'd take both bags with him, locking the door and leaving Tom in a distinctly disadvantageous position. What to do next?

From the kitchen came a high-pitched whistle. The kettle? Then came the insistent ring of the telephone and a strident hello, but Tom could make out no words, just low babbling. When the receiver was replaced, Simon's footsteps began clattering on the wooden floor, the sound getting closer and closer. Then he attacked the staircase with all his weight, taking two stairs at a time. At the top, he turned left and walked down the hall, passing the spare room en route. Tom saw a pair of Nike trainers fly past his vision, then heard them pad into the next bedroom along. The trainers came off and, by the sound of it, so too the T-shirt and shorts. Simon was changing clothes.

Time to act.

Tom inched his way out from under the bed on erect fingers and toes, now not breathing at all. His pace was agonizingly slow, but he dared not go any quicker lest he make a noise, inadvertently draw attention. Suddenly, the sound of the telephone broke the silence, like a pick axe on ice, and Tom froze, feeling inside as if all the blood in his body had made a beeline for his belly button and was now pouring out of him. This time, Simon's strident hello was closer, and Tom relaxed at the merciful realization that there must be an extension in the bedroom. He sprang soundlessly to his feet and tiptoed to the staircase, every bone in his body rigid with fear. From the open bedroom door, he could see Simon's pacing form, talking irrelevance into the telephone, oblivious to any presence but his own. Tom crept down the stairs and made it back into the living room where the bags still awaited collection. He outstretched his right arm, opened all fingers, and clamped down hard on the smaller bag's straps. Then he stood straight. It felt deceptively light, considering its contents.

But, once again, his entire existence then came crashing around his ears as Simon made his way back downstairs. The front door was now out of bounds, so Tom slipped into the kitchen and out the back door, fortuitously ajar as if expecting him. Sheer momentum helped him over the back wall and he found himself in a small communal passageway. He followed it until it took him back out onto the street. Dare he go back and fetch his car? He had, of course, no option, and as four impossibly tall school children ambled by, the air around them blue with teenage profanities, he slipped in step behind them.

By the time they'd turned into his road, Simon was out front, dressed now in an expensive casual suit, a look of all-consuming panic crumpling his handsome features. Almost perversely thrilled by the situation, Tom remained on the same side of the street, regardless that his car sat opposite, and followed the school children as they passed him. Tom kept the bag - thankfully, like those of the kids, just a regular sports bag, no easily discernible features - thrown casually across his shoulder as he approached.

"Excuse me," Simon asked them, "but you haven't seen anybody, um, a bag..." but here he trailed off, unsure of quite what to say next.

The boys laughed at him as if he were mad, and Tom took the opportunity to lock onto Simon's worried gaze and tutted. Kids, eh? Then he abruptly crossed the road, got into the car, and threw the bag onto the passenger seat. As he pulled away, he watched Simon skulk back into the house, his shoulders hunched, an air of devastated resignation around him.

Tom laughed to himself, turned the music up loud as he lit another joint, and punched a series of numbers into his mobile phone, then squeezed it into the space created when he brought one shoulder up towards an ear.

Nineteen. Aftermath.

Joe was ordered to continue driving south and follow her specific instructions. Carefully, on squatted legs, Katkin backed away from Dave, her gun still cocked, and instructed me to apply tape to his mouth, then secure both arms behind his back. Dave looked at me with pure malice and I offered him a helpless grin, suddenly aware that amid the adrenalin, I too was beginning to enjoy myself hugely. I stretched a length of brown tape across his mouth as tightly as possible, and began to pull more tape for his wrists. Upfront, Treeza was watching the drama unfold while swearing under her breath, and Joe kept one eye on the road, the other on the rearview mirror, on us.

"I don't know what the fuck you think you're doing," he said, calmly, "but I just hope you realize you're making a big mistake. A fucking colossal mistake. You're done for now, you know that, don't you? You won't get away."

Treeza joined in the oral assassination, but she had begun to practically foam at the mouth and the only discernible word I caught was fuck, repeated endlessly.

Katkin, meanwhile, said nothing, just aimed the gun squarely at Dave, whose own manic gaze was as heavy with profanity as Treeza's stream-of-consciousness verbiage. In fact, she appeared almost frozen in her dramatic pose - frozen, that is, until Dave suddenly grabbed me by the throat before application of tape, pulled me towards him, and physically threatened to break my neck unless she relinquish the gun. Without even missing a heartbeat, Katkin aimed and shot, the bullet whistling past me as the noise bounced off each side of the van like a bionic ping pong ball. Dave surrendered his grip immediately, although his brief stranglehold would cause pain for days after, and fell to the floor. He had a small hole, a perfect circle, a scarlet O, in the middle of his right thigh, and blood was pouring from it as if from a tap. How she'd aimed so directly and managed not to hit me, I'll never know, but I immediately felt huge gratitude toward her. Dave writhed around, unable to scream because of the tape across his mouth, but doing his utmost nonetheless. Tears of wrath streamed from his eyes which looked into Katkin's with profound shock, a complete lack of understanding. Just minutes earlier, Dave thought he was in there, a reciprocal Katkin enjoying the foreplay as much as he. And now this. Treeza was swearing again, literally jumping in the passenger seat, but Joe was very quiet indeed, both eyes now trained on the road ahead.

"Turn left here," Katkin said, "and follow it to the end, then take a right."

Joe did so, then pulled up and turned off the engine, as instructed, in what looked like a disused car park, a large stretch of ugly grey tarmac that was empty save for several abandoned cars dotted around the area like lost punctuation marks.

"Right, get out," she said harshly. "You too, fatboy."

Dave had managed to stem the bleeding by wrapping an oil-soaked rag around his thigh, but the repetitive throbbing of veins in his temples, coupled with the bright red hue of his face, suggested that the pain had yet to wane. He hobbled out of the back of the van, his entire aura a fair approximation of agony. They stood together up against a wall, the jewellry haul in a bag by Joe's feet.

"Throw that over to me," Katkin instructed.

The bag arced in the air and landed at Katkin's side.

"What now?" Treeza spat. "You going to shoot us, kill us all?"

"If I have to, yes."

"You haven't got it in you, bitch," she said.

Katkin asked whether she remember Leeroy St. Coke? Treeza did, and suddenly fell mute. She looked like a pan of boiling water suddenly transfered to a lower gas.

Joe, meanwhile, looked calm enough to scare us, or me at least, witless. Although we were the ones with the gun, I still felt that he ultimately had the upper hand. His expression was one of experience, sagacity, the kind that had seen and done everything many times before, and that this little episode, although unexpected and unwanted, was nothing but another hurdle. And Joe had spent a lifetime jumping, and clearing, hurdles.

Katkin dispatched a reluctant me to go and tape them up, and warned them that the trigger was a feather, and her finger a lead weight. As I approached Treeza, feeling an upsurge of revenge towards the woman who had so recently given me the beating of my life, she cleared her nasal passage loudly and spat into my face. I made sure the tape was stretched tight around her mouth, then attempted to cut off circulation at her wrists and ankles by bounding them together with as much ferocity as brown sticky tape would allow. Joe offered no resistance, just watched me without expression, while Dave whimpered, clearly praying that he'd never get shot again. Then Katkin approached, handing me the gun, and ushered Joe to one side, where there were remnants of an iron fence, and she bound him further still to that. She returned back to Dave and Treeza, smiled broadly at the latter before kicking her feet out from under her and watching her crash to the ground. She then did similar to Dave, and he tumbled like a felled elephant, his considerable weight cancelling out the possibility of a graceful fall. En route, he cracked his head on the ground, a heavy expulsion of air shooting through both nostrils, and he lost consciousness.

Jewellry, guns, keys to the van. It was time to go. The van, mercifully, started first time. With Katkin at the wheel, we high-tailed it out of there with a speed that left tyre marks, our collective adrenalin pounding faster than any engine.

*

It was at this point that I began to feel really nervous. Where was Tom? He was supposed to have been following me every step of the way, but even now my brother was nowhere to be seen.

Which just left me and Katkin, and me attempting to prepare

myself for whatever came next and gradually realizing that I too

was now solely at her mercy. Would she train the gun on me, deal

with me with as much severity as she had St. Coke or Dave? Or

would she go one step further still and drop the lead weight on

the feather with point-blank fatality? The conspiracy I'd had going

with Tom was there chiefly to destroy and outwit the conspiracy

she'd had with Simon, but with Tom now out of the picture, and

Katkin firmly in the driving seat, my life really was in her hands.

I turned my head very slightly to the right, and caught her

expression. Although unsmiling, she looked euphoric, the windows

down, a forty miles-per-hour gale in her hair, and a sparkle in her

eye which, although tiny, seemed magnified many times over and of

a high wattage. I thought I'd test the water.

"So," I began, "what now?"

Now, she said, we drive straight to Paddington, pick up our

bags, dump the van, and get the hell out of here. I thought about

asking after our own car, the Merc, but realized that of course we

weren't going back for it. Not only was it far too dangerous, but a car like ours never lasted a day left unattended in Deptford. By now it had probably already been spray-painted, had had the number plates and locks changed, and been sold for a straight, one hundred percent profit.

I was genuinely intrigued, fascinated to see what would unfold next. With my left hand, I surreptitiously dug around my trouser pocket to retrieve my mobile phone. I inched it out and snuck a quick look. The VoiceMail symbol was flashing urgently. Tom, maybe? It'd have to wait.

It was now late Saturday afternoon, the sun beginning its slow descent, and the traffic was picking up again for another busy Saturday night. To obliterate the silence, I reached over and turned on the radio. It was tuned to the same station we'd listened to days earlier, the sports programme lorded over by pundits extolling the kind of critical expertise only ever possessed by eternal laymen. They were currently fussing over the day's football fixtures. Chelsea, apparently, should have won.

Within half an hour we were over the Thames and back onto more familiar territory. Katkin visibly relaxed and re-tuned the radio to a station that played hits from decades past. She began humming lightly along to one of the eighties more abhorrent memories. At Lancaster Gate, she swung a sharp right and, on our immediate horizon, Paddington Station slowly emerged, then loomed large. My mind was on countdown mode, and possibilities, as few as there were for me, transformed from black-and-white into vivid colour. It now seemed quite unlikely that she was to turn the gun on me. More likely, she'd be happy to leave me in the dark and refrain from revealing her duplicity while making her own getaway. Although desperate to reveal to her my own cunning, I thought it ultimately unwise, just in case it made her panic, trigger-happy. So when she told me, as we pulled up outside the station, to go and retrieve the bags while she dumped the van in one of the backstreets, I didn't object. The engine was still running when I got out, and as I closed the door, our eyes met. I raised my eyebrows at her.

"Back here in five minutes," she said.

I nodded, but she didn't see, because she was already yanking the steering wheel and moving away from the curb at speed. I watched the van disappear around the next turn, quickly catching her profile, very probably the last glimpse I'd ever have of her.

Feeling more disappointment than surprise, I retrieved and

rooted around in her bag to find only a few T-shirts and shorts, no clothes of any real worth to her, and certainly no passport. This last, I guessed and later had confirmed by Tom, must have been with Simon, on the other side of town. So I left her bag, but took mine, and went back out onto the concourse where I fiddled anxiously with the mobile, switching the ringer back on and accessing VoiceMail. I had four messages, all from a hyper Tom.

The first was relatively relaxed. Hey, it's me. I'm in Fulham, outside loverboy's house. Been here all night actually, but I'm fine, fine. Buzzing, in fact. I've just watched him bring down some packed bags from upstairs, so it looks like he and she are going someplace. Then there's five, maybe ten, seconds silence as Tom' attention is stolen. Look, got to go. Loverboy's just gone out. I'm going in. The next was whispered, more frantic. You're not going to fucking believe this. Money! Thousands of pounds! It's all- shit! Then the line goes dead. The third was all over the place. Listen, I've been held up. He came back early and ... no, doesn't matter, I'll fill you in later. Anyway, I've probably missed you, so I won't be able to follow. And, Jesus shit, I've no idea where you're going! I'll, I don't know, I'll drive around Deptford, or something, see if I can find you. May take me a while to- The sudden sound of a blaring

horn -Look, I'll try and call later. Or you call me. The forth and

final message was left just twenty minutes earlier. Where are you?

Why the fuck isn't your phone switched on? Are you alright? Look,

I'm now back in Notting Hill, because I don't know where else to go.

I hope you're alright. I've got the money. Look, call me back as

soon as you get this message.

He answered almost immediately.

"Where the fuck have you been?" he cried.

Five minutes later, the unfamiliar hire car pulled up by my

feet, and I jumped in. As I attempted to locate my seatbelt, I

explained the afternoon's events to him rapidly and without pausing

for breath, while he drove with the kind of reckless abandon that

police just love to pull people over for. A familiar noise then

suddenly intruded into our personal space. The police were pulling

us over.

"Oh shit, this is all we need!"

I put two fingers on my pulse and felt a hundred galloping

horses. Sweat had soaked my back.

"I'll deal with this," Tom said, and wound down the window.

As he did indeed deal with this, with a professionalism that suggested this wasn't his first driving offense, I felt an overwhelming need to relax, not just from the activity of the day, but of the past few months. Although everything was still a blur in my mind, my senses, I felt a compulsion towards complete relaxation the way a junkie craves his next fix. Although I'd never actually seen one, I'd often read, and mused, about floatation tanks. They are, I understand, as blue as the bluest ocean, and as seemingly deep as the deepest sea. There's no salt in the water, but one is nevertheless able to float as if suspended by the wings of invisible angels. Music is distant, ambient, as soothing as honey, as warm as a loving heart. Colours are translucent and melt into one another like slow-motion cheese on toast right before the eyes, and the temples are massaged in a circular, clockwise motion forever. It's like a womb with a view. It's like sleeping on soft feathery down, like floating on plump air, the same sensation as having all your dreams come true at once. I wanted to dive in and luxuriate.

Instead, I blinked several times, then realized that we were back on the open road, driving without official assistance.

"What happened to the police?" I asked.

My brother handed me a piece of printed paper filled with scrawled blue biro marks, a fine for speeding and driving without due care and attention, and instructed me to rip it in half and half again. This I did, then placed the small squares of paper into the ashtray and snapped it shut.

Tom spoke. "So Katkin never knew we were onto her?"

I shook my head.

"And she got away with the jewellry, then?"

I nodded.

"Why didn't you take it?"

I said nothing, just offered him a loaded stare.

"Okay, okay, I suppose this will have to do." He patted the bag he'd taken from Simon's house, and I secretly marvelled at his tenacity. "Plus, of course, the money from the flat, which should set us up nicely wherever we happen to end up."

Twenty. Sidewalking.

London, of course, was history for us, a place to file in our past,

and perhaps eventually forget about altogether. This was plainly

clear to us as we drove further west from Notting Hill, keenly

aware that any second now Short Order could come crashing down

on us from any direction. His spies were everywhere, nothing was

outside his reach, his unerring ability to second-guess better

than most peoples' first. The only conceivable way for us to even

consider a possibility of safety, of anonymity, was to flee the

country. And in many ways, it made perfect sense to the entire

escapade, a fitting end to all the madness.

As we drove towards the airport, this time keeping well within

the speed limit, Tom lit himself a cigarette, then lit one for me. We

kept the windows tight shut and smoked with great compulsive

gulps, holding the smoke down in the lungs for several seconds at

a time, then releasing it like a gymnast throws a streamer,

funnelling it down through our nostrils and whistling it out of

pursed lips in long plumes, watching it dance and dissipate before

our watery eyes. When we'd finished these, we promptly lit another pair and repeated the exercise.

Tom returned the hire car and we then made our way into the nearest departure hall, looked up at the screens and tried to decide on a suitable location. For me, it seemed obvious. I didn't just want to separate myself from home by air miles, but in every possible way. I wanted culture shock on a grand scale, alienation, somewhere totally new, and anyplace that wasn't Paris, Rome, Barcelona. I wanted to lie back on a Thai beach, go trekking through the rain forests of Brazil, maybe travel India by train. But Tom, clearly, was already missing real life and wanted to start over, and quick. He began mumbling about his continued potential, financial riches, large apartments, city bars, nightlife, women. Sydney was too far - after our ordeal, twenty-four hours on an aeroplane was simply inconceivable. Los Angeles was too whacked out, Tokyo too foreign, and Toronto full of Canadians.

"Only one real contender, then," he said, and rubbed his hands together eagerly.

We approached the appropriate desk and purchased two club class tickets, paid for by overused credit card. We checked in two bags, but took the money on board as hand luggage. In the bar,

Tom showed me the two torn-out passport pages, which we set fire to and watched burn in the ashtray while toasting our success with a pair of double whiskies. In fact, we got so carried away with toasting, that we almost missed our flight. A small motorized buggy, driven by a crotchety old man in an airline uniform, was dispatched to carry us from bar to gate, and as my passport and ticket was checked for the final time, my mobile phone trilled.

"Sir, mobile phones are not permitted for use on aeroplanes," I was told. "And you really must board now."

Ignoring the advice, I answered the phone and offered it my most sober hello. The responding greeting managed to drain drunkenness from my very bones in an instant.

"Who is it?" Tom asked, noting my suddenly pale pallor.

Katkin, I mouthed.

At first she was friendly, and asked what had happened to me. She had returned to Paddington, she claimed, but failed to find me. As I was about to answer, a shrill female voice came over the tannoy announcing the final call for our flight. Katkin heard this, and immediately gave up on her pointless pretence. She screamed down the line, and I had to hold the phone away from my ear. Tom laughed uproariously.

"It was you, wasn't it? You bastard, you absolute bastard! You took the money, didn't you? You stole it from us!"

I pointed out to Katkin that the retrieval of my own money could hardly be described as stealing, something in fact she was guilty of.

"It was you who stole from me," I said. "But never mind, I forgive you. I've got my money back, and you've got the jewellry. We can go our separate ways now. I'm already well on the way. All you have to ensure is that Short Order doesn't catch up with you. Even without your passports, I'm sure you'll manage that." I then allowed a pregnant pause before continuing. "If I learned anything about you, Katkin, then it's that you're one determined lady."

"What do you mean?" she said, suddenly sounding panicked.

I waited patiently as she got Simon to check the passports, then held the phone even further away from my ear while she shrieked as if her belly were on fire.

Then came the threats.

"I'll get you for this," she said, sounding impaled on pure hate. "I swear I will."

*

During the flight, I watched a popular Hollywood comedy that I'd
missed when it had done the rounds at the cinema. I laughed all
the way through, picked at my meal of cardboard meat and plastic
vegetables, then fell into a delicious doze. When I was roused
several hours later, shortly before landing, I made my way
carefully to the toilet and peered at my tired face in the mirror,
an envelope of sleep beginning to open, a brand new day in
store.

*

Fall in Manhattan roasted under the kind of sun that refused to
believe the summer season was actually over. The blazing sun
bounced off buildings and churned out of the exhaust pipes of a
million poisonous cars and trucks, making the entire island
resemble the innards of an unclean furnace. People went shopping
just to escape the simmering heat and revel in a cold blast of

air-conditioning. Sweat clung to the body like a baby to its

mother's breast, and would it not have caused endless pile-ups,

then no one would have bothered with clothes at all. Tom and I,

honorary New Yorkers within weeks of our arrival, greeted the

eccentric temperature like every other city dweller: with an irascible

temper that flew off the handle at a moment's notice.

We'd recently moved to the Lower East Side, into an airy

apartment with high ceilings and a view of gridlock traffic, having

finally checked out of the hotel when Tom, still awaiting a fat

cheque from the sale of his Docklands flat, finally realized that the

bag of money was now sorely depleted and wouldn't, in fact, last

forever. And my credit card was absolutely frazzled. It was a

large place, the living room unfurnished save for one long sofa and

a glass coffee table. The floor was pine, the walls brick. A dire

example of modern art sat between two windows, and a perfect

example of Japanese technology - two hundred channels, Dolby

stereo - lay directly opposite. The acoustics were hollow; shout, and

your echo would shout right back. The kitchen was small but

efficient, while Tom's bedroom bristled with chaotic life. It was home

to a low futon, a large floor lamp, countless takeaway cartons, discarded pizza boxes, empty beer bottles and clothes strewn everywhere. Occasionally, there would also be a nameless one-night stand, history by the end of breakfast, who'd sit demurely on the edge of the bed, peering at a stain and wondering quite what it was. Mine, on the other hand, was as sparse as a prison cell: bed, neatly stacked clothes, alarm clock radio. The job I'd eventually landed kept me busy well into the night and the morning after; during the day I came here to sleep, deeply. Pretty soon, this spacious place, with its unruly neighbours and the constant roar from the traffic below, became home. And we became natives. We ate bagels for breakfast, viewed cab drivers with a grave mistrust even before they took that first erroneous U-turn, hit the park on rollerblades come Sunday, and never looked up, never made eye contact, never apologized in the perennial sidewalk jostle.

Prior to the resurrection of normality, however, we'd lived rather decadently. Upon arrival at JFK, we had taken a cab into the very centre of Manhattan and checked into a chic hotel two blocks north of Times Square. It was a discreet place that catered for people with more money than sense, but with an artist's eye for design. The foyer was habitually bathed in a haze of subtle sunset colour, the chairs were art deco and generally more comfortable on the eye than the backside. The rooms were compact but exquisitely designed, the television had cable, and the metallic bathroom was so luxurious that you felt you had to be either very famous or very rich merely to earn the right to stand under a shower with as many settings as this. The exquisitely tailored, sharply cheekboned doormen, who glided across the dusky foyer like swans on a lake, made it known that they knew people who knew people who could bring narcotics into the building, thereby minimizing the risk for indulgent guests, and for the first few weeks, Tom didn't leave his room during daylight hours at all.

But the honeymoon period soon waned, and Tom slowly transformed back into his old self once more. While, at first, we continued the bonding of our relationship - doing the tourist circuit, dining out, hitting the city's bars and waking up destroyed the morning after - it didn't last much beyond a buoyant four weeks. Gradually, it became obvious that our need for one another had now distinctly lapsed, and we quickly reverted to the roles we'd inhabited as teenagers, satellites around a common earth who rarely came into direct contact. He started going out alone, now intent on rebuilding his career, and made a beeline not to employment agencies but to the bars computer analysts hit after work. There, his foreign accent would quickly mark him out as a novelty, and his good looks a bonus. Within just a couple of days, he'd made several useful friendships, one of which helped land him an immediately well-paid job in a computer firm in the financial district, green card pending. Once he was settled there, we moved into the apartment east of Houston Street, and soon after that, the keenly-expected fat cheque arrived on the doorstep, securing our future for the foreseeable.

And me?

Well, I began the process of reacquainting myself with daytime talk shows on television, at first revelling in the amount of thrown fists and kung fu kicks, but soon tiring of the endless repetition of it all. So I watched the sickly-sweet Oprah instead, but soon felt the fillings fall clean out of my mouth and clatter onto the wooden floor, and I switched off altogether. I then attempted to join a temp agency but was informed that without appropriate government papers I was effectively an illegal alien and would do well to avoid instant deportation. I did get some casual work, washing dishes here, making coffees there, but nothing solid, nothing that ever really stretched from one Monday to the next. Bizarrely, I found myself nostalgic for the life I'd left behind, for Katkin despite or, perhaps worryingly, because of her chicanery. They were wild, wild times, and she a wild, wild woman. Often, I'd wonder whatever happened to her. Had they caught up with her? was she still with the ex-boyfriend? alive?

With ample time on my hands, and my hands thrust deep into the pockets of my baggy shorts, I traversed the streets of Manhattan getting to know my new home until I'd practically sidewalked every street and avenue on the island, much like I had every pavement back in London. I got off on the city's buzz, even though the city's buzz seemed intent on ignoring me. Daylight lasted an eternity here, and the only job I could find was the staving off of perennially encroaching boredom. It wasn't easy work. I had absolutely nothing to do with my life, and my only diversion was watching millions of people getting on with theirs.

Tom, by this stage, was fully set up. The new-found career was going very well, and he'd quickly become serious with a woman of refined stock, a strong nose, and a powerful family. Melissa

Bloomfield lived somewhere Uptown, with her prominent lawyer father and her keen socialite mother. Woody Allen was a neighbour, although she tended to side with her mother on that subject and prefered Mia Farrow. She agreed to move in with my brother into his boho neighbourhood on the condition that she could redecorate immediately, and that I would move out, which I duly did. From there, I dossed down with Gilbert McCarragher - Mac to his friends - from Dun Laoghaire, a stringy, pale young wannabe artist with painted-on eyebrows and bright ginger hair, who'd come to New York a year earlier for fame and fortune, but had since settled for anything he could get. Which, currently, wasn't very much at all. At the moment, he was a dog walker. Pooper-scooping was his business. He lived in a room in an apartment overrun with immigrants from all over the world, and very kindly offered me the floor. And it was thanks to him that I finally landed myself a regular job.

I became a barman in an Irish pub in Midtown where everyone, staff and customers alike, were all ex-pat and largely illegal, and, consequently, immediately friendlier with one another than normal - New York's dispossessed tend to cling together for support. The pay was lousy, and the hours long, but the tips weren't bad, especially late at night, and the subsequent social life flowed as easy as the Guinness. It was the kind of place where an American accent sounded foreign, almost unwelcome. It was always dark inside. The smoke alone could ruin the lungs in a night, and the collective vapours were practically one hundred percent proof. While I hardly needed the money - although often absent, Tom remained very generous, and I never found myself wanting - I certainly needed the diversion, and so I worked all hours, six days a week, right through fall and into winter. I was exhausted but occupied. Sundays, Mac and I would hit the park, go ice skating, meet girls, drink in bars and coffee houses, and attend the kind of Soho loft parties I thought only ever occurred in films.

New York's winter, I was to discover, was as extreme as its summer. The wind at this time of year had more bite. The rain was stronger, the snow thicker. But, unlike London, New York just kept grinding on. Work didn't stop, and the cold, if anything, brought more people into the pub than ever. High percentage alcohol tends to start prompt fires in the chest; we were rushed off our feet.

Along with Donal and Dolores, I elected to work right through Christmas, including Christmas Day itself when the pub was packed to the rafters with homesick nomads who had no place better to go.

Our festivities revolved around the creation of brand new drinks that doctors would tell you should absolutely never be mixed if you want the heart to continue its methodical rhythm, but they went down a treat with the drunken regulars who would consume anything that either looked or tasted like potent alcoholic liquid.

New Year's Eve arrived, and we were astonishingly busy. The doors opened at eleven in the morning, and people poured in immediately, some customers confusing day for night and convinced that midnight was imminent, despite such telltale signs to the contrary as sun in the sky. Voices floated through the air, some thick, others sweet, all demanding continuous refreshment. As the day progressed, the place became busier still, and by night, great droves of people were being turned away at the door by bouncers the size of Belgium.

As ever, in the rare moments I was actually able to look up from the pumps and view the night's clientele, I recognized practically everyone in the joint, most of whom were friends and dubious associates of the ebullient Mac, a man never backwards at coming forwards with strangers. I saw a dozen Danny Boys, a handful of Paddys, plenty of Micks, but not a genuine name among them. People who frequented this bar often wanted anonymity, reinvention, and they got it. I also saw Simon, Katkin's boyfriend, but only thought I saw Simon, and not for the first time, either. It happened quite a bit, my past lingering at the front of my mind and challenging my current status quo, teasing me by playing with my nerves for the sheer hell of it.

Midnight was fast approaching, the music throbbing, the roar of the crowd as loud as thunder, and Donal, Dolores and I were serving sixteen pints a minute, our hands flying over pumps, bottles and bags of pork scratchings like waves crashing over banks. Orders were barked, beer spilled, champagne flowed, salt licked, shorts knocked back, lime sucked. Burping was resonant, vocal, celebrated, and encouraged. Every other word was an expletive, and everyone wore green. The giant television screen above our heads was tuned to activities in Times Square, the cameras casting their eyes over a million different faces before panning out for the bigger picture, then up towards the ball which drops at the stroke of midnight. We behind the bar, however, were largely oblivious to all this, and were concentrating solely on the continuous delivery of the amber nectar, the liquid tar, and the formidable fire water that emanated from Eastern Europe, aware that every second we worked paid double time, and that afterwards, when everybody had drifted off into the arms of a brand new year, we too would then commence a celebration of our own.

Suddenly, cheers rose up and burst through the roof. An eruption of limbs flew into the air, alcohol took flight from glasses. Faces were red and ecstatic with the kind of happiness that must, by law, recede the morning after. But at this stage, the morning was still a long way off. From the corner of my eye, I saw utter pandemonium. Everyone was dancing and bouncing off everyone else. I saw Tom jump deliriously on the spot, his girlfriend looking awkward and slightly incredulous at this sudden burst of juvenile energy from someone who, by day, held a position of such importance. He grabbed her face and kissed it hard. Then he kissed everyone else around him. Laughter abounded. If communal felicity was the goal here, then everyone had just scored a hattrick. Donal, Dolores and I hugged and slapped one another's backs, but were quickly called back to the pumps as everyone suddenly became desperate to toast the new year in with a fresh drink. Hands, money, and empty glasses were thrust forward, and we collected, dispatched, and replenished wherever needed.

One hand reached further than most, proffering no money, no empty glass, but positioned as if to conjoin with another, in greeting. I looked at this hand, slender and delicate, nails manicured and painted red, and slipped mine into it to shake. I looked up, along the bare arm and up onto the face, and saw Katkin - blonde bob, black eyeshadow - looking back, with a mischievous expression that quickly gave way to sublime satisfaction.

"Got you," she said, and squeezed.

Epilogue.

Click.

Click.

Click.

Click - then, still alive, an overflow of exquisite relief ripples right through me.

All blanks.